Terminated [illegible]
with extreme prejudice.

George opened the door. "This one leads directly to the president's private office. Most people don't even know about it. This other door is the president's closet."

He opened the door, and McLeod noticed a woman's winter coat and an academic gown with an orange Princeton hood hanging from padded hangers.

Then she saw a woman curled in the fetal position on the floor.

What on earth is Melissa Faircloth doing hiding in her closet? was McLeod's first, absurd thought.

She looked at George, whose mouth gaped as he stared at the body. "It is—" she hesitated. "It is Melissa, isn't it?"

"It's Melissa," he said. "But why is she in there?"

"I expect it's because she's dead," said McLeod.

Praise for

THE PRINCETON MURDERS

"This book is a must-read. The premise and voice are fresh and entertaining. Waldron combines superb mystery, divine characters, and suspenseful storytelling."

—*Romantic Times Bookclub*

Berkley Prime Crime
Titles by Ann Waldron

THE PRINCETON MURDERS
DEATH OF A PRINCETON PRESIDENT

Biographies

EUDORA: A WRITER'S LIFE
CLOSE CONNECTIONS: CAROLINE
GORDON AND THE SOUTHERN RENAISSANCE
HODDING CARTER: THE RECONSTRUCTION OF A RACIST

Children's books

GOYA
MONET
TRUE OR FALSE? THE DETECTION OF ART
FORGERIES
THE BLUEBERRY COLLECTION
THE FRENCH DETECTION
SCAREDY CAT
THE LUCKIE STAR
THE INTEGRATION OF MARY-LARKIN
THORNHILL
THE HOUSE ON PENDDLETON BLOCK

DEATH OF A PRINCETON PRESIDENT

Ann Waldron

BERKLEY PRIME CRIME, NEW YORK

DEATH OF A PRINCETON PRESIDENT

A Berkley Prime Crime Book / published by arrangement with the author

PRINTING HISTORY
Berkley Prime Crime mass-market edition / February 2004

Cover design by Jill Boltin.
Cover art by Grace DeVito.
Interior text design by Julie Rogers.

For information address: The Berkley Publishing Group, a division of Penguin Group (USA) Inc., 375 Hudson Street, New York, New York 10014.

Visit our website at www.penguin.com

ISBN: 0-425-19462-0

Berkley Prime Crime Books are published by The Berkley Publishing Group, a division of Penguin Group (USA) Inc., 375 Hudson Street, New York, New York 10014.

PRINTED IN THE UNITED STATES OF AMERICA

10 9 8 7 6 5 4 3 2 1

But Princeton drew him most with its atmosphere of bright colors and its alluring reputation as the pleasantest country club in America.

—F. Scott Fitzgerald, *This Side of Paradise*

Acknowledgments

I'd like to thank many people who provided information and advice.

The Reverend Sue Ann Morrow, associate dean of religious life at Princeton, and Bernie La Fleur, the sexton of the chapel, took me on a wonderful tour of the towers and nooks and crannies of the Princeton Chapel. If I got anything about that wonderful structure's geography wrong, it's my fault, not theirs.

Marcia Snowden was most generous again with facts and advice about life at Princeton. Kim Otis answered tons of legal questions with his usual patience and courtesy. Lieutenant John Reading of the Princeton Borough Police was also forthcoming and helpful about police procedure.

Carl Reimers and John McPhee provided useful bits of information in answers to my questions, as did Jim Merritt, Justin Harmon, and Henry Martin.

I owe a huge debt to Amanda Matetsky, who read the

manuscript more than once, made invaluable suggestions, and provided unflagging support and encouragement.

I couldn't ask for a better editor than Susan Allison or a better agent than Elizabeth Frost-Knappman. I'm lucky to have them both.

Prologue

MCLEOD DULANEY WAS *awed and bored at the same time on that February morning. She was sitting in Princeton's Alexander Hall, part of the audience for the installation of Melissa Faircloth as president of the university, and she was awed by the pageantry and the setting.*

Alexander Hall was a horseshoe-shaped Victorian confection of granite and brownstone, surely the least graceful edifice on campus, and adorned within by glittering mosaics. Legend claimed that an alumnus had given the money to build it on condition that his failed senior thesis in architecture be used as the plan.

McLeod was also impressed by the regalia displayed in the academic procession. Faculty members from Princeton and presidents of other colleges wore mortarboards and robes with the colorful academic hoods of universities from all over the world (for example, crimson from Harvard, blue from Yale). The elderly professor of classics who led the procession wore, instead of a mortarboard, a curi-

ous medieval-looking orange velvet hat (McLeod found out later it was called a biretta) and carried before him the huge mace, a gift from town (the Borough of Princeton) to gown (the university) a hundred years before.

So much for the awe. As for the boredom, the speeches were tedious, even the one by the newly installed president Melissa Faircloth herself, although McLeod liked Melissa's looks—trim and graceful, her thick, straight dark hair cut so beautifully that it swung around her head beneath the mortarboard.

Things got livelier when Mystique Alcott, who taught creative writing, came forward to read the poem she had written, commissioned for the occasion by the trustees. Mystique, McLeod thought, actually looked better than she ever had—a loose-flowing black academic gown was flattering to her heavy figure and her long blond hair was wound into a becoming knot instead of spreading around her shoulders. Her poem referred to the university as an outhouse, to its faculty as asses, and its students as morons. Mystique was apparently working hard to outrage, but didn't succeed. Most people in the audience had heard worse, and the people who might have been upset had long since dozed off. Mystique was quite smug about it later, saying that it was good for the old farts to be shaken up. "Melissa loved the poem," Mystique was to tell McLeod. "And the Sewanee Review *is going to publish it."*

One

WHEN MCLEOD DULANEY'S nonfiction writing class at Princeton University filed out at five o'clock on a March afternoon, Sophy Robbins stayed behind. Sophy was one of McLeod's favorite students, and they went back to her office to talk.

In the office, McLeod took a good look at Sophy. Her hair was thick and dark and shiny. Like most women students, she pulled it back and fastened it in a ponytail. Her dark eyes looked enormous in her pale face. She wore jeans and a sweatshirt. She was beautiful, the way all young people are beautiful. But there were signs of strain that McLeod hadn't noticed in the classroom.

It might be spring, but to McLeod it was still cold, and she asked Sophy if she was warm enough. "Don't you need a jacket?"

Sophy looked surprised. "No," she said. "I'm fine."

"And what can I do for you?" asked McLeod after a silence, since Sophy apparently had no paper to turn in.

"You're doing very good work," she added, after another silence. Sophy was from Princeton—she was a townie but lived in the dormitory. She was majoring in classics and wanted to go to graduate school and get a Ph.D. in classical archaeology. Nothing in her academic background explained all these silences.

"Ms. Dulaney, I want to ask you a favor," she said finally.

"Sure," said McLeod, relieved.

"I want you to find my mother."

"Find your mother?" McLeod was bewildered.

"Yes. She's missing."

"Where does she live?" asked McLeod. "I think you're from Princeton?"

"She lives in Lowrie House," said Sophy, speaking patiently. McLeod's brain worked furiously. Lowrie House was the Italianate mansion that served as the official residence of the presidents of Princeton University. "Your mother is Melissa Faircloth? The president of the university?" McLeod knew that the new president was divorced, but had never heard her ex-husband's last name. She now presumed it was Robbins.

"Yes, my mother is Melissa Faircloth," said Sophy. "And she's been missing for three days."

"She has?" McLeod was astonished. "George Bridges is a good friend of mine and he has never mentioned it." George Bridges was assistant to the president of the university, and McLeod privately thought of him as a very good friend indeed.

"George is so discreet," said Sophy. "Everybody in Nassau Hall is. They want to keep my mother's disappearance quiet until she turns up. They all think she slipped off just to get away for a while, that she's having a nervous breakdown or something. But I don't think she would ever do a thing like that. She would tell me, even if she didn't tell George or Kenneth Coales—he's the provost—or her secretaries. We always keep in touch."

"When did you last see her?"

"I saw her on Sunday," Sophy said. "But I tried to call her Monday night—I left a message on the voice mail—and she never returned my call. And she wasn't in her office on Tuesday. Finally, George admitted he didn't know where she was. Neither did Mrs. Linley, the housekeeper at Lowrie House."

"But how can I help find her?"

"You solved those murders when you were here two years ago," said Sophy. "I know your class worked on it, too. I thought our class might help find Mom. They're a great group, you know."

"No! No! No! I absolutely and irrevocably refuse to involve the class in any detective work. That was a mistake. I should never have let them dabble at solving a murder. And I simply will *not* have anything to do with a project involving a class again."

Sophy seemed stunned. "You'd still be perfect to do some investigating on your own," she said. "You could make some quiet inquiries, and everybody likes you and . . ."

"No," said McLeod. "Have you been to the police?"

"No. The provost doesn't want to call in the police. He's afraid of the scandal."

"That sounds crazy," McLeod said. "Your mother is a smart woman, and you don't think she would go incommunicado without getting in touch with you. Then the police ought to know."

"I guess the provost's attitude is odd," said Sophy. "But I took him at his word. I thought you might be able to find out something. I bet people would talk to you."

"What people?" asked McLeod. "I wouldn't know where to start."

"I can tell you some people to start with," said Sophy.

She knew better, but McLeod was hooked. "Who?" she asked.

"My mother's best friends are the Cowans—he teaches economics—Bruce and Martha Cowan. And then there's my father."

"Your father?"

"My father," said Sophy. "He was in town, and I think he may be the reason she's missing. He drives her crazy. He knows how to push all her buttons. I think maybe she's gone underground to avoid him. Although that's not really like her, to avoid a fight."

Sophy stopped talking and clenched her fists on her knee. "I know I'm rambling," she said. "I'm just so worried, and I haven't had anybody to talk to."

"Have you talked to your father?" asked McLeod.

"I talked to him yesterday. Wednesday."

"What did he say?"

"He said women were just like that. He wouldn't say whether he'd seen Mom or not."

"Where does your father live?"

"He moves around a lot," said Sophy. "He was living in Austin most recently."

"Is he a professor, like your mother?" asked McLeod.

"Oh, no. He's a businessman."

"What kind of business?" asked McLeod.

"Oh, different things," said Sophy vaguely.

"And he's in Princeton?"

"He was here yesterday. I don't know when he got here. He's staying at the Nassau Inn. He can't really afford it, but he said that if he stayed at a cheaper place on Route 1, he'd have to rent a car."

"And you want me to talk to him? Sophy, I don't even know his name. Would he really talk to me? I doubt it."

"His name is Clarence Robbins, and he'll talk to you. I'm sure of it. He thinks I'm a baby, his little Sugar Baby. But he'd take you seriously since you're o—" Sophy broke off.

"You mean he'd talk to me because I'm old?"

"You're not old," said Sophy. "I didn't say that."

"But my hair is white," said McLeod. "People are always saying things like that to me. My colleagues, the other reporters in Tallahassee, say the people I interview tell me things because of my white hair. Don't worry about that. But let me think about this business of your mother, Sophy. Right now I can't see how I have an excuse to call the Cowans or your father. I'm not exactly shy, but I can't see what I can do right now. But let me think about it. And don't involve the class, whatever you do."

"All right," said Sophy.

McLeod reflected that a young Southern woman would have said, "Yes, ma'am." But she let it pass, and Sophy left looking at least a bit relieved.

As she prepared to walk to her apartment, McLeod thought about Sophy—and her mother. She knew that Melissa Faircloth had taught economics at Princeton for years before she was named president. She was a crackerjack economist, everybody said, who was sure to get a Nobel Prize someday for her work on the sustainability of the human population. McLeod had never met her but had heard a great deal about her, none of it bad. When Melissa chaired the Economics Department, she had demonstrated that she was a first-rate administrator. She had been good on committees; she had served on an advisory council to the president of the United States. In the short time she'd been president, she had already proved to be an effective fund-raiser. She liked students and she still walked to work nearly every day. She seemed to be universally popular.

Universally popular, except with some of the crankier old alumni who wrote frequent letters to the alumni magazine protesting that Princeton, which in their day had been all male, not only had gone coeducational, but now had a female president. "Why not make it a single-sex college again, this time all women?" grumped one Old Tiger. Other alumni letter writers complained that the new president was divorced (nobody seemed to know who her ex-husband was) and that she had confessed to reporters that although she had grown up in a fundamentalist Christian household in Abilene, Texas, she was now an atheist. An atheist running a college originally founded by Presbyterians to train preachers? It wasn't right, the old guys said.

Why was Melissa Faircloth missing? Where was she?

MCLEOD WALKED HOME on a sidewalk that was cleared of ice but bordered by snow. Spring term! she said scornfully to herself. This was not spring. This was winter. She had been forced to spend a fortune on warm clothes after she arrived at Princeton for her second tour of duty as a visiting lecturer, teaching nonfiction writing under the auspices of the Humanities Council. (The other had been in the fall term year before last.) She wore her purchases today—down coat, shearling boots and gloves, warm hat that came down over her ears, and a long bright orange scarf. She would be able to wear none of them back home in Tallahassee, where she worked as a reporter for the *Star of Florida.* The weather in Princeton this semester had been a shock to her. Still, it was great to be back.

I'm lucky, she thought. She had lived in Tallahassee for thirty years; for twenty of those years she had been a widow and raised two children on her own, supporting them while she worked as a reporter. Her friends in Tallahassee had been like an extended family.

Now that her two children, Harry and Rosie, were grown and more or less on their own, she could do things like teach at Princeton for a semester now and then. Her indulgent boss, Charlie Campbell, owner and editor of the *Star of Florida*, had twice given her a leave of absence to teach at Princeton, this time in the spring—there was that misleading word again—when the Florida state legislature was in session. McLeod's years of experience made her an especially valuable asset to the paper when the legislature was meeting, and she had been afraid Charlie wouldn't let her go this time.

He had sighed noisily. "But you really want to go, don't you?" he asked her as they sat in his cluttered office. Charlie, an ardent saltwater fisherman, was always tanned and his blue eyes seemed to be the color of the Gulf of Mexico, where he spent his happiest hours fishing.

"Yes, I do really want to go," McLeod said to him. "I'm surprised at how bad I want to go. I think I'm tired of covering the legislature, to tell you the truth. I've done it for more than twenty years, and my heart sinks at the prospect of another session. Of dealing with that old fool from Escambia County and that jerk from Tampa. I used to remember what Toe Sack Burlap told me years ago. 'They're rogues, but they're our rogues.' He said just relax and enjoy their antics and their buffoonery, but Charlie, now I'm sick of it."

"You've seen Paree," said Charlie sadly. "And now we can't keep you down on the farm."

"I don't want to live up there. And I may hate it if I go back. I thought it was cold that fall I was up there, but everybody says that's nothing compared to what happens in February. I'll be back on the farm."

In the end, of course, Charlie Campbell had acquiesced and said she must go to Princeton for another semester if she wanted to.

I hope they do miss me, McLeod thought as she reached her apartment, rented from the university for a semester. It would be awful if they got along just fine without me.

She had a different apartment this time—no lake view, but a patio and a fireplace. She decided not to light a fire in the fireplace since she was going out to dinner, and turned up the thermostat instead.

McLeod continued to think about how lucky she was as she got ready to go out. She had discovered that she had made more friends in Princeton during that earlier tour than she had realized. People in the English Department remembered her and asked her out. She had kept in touch with Stephanie West, the department administrator, who was a marvel of efficiency and knowledgeable about everything on campus—a gold mine for someone like McLeod, who was always curious about everyone and wanted to know everything.

And she had met George Bridges soon after she arrived this semester. They met cute, as the movie people say. They were both looking at the shelves of Penguin Classics at Micawber, the wonderful bookstore on Nassau Street, late one afternoon. It was a bitterly cold day, with a north wind howling through town like a pack of wolves chasing a dog sled in the Arctic. They each reached for the same Anthony Trollope book at the same time, and each tried to hang on to *The Way We Live Now.*

McLeod withdrew first. "Go ahead, it's yours," she said, loathing this greedy man at sight.

"Oh, no, I beg your pardon," he said. "Take it. I'm sorry."

They continued to apologize, each insisting that the other take the book. Finally the man won and McLeod took it. "I'll read *He Knew He Was Right*," he said. McLeod decided he wasn't greedy and she no longer disliked him. "I wanted to go home and light a fire in the fireplace and read Trollope," she explained.

"It's the only thing to do on a night like this," said the man. "But why not have a cup of coffee with me before you go home? I prefer Small World, but Starbucks is so close let's go there."

He had an untidy mop of black hair and wore glasses with heavy black rims. He had on a broad-brimmed felt hat and an old navy overcoat. When they got to Starbucks and he took off his overcoat, she could see that he was impeccably dressed in a dark suit, white shirt, and tie. He introduced himself: His name was George Bridges and he had worked at Princeton University for decades as assistant to the president.

"I'm McLeod Dulaney—that's pronounced McCloud but spelled M-C-L-E-O-D—and I teach a writing course. I taught here once before and I didn't meet you, I'm sorry to say," McLeod said.

"I knew you were here—I read about your Pulitzer and then your appointment—but I never met you. I'm sorry, too," George said.

When they had finished their coffee, George invited McLeod to come home with him. "I'll build a fire and cook us some dinner," he said.

McLeod, feeling daring, accepted, and had a good time. They became friends, and managed to see a good bit of each other in spite of the long hours George worked. Melissa Faircloth was the third Princeton president for whom he had served as right-hand man. He wrote speeches and important letters, organized her schedule, served as doorkeeper, and often as spokesman. He supervised the secretaries and the staff in the president's office. He was also an amusing man who took his work seriously, but not himself. George was the soul of discretion about the confidential aspects of his job, but when he could talk about something, he did so very amusingly.

George liked Melissa Faircloth. "She's good to work for," he said.

"I like Charlie Campbell—my boss—but not many people like their bosses. Have you noticed?"

"You're right," George said. "In academia, there's that mentor-protégé relationship that can be very close but is usually fraught with tension. Melissa's not my mentor. She's just a good boss."

As time went by, McLeod liked George more and more. He did the *New York Times* crossword puzzle every day, and could always finish Friday and Saturday's puzzles. (She couldn't.) He liked the novels of Anthony Trollope, but he read modern fiction, too. He was divorced and had no children.

"He's always been a loner," Stephanie West told McLeod. "You've made quite a conquest."

"Fancy that, at my age!" said McLeod.

"I'm beginning to think white hair is sexy," Stephanie said.

Two

"WHY DIDN'T YOU tell me Melissa Faircloth was missing?" McLeod asked George Bridges as soon as she got to his apartment, as arranged, for dinner that night.

"How did you find out she's missing? It's supposed to be a secret."

"A secret! The president of the university is missing and it's a secret?"

"How did you find out, McLeod?"

"Sophy Robbins is in my class and she asked me to help find her mother. I didn't even know she was Melissa Faircloth's daughter. Sophy wanted to get the whole class to work on it. I flatly refused that proposal. I didn't want to repeat the experience we had when it seemed as if half the English Department was killed."

"I remember that," said George. "Everybody was talking about you and your class. Let me fix you a drink."

"I'll have a martini," McLeod said. "Can I help you with dinner?"

"No, it's all done. Or will be. It's simple—grilled salmon."

"Tell me why it's supposed to be a secret that the president of the university is missing."

"Everybody in Nassau Hall—the provost mainly—decided we should keep it under our hats," said George.

"This has aroused my curiosity. Tell me everything that happened."

"It started Tuesday," George said. "Melissa is usually the first person to get to Nassau Hall in the mornings, and the last person to leave in the evenings. And on Tuesday, she simply failed to show up for work." He sipped his drink.

"The dean of the graduate school, Melissa's first appointment, showed up," he said. "The receptionist came in and asked me what to tell him. I said to tell him Melissa's been delayed. I told her to tell him I'd come out and reschedule him."

George said he had to wait until the dean could get back to his office and could look at his own calendar before they could settle on another date for him to see the president. They finally made it for a week later. George called Lowrie House; she wasn't there, the housekeeper had not seen her.

"Then I looked at the appointment book and saw Melissa was supposed to have lunch with a big potential donor from Philadelphia in the president's dining room at Prospect. To be on the safe side, I called the donor and arranged another lunch. The donor seemed to be only mildly annoyed. But just think—it probably saved him millions. Melissa was counting on him to fund the new science library."

George took time out to grill the salmon and put it on a platter with sliced roasted potatoes. He dressed the salad and brought it to the table, then poured white wine.

"Anyway, that's how I managed things," George said when he finally sat down, "putting off appointments and rescheduling meetings for three days and nobody—until now—knew that the president of Princeton was not around. Do you remember the time when the president of Harvard simply would not get out of bed? It was several years ago. He hadn't been president very long, and he was apparently just overwhelmed by his job. He had an appointment for a big fund-raising lunch that day, and he just couldn't go. He wouldn't get up. It was a kind of nervous breakdown, and it was in all the papers. He and his wife went away to the Bahamas or someplace for a long vacation, and he was all right after that. I guess we all thought Melissa was going through something similar, and we wanted to avoid that negative publicity. But now I'm worried. The housekeeper has finally decided Melissa has not even been home since Monday."

He paused. "Next week will be impossible. I can't think up any more excuses."

"When did you actually see her last?"

"Monday afternoon. I usually stay as long as she does, but that day I left about six. I went to the dentist and had a root canal done. Everybody else in the office had already left. I asked her if she would need me for anything else, and she said no, she was working on a speech she had to give and she would be fine by herself. I made sure all the doors were locked and left."

"So you haven't seen her since you left the office on Monday? Where could she be?" McLeod asked. "It's impossible for anybody to just drop out like that. And a college president—I'm amazed that there hasn't been more of a hue and cry. Poor Sophy. I like her. Melissa has certainly kept her out of the limelight, hasn't she? But she—Sophy, I mean—must be worried sick."

"She doesn't see all that much of her mother," George said. "At least, I don't think she does. She was already a student at Princeton before Melissa became president."

"And she doesn't live at Lowrie House?"

"No, most Princeton undergraduates live on campus. Freshmen are required to, and most others prefer it—that's just the way it is. The university regards it as a necessary part of the college experience. And you'll notice that students whose parents live in town don't go home any more often than students whose parents live in New York or Philadelphia. Sophy probably goes over to Lowrie House more often than she went home when Melissa taught economics and lived on Robert Street. Melissa said that Sophy loves the luxury of Lowrie House and all the servants—it's a really grand old mansion and the university provides lots of household help."

"Do you have any idea yourself where Melissa might be?" asked McLeod.

"I don't," George said.

"Did she take anything with her? Any clothes?"

"I don't know. The housekeeper hasn't said anything," said George.

"Where's her car?"

"It's at Lowrie House."

"So she went home Monday night, right?"

"Not necessarily," said George. "She often walks to work, if the weather's not too bad. She doesn't mind the cold, but she is leery of icy sidewalks. She doesn't want to break a bone."

McLeod shivered at the thought. "Has she ever done anything like this before?"

"Not that I know of, certainly not since she became president."

"Who knows that she's missing?"

"You'd be surprised at how few people are aware of it. She's been out of the office for three whole days, but it's not unusual for the president to be gone a few days. But by now the people in the upper echelon in Nassau Hall know—the provost and the deans of faculty and the graduate school. I don't think anybody outside Nassau Hall knows. The people she had appointments with this week and didn't keep—they might guess."

"Sophy asked me to help find her," McLeod said. "She said Melissa might have gone under cover to get away from her father—I mean, Sophy's father. He's been in town some time and she said that he drives her mother crazy. She seems to care about her father and can't understand her mother's reaction—she called it 'allergic'—to him. Who is he?"

"His name is Clarence, and they've been divorced for years. Let me tell you, I'm allergic to Clarence myself. Any normal person—except possibly a daughter—would beware of him."

"What does he do?"

"I don't think he does much of anything," said George. "Nobody knows much about him. He turned up last September when Melissa took over as president. He came back last week. He once worked as a toll bridge operator on the eastern shore. Just sat there and opened the bridge maybe twice a day. Then he did some day trading and based on that vast experience he tried to publish a newsletter on stocks. One time he rented a truck to go into the hauling business. Not long ago, he was reduced to working in a filling station and after that he set himself up as a consultant on energy problems. Long ago, he wrote a book but never found a publisher—so he went into business as a literary agent. You might say failure goes to his head."

McLeod mulled all this over for a minute or two. "I don't have any idea how I can find out where Melissa Faircloth is," she said. "Sophy overestimates my detective skills."

"If you do figure out how to find her, let me know," said George.

"Sophy suggested I talk to some friends of hers—I wrote down their name." She rummaged in her purse and pulled out a crumpled piece of paper. "The Cowans. He teaches economics and they've been friends for years."

"That's a good idea. I thought about calling Bruce Cowan myself but I didn't want to spread the word we don't know where Melissa is. But go ahead. He'll be discreet—I hope."

McLeod stayed late at George's apartment. He was leaving the next day to visit his parents in Florida and would not be back until Sunday.

Three

MCLEOD DULANEY REALIZED she had no good reason to talk to Clarence Robbins, but her inordinate curiosity about the mysterious man who was Sophy's father and Melissa Faircloth's ex-husband impelled her to take action. On Friday she called Clarence Robbins at the Nassau Inn. He wasn't in his room, but she left a message, and he called her back shortly before noon.

"Thanks for calling me back," McLeod said. "Your daughter Sophy is in my writing class and she's a wonderful student."

"She's a sweetheart," said Robbins.

"I wonder if I could talk to you for a little while. Can I take you to lunch?"

"Sure. How about Prospect?"

McLeod liked to go to Prospect, another old Italianate house that served as the faculty club, but she did not feel entirely comfortable about appearing there for lunch with the ex-husband of President Melissa Faircloth. She hesitated, trying to think of a reason to go somewhere else.

"You do have Prospect privileges, don't you?" Robbins said.

"Yes," she said, "I do." She gave up. "Prospect's fine. Shall I meet you there?"

They discussed logistics for a minute, and at last agreed that McLeod would come by the Nassau Inn—it was on her way to the campus—and meet him in the lobby. They'd walk together from there. "You can recognize me. I have white hair and I'll be wearing an orange muffler," she said.

Robbins turned out to be a battered-looking man in his sixties wearing clothes that were on the verge of downright shabbiness. Graying wavy hair framed a wrinkled tan face. His smile never reached his dark brown eyes, and McLeod thought that a smirk lay just underneath it.

"How do you do?" Robbins said as they shook hands. "I'm glad to meet you. Your muffler is very orange. Is that a symbol of your loyalty to Old Nassau?"

"I didn't intend it that way," said McLeod. "I just like bright colors."

"Good for you," said Robbins. "I certainly have no loyalty to Princeton. I feel no connection, really, even though I have a daughter who's a student there. And of course, I guess I'm an ex-faculty spouse in a way. You probably don't know that my ex-wife is president, and still ranked a full professor."

They left Palmer Square and crossed Nassau Street to the campus. Robbins was clearly trying to be charming as they walked around Cannon Green and into Prospect's gate.

When they were seated at a table by one of the windows overlooking the Prospect garden, which was planned by the wife of Woodrow Wilson when he was president of Princeton, Robbins looked around the room. "Don't see anybody I know," he said, and ordered a martini. "But then, I don't spend much time in Princeton."

McLeod said she'd just have tomato juice.

"Oh, you're like that?" asked Robbins. "I don't trust people who don't drink." He winked at her and smiled in what he must have thought was a winning way. "I'm kidding, of course. People who don't drink are the ones to trust, aren't they?"

"I don't drink at lunch," McLeod said. "It just makes me sleepy and I have to take a nap."

"And what's wrong with that?" asked Robbins.

"I guess you have a point," she conceded, studying the menu, but she stuck with tomato juice.

When they had ordered lunch, Robbins said, "You wanted to talk to me, you said."

"Sophy spoke to me about her mother," McLeod said. "She's worried. She suggested I talk to you."

"Why would she suggest you talk to me, if she's worried about her mother?" Robbins was still smiling that curious, fixed smile, but his eyes were hard.

McLeod suddenly remembered the old flat, round containers of brown shoe polish she had known in her childhood. Clarence's eyes weren't that big, but they were flat and round and brown.

"She was afraid, I think, that you don't take her seriously, don't regard her as an adult. She wants to know where her mother is and she wonders if you know." McLeod spoke firmly.

"Isn't that interesting?" Robbins said, leaning back, his arm over the back of his chair, and waving to the waiter with the other hand. "Another martini," he said, too loudly.

McLeod's heart sank. Nobody she knew had ever begun lunch with two martinis and remained lucid throughout the meal. Other lunchers were casting glances at them. How many of these people knew who Clarence Robbins was? McLeod wondered. And how much time did she have before he was too drunk to talk sense? Might as well be blunt, she thought. "Do you know where she is?"

"In class, I guess, or in her dormitory room," he said. "Or the library. Or the computer center. Wherever students go."

"I don't mean Sophy, Mr. Robbins. I mean her mother."

The waiter brought Clarence his second martini and he swallowed a huge gulp of it. "Oh, you mean Melissa. Melissa Faircloth. My wife, or my ex-wife, the president of Princeton. Where is she—that's what you're asking? In Nassau Hall, Number One Nassau Hall. Or maybe at Lowrie House, or maybe even right here in Prospect. Isn't that the President's Dining Room right next door? Have you looked in there?"

Robbins was being oafish, McLeod thought, but whether from genuine ignorance, duplicity, or two martinis, she couldn't tell. Surely he knew Melissa had been missing four days. Hadn't Sophy made it plain? If he didn't know Melissa was missing, McLeod didn't want to be the one to tell him, mainly because George Bridges was still trying to keep it quiet.

The waiter brought their lunches, and Robbins asked for a glass of red wine. At least he wasn't having a third martini, McLeod thought. She decided to change the subject and try the technique she had used in many a newspaper interview. "Tell me about you," she said. "Where did you grow up?"

Robbins finished off his martini and attacked his roast lamb. After he had chewed a bite, he smiled his dreadful smile again and answered. "I was born and raised in Missouri. Springfield, Missouri." He pronounced Missouri as though it ended in an "a" instead of an "i."

"Where did you meet Melissa Faircloth?"

He drank some more wine. "I met her in Chicago—she was almost through with graduate school, finishing up her dissertation."

"Were you in graduate school, too?"

"No, I was just hanging out in Chicago. I had dropped out of art school at the Institute. And we met—met like two wild beasts in the jungle—it was love at first sight, a *coup de foudre*, as the French say." He paused dramatically. "It was a one-night stand," he said.

"A one-night stand?" repeated McLeod with some astonishment.

"You have to understand that Melissa grew up in this strict, fundamentalist family. She was as smart as she could be. She was so smart that when she went to the University of Texas, she stood out like that tower they have there. She was so smart that her professors insisted she go to graduate school. She wanted to do economics and she decided to go to the University of Chicago to get her Ph.D. She didn't have any trouble getting in.

"But smart as she was, she had not completely gotten away from that strict, religious upbringing of hers. She had learned to drink a little, though she never was a heavy drinker, and she had even learned to enjoy sex—'fornicating,' the preacher called it when she was a little girl. But when she got pregnant, she couldn't bring herself to have an abortion, and she refused to have a baby when she wasn't married. She told me we had to get married. That wasn't a new concept for me, and I said, 'Sure.' I'm easy."

"And you weren't in school? Were you working?" McLeod asked.

"In a way, I was. I had realized I wasn't ever going to make money at art, and I couldn't find a job that really interested me, so I started showing tourists around the Frank Lloyd Wright houses in Oak Park. Nothing official. I just helped them find the houses listed in the walking tour brochure they got at the tourist office. And then if they wanted me to, I'd tell them a little bit about each house. And they'd usually tip me, a little something."

"How did you get interested in Frank Lloyd Wright? Did you study architecture?"

"Never. I really never studied anything. I mean, I took courses in college, but I never really studied anything. You see what I mean? Melissa said I was a fraud, showing people around those houses and making up what I told them. But it kept me on my toes, so to speak, not knowing anything." He smiled an aren't-I-a-devil smile at McLeod. "You know what I mean."

He looked around, caught a waiter's eye, and held up his empty wineglass.

"I see what you mean," McLeod said. "But you must have been good at it, supporting a wife and baby on tips for making up things about Wright houses."

"Oh, I wasn't supporting a wife and baby. Melissa didn't want a husband. She just wanted a marriage license. We never lived together. I told you it was a one-night stand. She was independent as hell. She wouldn't have anything to do with me—divorced me before I knew what was going on. She had enough from her fellowship for her and the baby to live on while she finished her dissertation. I went to New York and tried to get a job in publishing. I've always been sorry I gave her up so easy. I really loved her, and I never got to know Sophy."

The waiter had brought him another glass of wine; Robbins drank it down and held up his empty glass for the waiter's eye. "And as a matter of fact, Melissa was right. I didn't know enough about Frank Lloyd Wright to tell the tourists anything that was true. She was right, dammit. Right as rain. She always was."

To McLeod's horror, tears began to roll down Clarence's cheeks. His eyes no longer looked like shoe polish, but like pools of chocolate sauce. Martinis were hell, she thought, especially at lunch. She remembered the barmaid in a north Florida roadhouse, where she and her husband had stopped on the way from Tallahassee to Jacksonville, who said solemnly. "We don't serve no martinis here no more. They cause too much trouble."

Robbins was dabbing his cheeks with his napkin.

"I'm sorry," he said. "I guess I show my feelings." He choked on a sob.

McLeod tried to bring the conversation back to a lower emotional pitch. "Where do you live now, Mr. Robbins?" she asked.

"I go where the opportunities are. I've been living in Austin, Texas. I guess I'll go back there, maybe tomorrow.

I was hoping to see more of Melissa and Sophy, but I'll go back to Texas. Might as well. Might as well."

"But you've seen them both, haven't you?"

"Oh, yes, I saw them both. But not for long. Not for long." His brown eyes looked at her woefully. He tried to display another of his smiles, but gave it up.

"Where did you see Melissa?"

"In her office, in her office."

"When was that?"

"The day I got here," said Robbins. "The first day I got here."

"What day was that?"

"I got here Monday. Monday."

He was fading fast. McLeod only hoped she could get him out of Prospect before he passed out.

Robbins, who seemed to be really hungry, roused himself when the waiter came. He said he wanted dessert, and chose a hot fudge sundae. McLeod ordered coffee for them both and hoped Robbins would drink his. After he'd finished his ice cream, Robbins complained that his coffee was cold, and McLeod asked the waiter to bring two cups of hot coffee.

Robbins burped, hiccuped, and finally drank his coffee. After McLeod had signed the check, he managed to walk out beside her. He left McLeod outside Prospect and wobbled off toward Nassau Hall. "Just going to look in on Melissa," he said, waving a hand at McLeod and smiling his awful smile. Does he really not know that Melissa is missing? wondered McLeod.

Four

SINCE GEORGE WAS out of town, McLeod was glad she was invited to a party at Mystique Alcott's house Friday night. Mystique was known for giving lavish parties in her big house on Hodge Road.

McLeod had sometimes found Mystique hard to take, but she was so outrageous it was hard not to be amused. She greeted her hostess warmly. "I haven't seen you, Mystique, since Melissa Faircloth's installation. I was quite struck by your poem."

"Thanks, McLeod. It's great to have you back."

"It's good of you to have me tonight," said McLeod and, as Mystique moved on to the next guest, looked around for familiar faces. But she was elated to see Max Bolt there. Bolt was the producer and cowriter of a movie based on F. Scott Fitzgerald's novel about Princeton, *This Side of Paradise.* He had arrived on campus in January, when McLeod did, and had rented a house. Two location researchers, who arrived soon after, had been scurrying around with huge clipboards, making notes on likely settings for scenes.

After somebody had pointed Max Bolt out to McLeod, she had seen him eating at Prospect, striding across Cannon Green, and using the on-line catalogue in Firestone Library. Good-looking, with long blond hair, he always wore jeans, a shearling jacket, and a baseball cap. McLeod had stayed in Princeton during spring break and had seen Max Bolt's movie company move onto campus. On the Friday that students left in droves, trailers had been parked everywhere—a trailer for costumes, a trailer for makeup, a trailer that served as a canteen. Tents mushroomed on the quadrangles so the stars, Billy Masters and Temple Jones, could pop inside briefly when they were shooting outdoors. Miles of cable seemed to stretch across campus, and cameras hung perilously on booms. To shoot some scenes outdoors, they draped the modern sculptures, erected long after Fitzgerald's day, in false foliage to hide them from the cameras.

McLeod had even managed to slip inside McCosh Hall when they were getting ready to film a classroom scene. Coils of cables stood around the entries and halls, and more cables ran across the floor among booms, lights, cameras, folding chairs, and boxes of electronic equipment. Electricians climbed over the seats in the lecture hall and hung over the rail of the balcony. Workers were attaching cameras to booms and putting up more lights. McLeod stared until somebody chased her out.

At Mystique's party Bolt had on blue jeans as usual, but was without the baseball cap and shearling jacket. He wore an elaborately fringed cowboy shirt. McLeod thought he looked quite exotic among the Princeton academic types. As soon as Mystique introduced them, McLeod began to question him about the movie.

"It's loosely based on Fitzgerald's novel about Princeton, *This Side of Paradise*," said Bolt, "but it's really a movie about Fitzgerald himself."

"Amory Blaine, the hero of *This Side of Paradise*, is

supposed to be Fitzgerald himself. Since the book is just about Amory Blaine and Princeton in 1913 and Amory's social climbing and his boredom with schoolwork, I should think it would be a tough book to film. Is it?"

"We're going to have to deviate from the book a little," admitted Bolt, grinning.

"Are you going to have a happy ending?"

"Oh, sure. Amory Blaine's going to make Cottage Club. He's going to get the lead in the Triangle Show, which he writes himself, and he may play football for Princeton. I know, I know. Neither Fitzgerald nor Blaine made the team, but still, football was so important to the student body back then."

"What about romance? The girl in the book is Isabelle, but did she ever come to Princeton? Weren't the love scenes all off-campus, at girls' houses in New York or Long Island?"

"That's another thing we're changing. We're going to have a Zelda-like girl, a Southerner, come to Princeton for Houseparties weekend."

"Girls were actually very chaste in that book," said McLeod. "Kissing a boy was pretty daring."

"We may change all that, too," Bolt said. "The script right now is fluid."

"Where all are you going to film?" asked McLeod. "I saw you at work in McCosh."

"That's pretty fluid, too," Bolt said. "We're negotiating with the university, and they can be extremely difficult. They're very particular about shots of Nassau Hall—it's registered as a trademark, or something. But we want to use Cottage Club, of course, and exterior shots at Blair Arch, the classroom in McCosh, as you know, the auditorium in Alexander Hall, and student rooms in some dormitory that was built before 1913. We need someplace to do Triangle Show rehearsals—McCarter Theater wasn't built then. It all depends on getting a green light from the Princeton guys."

"I'm reading a biography of Fitzgerald by Andrew

Turnbull," said McLeod. "Fitzgerald lived in a rooming house on University Place his freshman year, then in Patton the next year, Little the next, and Campbell the next."

"We should hire you as a consultant," said Bolt with a smile.

"I'm no expert," said McLeod. "But you ought to read the Turnbull book."

"I read the Mizener biography, but he never says where Fitzgerald lived when he was at Princeton." Bolt whipped out a small notebook. "Can I have your telephone number?"

McLeod gave it to him, protesting once more that she was no expert.

Bolt gave her his card. "That's our office out at the Residence Motel on Route 1," he said. "But here's my home phone number." He took the card back and wrote on it. "I've rented a house in town for six months," he explained.

Other people came up to talk to Bolt, and McLeod discreetly slipped away. Sometime later she heard raised voices and turned to see what was going on. Bolt was berating Jim Macy, the university's director of public relations.

A hush fell over Mystique's crowded living room as everyone stopped talking and swiveled to stare at the two men. Macy, a tall, dark young man, was obviously embarrassed, but Bolt seemed to be enjoying himself as he roared at Macy: "You don't understand that you're interfering with the creation of a work of art, you—you—you Philistine!" He hissed the last word, then began to roar again. "And Princeton is supposed to be a beacon to the arts and learning. That's total bullshit! Princeton does nothing but put up roadblocks to creativity."

"Our first concern has to be educating our students. You must see that," Macy said. "We can't allow anyone's creative endeavor to interfere with that duty."

"Fine talk from the Grove of Academe," said Bolt. Childishly, he made a face at Macy and stalked over to the bar.

"What was that all about?" McLeod asked Macy, whom she knew from her previous visit, and liked.

"It's all about his shooting schedule. He wanted to film during the semester, when classes are going on. We told him it was impossible. He insisted and we finally agreed to let him on campus during spring break, but told him he had to be off by the end of last week. Well, he's not off. I knew they couldn't finish during spring break. And they're still on campus and driving everybody nuts. It's a real bone of contention."

McLeod started to ask Jim if he knew the president was missing, but decided she had better not.

Five

ON SATURDAY, MCLEOD called the Cowans at home. She explained to Martha Cowan that Sophy Robbins was in her writing class and had asked her to talk to the Cowans about a personal matter. Could she come around to their house this morning? Martha consulted briefly with her husband and came back to the phone to ask McLeod if she could come by at eleven.

McLeod said she'd see them at eleven.

The Cowans lived in a very nice house on Boudinot Street and Martha answered the door almost as soon as McLeod rang the bell. She was an about-to-be-plump, rosy, and pleasant-looking woman with short hair and glasses. She led McLeod back to the living room, where a newly lit fire blazed in the fireplace, and introduced her to Bruce Cowan, who stood up when she came in.

He, too, was almost plump, rosy, and pleasant looking—they were like a pair of baked apples, McLeod thought—and they both wore blue jeans. Martha brought coffee and offered McLeod cookies. "The children love these cookies," Martha said. Bruce inquired about her class and Martha asked her how she liked Princeton. In turn, McLeod asked Bruce about his classes and found out from Martha that she taught math at Princeton Day School. The Cowans had two children, who were watching television in another room.

It was all nice and jolly. Then the Cowans looked at her expectantly. "You wanted to talk to us," said Bruce.

"Yes." McLeod took a deep breath. "As I told you, Sophy Robbins is in my class, and she asked me to talk to you. She's quite worried about her mother."

"Oh, so there is something wrong," said Martha. "We've heard rumors. Is she really missing?"

"I'm afraid she is," said McLeod. "She didn't show up at the office four days in a row and neither George Bridges nor Mrs. Linley at Lowrie House know where she is." It was a relief to find that her news did not seem to shock the Cowans.

"Has anyone talked to the police?" asked Bruce.

"I don't believe so," said McLeod. "The provost wants to keep it quiet, Sophy tells me."

"Ken Coales is an idiot!" said Martha Cowan.

"Martha!" said Bruce Cowan. "He's our beloved provost." His voice was heavy with irony. "Well respected, affectionately regarded."

"Really?" said McLeod, who knew only that he had vetoed calling the police about Melissa Faircloth, a line of action that she thought demented.

"No, of course not," said Martha. "Bruce is just teasing you."

"Actually, Ken was indeed respected and well regarded when he was a professor of molecular biology, but since he became provost several years ago, he has been the most unpopular man on campus. His days are numbered, though; Melissa plans to get rid of him."

McLeod was fascinated with this bit of gossip. Why did George never divulge things like this?

"Oh, yes, everybody knows it," Bruce continued. "If Ken Coales had any grace or tact or sense, he would have resigned when a new president was named. But no, he's forcing her to ask for his resignation."

"If he resigned as provost, could he go back to teaching molecular biology? Would everybody like him again?" McLeod asked.

"I think he's burned too many bridges," said Bruce.

"Too bad," said McLeod. "But I really have to ask you this: Do you have any ideas about where Melissa Faircloth could be?"

"I don't," said Martha, looking at her husband.

"I don't either," Bruce said. "We don't see nearly as much of her as we did before she became president. When we were colleagues in the economics department, we were best friends. She and Sophy used to go on vacations with all of us."

"We're still friends," said Martha. "We're very fond of her. It's not just that she's in a different circle now, but that so much of her time is taken up with the work of being president, with official and ceremonial duties. As for where she is now, I can't imagine. I do think somebody ought to do something, don't you, Bruce?"

"Of course I do. I'm racking my brains to figure out where she might be."

"She doesn't have a second home anywhere," said Martha. "No little hideaway in the Adirondacks or anything like that. Of course, there's the beach house on the Jersey shore that goes with the presidency. Has anybody looked there?"

McLeod made a note. "I'll ask Sophy," she said. "What about relatives?"

"She has a sister, who still lives in Texas—Abilene, I think," Martha said. "And there are some cousins. That's about it. Sophy would know how to get in touch with them. And that scamp of a husband of hers—she can't abide him. I can't imagine how those two ever got together. As smart as she is. And he's been married three other times, once before Melissa and twice since then. I think he lives in Austin."

"He's in town," McLeod said. "I talked to him yesterday. Sophy asked me to see him."

"He doesn't turn up often, but when he does, there's always trouble," said Martha.

"Why doesn't Sophy ask us questions herself?" asked Bruce. "She knows we won't bite."

"I think she thought an older person might carry more weight," said McLeod.

"We've known Sophy since she was a baby," said Martha. "Well, we won't be cross with her no matter what she does. She must be out of her mind with worry. She and Melissa have always been very close—it was always just the two of them, you see."

"You've been wonderful," said McLeod. "I really appreciate it. I'll urge her to come and talk to you herself." She rose to go. "Thanks so much."

WHEN SHE GOT home, McLeod e-mailed Sophy and told her she had talked to her father and to the Cowans and had one or two suggestions to make about locating her mother. She felt she was in a difficult position; she wanted to urge Sophy to go to the police, but she hated to do something that George didn't want done. She would certainly try to persuade Sophy to talk to the Cowans, hoping they might push her to call the police.

Sophy called almost immediately to ask about the suggestions.

"Well, there's the beach house," said McLeod. "The Cowans mentioned it. And relatives. What about her sister?"

"Aunt Claudia and Mom aren't close at all, but I should call her. And I never thought of the beach house. That's a good idea."

"And you should go talk to the Cowans," McLeod said.

"They obviously think the world of you. They're such good friends—I think they'd be more help than I can be."

"I will," said Sophy. "Maybe she's hiding out over there."

Somehow, McLeod did not think Melissa Faircloth was hiding out at the Cowans' cheerful home, but she didn't voice her fears, just told Sophy she'd talk to her the next day.

She got out her knitting and worked on a sweater for her son, Harry.

TO KILL TIME until George got home from Florida, McLeod went to church on Sunday. At the coffee hour reception after the service, she stood around wishing she knew somebody to talk to, when Margie Kinkaid walked up.

McLeod had met Margie during her previous semester at Princeton, but under terrible circumstances—Margie's husband had been murdered. Now McLeod grasped her hand warmly.

"Margie, how are you?" She could see apprehension in her friend's face, and decided that she would not be the first to mention the painful past.

"I'm fine, McLeod, and it's so good to see you again."

"You promised to take up painting," McLeod said. "Please tell me how things have gone for you—it seems like such a long time ago."

Margie laughed, seeming relieved. "You won't believe it, but I took up sculpture instead. I do these enormous metal things. You must come by and see them." She sipped a cup of weak Presbyterian coffee. "My son, you know, the one who was a carpenter, came back home after Dexter passed away"—McLeod noted that Margie was still unable to face the fact that Dexter Kinkaid had been murdered—"and he knocked out walls in our old house and cut a hole in the floor of one second-story room. So I have an enormous studio where I can work on really big pieces. I use a welder and everything. Please come over and look at them."

"I'd love to, Margie," said McLeod, trying hard to visualize stout, gray-haired Margie working on a metal sculpture more than nine feet tall. Margie had turned to talk to a white-haired, red-faced man in a dark suit with a vest and a white shirt. He was portly with, like Trollope's Dr. Fillgrave, a "little round abdominal protuberance," which McLeod supposed indicated a fondness for good food and good drink.

"McLeod, this is Fletcher Prickett," said Margie. "Fletcher, this is McLeod Dulaney. She's teaching nonfiction writing at the university this semester."

"How do you do, my dear," said Fletcher Prickett. "So you're teaching at the 'best old place on earth,' are you? And you teach writing? Well, you're a charmer, I'm sure, but why don't they ever hire any men anymore? Nothing personal, love, but it's true, isn't it? They don't hire men at Princeton anymore."

"Not entirely true," said McLeod. "They hire a lot of men. In fact, the faculty is predominantly male, especially senior faculty. Anyway, I'm glad they hired me. I love to teach here."

"That's good, that's good. I like to hear you talk like that. And you come to church. That's unusual for a Princeton faculty member. In the old days, they all used to come here, or to Trinity, you know, the Episcopal church. But now they all do something else on Sunday mornings. Lord knows what."

McLeod—for once—was at a loss about what to say, so said nothing.

"And they have no standards, no morals," Prickett went on. "Did you hear the poem that other writing teacher read at the inauguration of That Woman?" (McLeod could hear the capital letters.) "Disgraceful. I couldn't believe I was hearing language like that in Alexander Hall. And she calls herself a poet. What would Booth Tarkington or Henry Van Dyke have to say about that?" McLeod struggled to remember enough about either of these Princeton alumni writers to say something intelligent, but as Prickett rumbled on, she realized gratefully that no insight from her was going to be required. "Not even Scott Fitzgerald would have used that kind of language," Prickett continued. "It's appalling. I can assure you that no other president of Princeton would have allowed that kind of thing to go on at an official occasion."

"Melissa Faircloth probably had no idea what Mystique was going to read," said McLeod.

"She should have made it her business to have an idea," said Prickett. "And note that you don't see her here this morning."

McLeod, who found Prickett amusing, if somewhat illogical, rather timidly suggested that neither of the two previous presidents, one of whom was Jewish, would have been at Nassau Presbyterian Church on a Sunday morning.

"Aha! That's the problem," said Prickett triumphantly. "The moral decline began sometime ago. But it has reached its apex with That Woman in Nassau Hall. I should say, Those Women, because women are all over the place now . . . women deans, women directors of this, and women directors of that. And it's That Woman who sets the tone, who has been the moral arbiter, or the Immoral Arbiter, I should say, since she is so lacking in moral leadership." He paused to take a sip of his coffee and gazed out at his fellows in morality.

Margie nudged McLeod and murmured, "Do you think he has a bit of a point?"

"No, I must say I like everything I've seen and everything I've heard about Melissa Faircloth," McLeod said.

"Oh, you do, do you?" said Fletcher Prickett, eyeing her grimly over the Styrofoam coffee cup.

"Have you seen her lately?" McLeod asked on an impulse.

"Why, no," said Prickett. "I see her as little as possible. She has ruined the campus for me. Why do you ask?"

"I don't know," said McLeod vaguely, seeing that

Melissa's disappearance was still unknown in these quarters. She changed the subject. "Did you go to Princeton, Mr. Prickett?"

"Of course I went to Princeton. I'm a member of the great Class of 1940."

"You must be a loyal alumnus," said McLeod, sensing that the conversation had gone in Prickett's favorite direction.

"I certainly am! I'd do anything for Princeton."

WHEN GEORGE GOT home late Sunday afternoon, he and McLeod went out to eat Indian food. Over the lamb sag, McLeod asked George if it was true that Melissa was going to fire Kenneth Coales.

"Yes, it's true," said George. "How did you hear about it?"

"Bruce Cowan. I talked to him and his wife yesterday. You are the world's most discreet man. You didn't tell me Melissa Faircloth was missing. You didn't tell me she was going to fire the provost."

"There are ten million facts I could tell you about my job, most of them boring beyond belief. But I learned long ago not to tell anybody anything about what goes on in the president's office. It really is necessary that somebody keep his mouth closed around here. If I told anybody anything, it would be you. But it's best if I don't." He paused. "So you really did go talk to the Cowans?"

"I did. Sophy asked me to. They are as nice a couple as I've ever met. And I talked to Sophy's father Friday, too."

"And how was that creep?" George asked.

"He was creepy, all right. He got drunk at lunch at Prospect and wept. He said he still loved Melissa."

"I don't think he's tending an undying passion for her. He's been married two or three times since they got divorced. Did any of them have any helpful information about Melissa's whereabouts?"

"Clarence Robbins got so drunk at lunch he became incoherent, but the Cowans suggested checking with Melissa's relatives and wondered if she might be holed up at the president's house on the Jersey shore."

"Hmmm," said George. "We never called Melissa's sister."

McLeod changed the subject. "I met an eccentric old man at church this morning. His name is Prickett. He's quite charming, but he hates women, women at Princeton anyway. He says the university hires nobody but women and he thinks it's awful. He says feminism is just a fad."

"That's Fletcher Prickett, Class of 1940. He's an ardent alumnus who weeps when he sings 'Going Back.' He's a loyal Princetonian, but he thinks it should never have gone coeducational. He never quite approved of letting Jews in the eating clubs, either."

"Is he the one who writes those letters to the *Princeton Alumni Weekly*? Objecting because Princeton has a woman president?"

"He's the main one," George said. "He hates Melissa because she's a woman, because she's divorced, because she didn't go to Princeton, and because she says she's an atheist."

"I've noticed that several people have written to the *Princeton Alumni Weekly* to point out that John Witherspoon, the illustrious president of Princeton who signed the Declaration of Independence, never went to Princeton," said McLeod.

"I know," said George, "but Prickett goes on and on. He's an embarrassment."

"I think he's a character," said McLeod. "I never saw anybody like him."

"Be glad of that," said George.

When they had eaten all they could and finished the bottle of wine they'd brought, George asked, "Do you want to go back to the office with me? I've never given you a tour of the president's suite, and I should go by and see if anything important came in while I was away."

McLeod said she'd love to, and so they walked down

Nassau Street to the west end of Nassau Hall, where George opened the old wooden door with a key that fit a very new lock. They followed the stone-floored corridor past the main front door to the building in the formal entrance hall, to One Nassau Hall, where a small sign indicated that to be found within were MELISSA FAIRCLOTH, PRESIDENT and GEORGE BRIDGES, ASSISTANT. George used another key to let them into the suite of offices.

He stood aside and showed McLeod into a big room with a receptionist's desk. He turned on lights and opened the door to a small office. "This is my lair," he said. "It's tiny, but it has a window facing Cannon Green." Next came a big room where several secretaries worked. "They have windows, too," George said. He showed her offices where two lesser assistants and more secretaries worked.

Then he led her into Melissa Faircloth's own office.

"It's huge," said McLeod.

"It is," said George.

"It's freezing in here," said McLeod, shivering.

"It is," said George. "Melissa likes it cool. Building Services came over and did something to get this room cooler than the rest of the suite."

"It has lots of windows," said McLeod.

"It does," said George.

Melissa's desk was big, too. Down-cushioned chairs and a sofa were grouped around a coffee table at the end of the long room nearest the entrance.

"I love the pictures," said McLeod.

"The Art Museum lent the paintings to us," said George. "They are nice, aren't they? One's a Reginald Marsh and one is by a woman painter, Lilla Cabot Perry. She painted in Giverny with Monet."

"Where do all the doors go?" asked McLeod.

"I'll show you. This one we just came through leads from the reception area to the president's office. This one goes to my office. That's so I can come in without going through the reception area. Then this door over here is the president's escape hatch. It goes out to an anteroom on the east side of the building." George opened the door. "See how the old outside door opens right into this vestibule. There are only the two doors opening out of the vestibule, and they're both always locked. This one, as you have seen, leads directly to the president's private office. Most people don't even know about it. And the other one opens into the corridor inside the president's suite—it's very handy. I started to bring you in this way, but I wanted to give you the full effect of coming through the marble foyer to One Nassau Hall."

George beckoned her into the office and shut the door. "This other door is the president's closet," he said. He opened the door, and McLeod noticed a woman's winter coat and an academic gown with an orange Princeton hood hanging from padded hangers.

There was a woman curled in a fetal position on the floor.

What on earth is Melissa Faircloth doing hiding in her closet? was McLeod's first, absurd thought, before the horror of the body sank in.

She looked at George, whose mouth gaped as he stared at the body. "It is—" She hesitated. "It is Melissa, isn't it?"

"It's Melissa," he said. "But why is she in there?"

"I expect it's because she's dead," said McLeod.

"Dead?"

"I thought there was a bad smell in here, but I didn't want to say anything." McLeod knelt down and felt a wrist. "I'll call 911," she said. "I'll go to the outer office to do it. Don't touch anything in here." She glanced behind her to see George still standing motionless.

When she dialed 911, the Public Safety Office on campus answered. The dispatcher who took her call almost refused to believe her, then gave in, and said someone would be there immediately.

George came into the reception area and said, "I'm sorry. I'm catatonic. What else should we do?"

"Sophy?" asked McLeod.

"I'll call the Cowans," said George. "Let them tell her."

He went into his own office and sat down, reaching for his Palm Pilot. As he dialed, McLeod heard a knock on the main door to the suite and then a key turn in the lock. The door opened to admit a proctor from Public Safety, who was followed by two uniformed men from that office.

George was still on the phone, so McLeod led them to the president's office. The proctor knelt down and looked at the body.

Without getting up, he spoke over his shoulder to the two uniformed men. "Call the Borough Police."

During the following cacophony of sirens and flashing lights outside and the tramping of what seemed like hordes of law enforcement personnel inside, McLeod sat in George's office.

George was in the reception area, talking to the police. Peering out, McLeod recognized bald, blue-eyed Nick Perry, lieutenant and chief of detectives with the police of the Borough of Princeton.

After a while, Perry spotted her and came in to speak to her. She noted how he fitted in on campus, wearing as he did the male uniform—gray flannel trousers and navy blue blazer. "Hello, Lieutenant Perry. Glad to see you."

"What are you doing here?" he asked. "Are you still teaching?"

"I was lucky enough to be invited to come back for this semester," she said.

"I understand you were with George Bridges when he found the body."

"That's right," she said.

"Do you know anything about this business?"

"Not a thing," she said. "I never met Melissa Faircloth. George is a friend of mine and we had dinner together. He came over to check his messages and I came with him. I've never been in the president's office before."

"Did he tell you she was missing since Monday?"

"He did not," said McLeod. "The president's daughter is in my class and she told me. I don't think many people knew."

"Were you investigating the disappearance? You and your class?" Perry's voice was sharp.

"We were not," said McLeod. "We never mentioned it in class. In fact, Sophy asked me to have the class try to find her mother." McLeod felt virtuous as she added, "And I refused."

Perry looked at her searchingly with his blue eyes. "And did you do anything on your own?"

"Of course not," said McLeod. She hesitated. "For Sophy's sake, I did talk to Melissa Faircloth's ex-husband and two of her friends. But they could shed no light on her disappearance. I didn't do anything else." And she added, "In all fairness, I couldn't think of anything else to do."

"Who is her ex-husband? Does he live here?"

"His name is Clarence Robbins, and he lives in Austin, Texas. He's staying—or he was Friday—at the Nassau Inn."

"And the friends you talked to?"

"Bruce and Martha Cowan. He teaches economics at the university and she teaches at Princeton Day School."

"Why didn't you call the police?"

"George said the university wanted to wait, to avoid bad publicity. I thought they should have called you in, but I didn't feel that I could call the police on my own."

"McLeod, a citizen can always call the police," Perry said. "Now I guess you want to go home. I'll get Culkin—he's with the campus police but he's helping us—and he can get your telephone number and address. Can you get home on your own? I expect George Bridges will be here a long time. Or would you rather wait for him?"

"I'd rather walk home," she said, smiling at him as she got up. "It's good to see you again."

"Good to see you, too. Even though it does seem you're always around when there's a murder at Princeton University."

"Thanks for letting me go," she said. "Could I see George just to tell him I'm leaving?"

"He's answering questions right now. I'll tell him we let you go home," Perry said.

"Ask him to call me when he can," McLeod said.

Culkin came in with a notebook and Perry left. After he'd gotten his information, Culkin led her to the outside door on the east side of Nassau Hall and told the two policemen on duty there that Ms. Dulaney could leave. One of the policemen walked over with her to the yellow tape bounding the area around Nassau Hall and lifted it for her.

She thanked him, wished him good night, and walked home.

At home she found an e-mail from Sophy Robbins, who said she had driven over to the Jersey shore with some friends and made certain her mother was not in the beach house. Poor Sophy, thought McLeod, and went sadly to bed.

Six

GEORGE CALLED AT eight o'clock on Monday morning. "I hope I'm not too early," he said. "I'm sorry about last night; I had to stay. You got home all right?"

"I did and I certainly understand. Did Nick Perry give you my message?"

"He did, but I couldn't call before. I'm back at the office now. I was here last night until three o'clock in the morning; the police wanted information about every person Melissa Faircloth has talked to in the past six months. I went through her calendar, every address book, both her computer address file and mine. It was endless. Then I went home at three and lay in bed for a couple of hours—you know, stiff as a board, eyes wide open—then I gave up and took a shower and shaved. I was back here by seven."

"What do the police think happened? The Trenton *Times* said Melissa Faircloth was strangled."

"She was strangled—and then stuffed in the coat closet. Sometime Monday or Tuesday. Look, can you have dinner tonight? Surely I can get away by then. And I'll tell you everything."

"Come here for dinner," McLeod said. "I'll cook for you. You deserve a little mothering."

"It's not a mother I want you to be," said George.

"I understand. At least I hope I understand."

"I'll see you at six. How's that?"

"Six is fine." There was an embarrassed pause as they absorbed what they had just said to each other. George recovered first.

"The Cowans found Sophy, by the way. That took some doing. Nobody answered at her dormitory room. They went to her eating club and people said she had left to go back to the dormitory. They finally found her with the crowd outside Nassau Hall. Like a thousand others, she had heard the sirens and seen the lights and she stopped by to see what was going on."

"The poor thing. What a way to find out. How did they find her in that crowd?"

"I guess it was as much luck as anything. Anyway, they found her and went back to her dormitory to pick up some clothes, and then they took her to Lowrie House. Martha stayed there while Bruce went home to pick up their children and they all spent the night at Lowrie House. Everybody seemed to think Sophy should stay there for now—the Survivor in Residence, so to speak. She has a police guard."

"Can I call her?" asked McLeod. "Can I get through on the phone?"

"Wait a minute. I'll give you the number for a private line you can use. Look, I've got to go. I'll see you tonight."

It was still only eight-thirty—too early, McLeod thought, to call anybody, especially a college student. Should she take Sophy flowers? No, Lowrie House was probably full of flowers; she would make Sophy a pound cake. Of course, she'd have to buy eggs and butter, but she needed to go to the grocery store anyway to get the things for dinner. Back home, she quickly stirred up the cake. While it baked, she cleaned house.

McLeod finally got through to Sophy after lunch. "I'm so sorry about your mother," she said. "Can I do anything? Can I come over to see you?"

"I'd love to see you," Sophy said.

"I'll be right over," said McLeod.

She took off her jeans and put on a skirt and sweater—a skirt seemed more appropriate than jeans for the splendors of Lowrie House. On the way, she stopped at Thomas Sweet's for a quart of chocolate chip ice cream.

A policeman stood at the driveway entrance at Lowrie House, and a man from the Public Safety Office at the university was at the front door. She explained to each of them that Sophy had asked her to come by.

When McLeod finally got in, Sophy came down the big staircase to greet her. She looked ravaged, McLeod thought, and her face, with her hair pulled back tightly, looked gaunt. She also looked about ten years old. She was a small woman and she seemed to have lost weight in the two days since McLeod had seen her.

"Ms. Dulaney, I'm so glad to see you. Come in and sit down."

"I brought a pound cake and some ice cream," said McLeod. "I know it sounds idiotic, but ice cream slides down when nothing else will."

Sophy managed a weak smile. "The cake is beautiful. Did you really make it yourself? Let me put the ice cream in the freezer," she said. McLeod followed Sophy's jeans-clad figure into the kitchen, where a woman in a white uniform took the cake and murmured approvingly.

"Mrs. Linley, this is one of my teachers, McLeod Dulaney. She's from Florida."

Mrs. Linley smiled and took charge of the ice cream. "Would you like some coffee, Ms. Dulaney?" she asked.

"Sophy? How about you?" asked McLeod.

"No, thanks."

"I won't have any either, thanks, Mrs. Linley."

Sophy led McLeod to the big drawing room with its French furniture, all done in yellow. They sat on a puffy down sofa. As McLeod had expected, the rooms were all full of flowers and the air was heavy with their scent.

"Ms. Dulaney, my mother was murdered. Murdered." Tears rolled down Sophy's cheeks.

"I know, Sophy. It's ghastly."

"You have to help find the murderer."

"Sophy, the police will go all out on this, believe me. They can do so much these days. There's no need for me to go messing around." McLeod paused. "If there's some specific thing I can do for you, I'll gladly do it, but I can't start investigating your mother's murder when the police are already active."

"You could talk to my father again. Don't take him to lunch. At least, don't let him have any alcohol. Talk to him again."

"Sophy, you don't think he had anything to do with your mother's murder, do you?"

"He probably knows something." Sophy's lips were fixed in a hard line; she looked stubborn. "He always knows something about everything."

"Sophy, believe me, the police will talk to him. They'll talk to the Cowans, too, of course, and anybody else whose name you or anybody else suggests. Did you talk to the Cowans about this last night?"

"Just a little bit," Sophy said. "They found me. Did you hear about that? They're going to stay here awhile, I think."

"When you feel ready to talk about it, tell the policeman in front of the house you want to see Captain Perry," McLeod said. "I'm sure he's in charge, and he's very nice." A thought occurred to her. "What about your aunt?"

"She's coming. I don't know when. Martha Cowan and I called her. And my uncle, too."

"Oh, good," said McLeod. "I hate to think of you in this big house with no family."

Again a small smile appeared on Sophy's face. "It's

weird, isn't it? Actually, I guess I can't stay here too long, can I?"

"I don't think the university will kick you out immediately."

MCLEOD, GLAD SHE had no student conferences scheduled, spent the rest of the day cooking for George. She made ginger chicken with olives and prunes for the main dish, and smoked salmon and sour cream canapés. In a final effort, she made crème brûlée. She had first made it not long ago in Tallahassee and her daughter Rosie had given her a miniature blowtorch for burning the brown sugar crust on top. She had not brought the little torch with her to Princeton, but she had used the broiler before and could do it again.

She went to the liquor store and stopped on the way home to buy flowers. She arranged the flowers and then took a shower.

George arrived promptly at six. "I'm exhausted," he said after he'd kissed her.

"Sit down," she said. "You should be exhausted. What will you have to drink? I have everything—gin, vermouth, scotch, bourbon, sherry, red wine, white wine."

"One of each." He followed her to the table that served as her bar. "If I have anything alcoholic, I'll probably pass out. But that doesn't mean I'm going to abstain from anything alcoholic. In fact, I'll have a martini."

"I'll join you," McLeod said. "Dinner's all ready—except for the rice. That won't take but a few minutes more. It's just something plain to go under the chicken."

When they sat down, drinks in hand, McLeod said, "Tell me everything. Everything you can remember. Go back to Sunday night. Tell me word for word what they said and what you said."

"The police came and you saw how it was. It got even more chaotic, but they did seem to know what they were doing. They wanted to know when I had seen Melissa last and I said Monday afternoon. They were puzzled and irritated with me because Melissa had been missing several days and nobody had reported it to the police. They couldn't get over it."

"It's not a crime not to report a missing person, is it?" said McLeod.

"No, I don't think so. You always read in the paper how they don't get excited about missing persons."

"I think it's teenagers who have run away from home," McLeod said. "Not the presidents of Ivy League universities."

"Well, the police *were* upset," George said.

"When do they think she was killed?"

"I don't think they know. The office is so cold that the body didn't decompose the way it would have in a warmer room. I don't know."

McLeod checked the rice and pronounced it done. She served the plates and they sat down at her small table in the "dining area" of her apartment. She poured wine. "What happened then?"

"They finished taking pictures of the body and the closet and the office, and they could tell definitely that she'd been strangled. And she had fought back. Her clothes were torn, they said. Then the murderer folded her up so neatly that when we found her in the closet, we didn't notice all that." He took a gulp of wine.

"What was she strangled with?" asked McLeod.

"They don't know yet. Fabric of some kind. They wanted the name of every person who had seen Melissa recently. That took forever."

MCLEOD CLEARED THE table and made coffee. "What else?" she asked when they were sitting on the sofa with their coffee.

George asked if he could have a little brandy. "For somebody who ought not to drink anything alcoholic, I'm sure not adhering to principle," he said, accepting the glass and getting back to the story.

"The police had a press conference this morning in Alexander Hall. We couldn't have it in the Faculty Room since Nassau Hall is under siege, and the Faculty Room wasn't big enough anyway—hundreds of newspaper and television people were there. I didn't go to the press conference. Kenneth Coales went, as provost, and the vice president for public affairs, but I stayed in the office. At least the chief and Captain Perry were out of our hair for about an hour. This is a big story, a very big story. It was a long press conference. I understand they talked about an 'attacker' and a struggle. You know, we didn't see any signs of a fight when we went in her office on Tuesday morning. The murderer must have tidied up."

"And she was folded up so neatly . . ." said McLeod.

George sipped his brandy and drank his coffee and McLeod did not ask any more questions for ten whole minutes. She wondered, in fact, why her friend Oliver Hunt, who covered crime for *The New York Times,* had not called her about helping him. Then she realized he probably didn't know she was in Princeton again. "Where is the press hanging out?" she asked.

"They've improvised a press room in the ambulatory at Alexander Hall. Fortunately, the movie crew had just cleared out of there and now it's full of tables and telephones and connections for computers."

"It's a big story when the president of an Ivy League university is killed," said McLeod wistfully. She forced her attention back to George. "How did things go at the office the rest of the day?"

"Thank God the staff was all there," George said. "And we called in some reinforcements—people who used to work for us—to help deal with the phone calls. We have to deal politely with everyone who calls and be sure that the right people get through to us. Then flowers poured in."

"Lowrie House was packed with flowers, too," said McLeod.

"And it's only just started," said George. "And the notes. Think of the letters that are going to come in, letters and notes that have to be answered."

They sat silently, contemplating what lay ahead. "The trustees will have an emergency meeting tomorrow. I don't know whether they'll have a quorum on a Tuesday with one day's notice, but the executive committee will be here," said George.

"Will they name an acting president?" asked McLeod.

"I really had better not talk about that," said George. "I can tell you what the police did, though. They started talking to people right away. They have debriefed me thoroughly, let me tell you. I think I like your friend Nick Perry. He's a tiger, but he's a good guy. A gentleman, as Fletcher Prickett would say.

"Then they started talking to all the rest of the administration, the provost, and all the vice presidents. They gave us passes to get in and out of our offices. Nassau Hall is really shut off from the world. And they're combing the campus, looking for whatever was used to strangle Melissa. They've called in help from the township police and I believe some neighboring boroughs. I know Lawrenceville is involved. It is really a huge undertaking."

"Who could have done it?" asked McLeod. "What motive could anybody have for murdering the president of Princeton? And she was popular, wasn't she?"

"She was, except for a few Old Tigers," said George.

"Could it possibly have been a robbery?"

"Nothing is missing that we know of," George said. "I don't see how it could have been random violence, either. It had to be somebody who had a key to the president's suite or somebody Melissa knew well enough to admit to her office after everybody had gone home."

"The husband comes to mind, always," McLeod said.

"He certainly does," George said. "I'm sure the police are talking to Clarence Robbins. They know he's staying at the Nassau Inn."

"Could it have been an assistant professor, angry because he didn't get tenure?"

"Who knows? Maybe it was a really rabid Yale supporter." George was making fun of her, and she thought that was a good sign. The brandy was working.

"What about the provost?" asked McLeod.

"Ken Coales?" asked George, obviously astonished.

"Well, Melissa was going to fire him. Maybe he took drastic action to stop her."

"I don't think that's very realistic," said George. "Still . . ."

"Is he as bad as the Cowans say?" asked McLeod.

"I don't know how bad they say he is," said George.

"Please don't always be so discreet," begged McLeod.

"He's not Miss Congeniality. But murder? Come on. Anyway, the police will certainly talk to him."

"Will they talk to him as a possible suspect? Or just as a respected provost?"

"Surely they know their job," George said.

"And then there's Max Bolt," McLeod said. "You said he shouted at her."

"He was angry because she refused to let him film on campus during term time."

"Would that be enough to make him kill her?"

"I don't think so," said George.

"I know he had a bad temper. I heard him yell at Jim Macy at Mystique's party."

"He was hard to deal with. He was fighting the Borough of Princeton as well as the university. He wanted to shoot on University Place and Nassau Street. He wanted them to take up the paving and get back to the dirt surface that was there in 1913, but he gave up on that one in the face of the Borough's adamant refusal to consider it. Then he wanted to put dirt on top of the pavement and close University Place. But the Borough was being difficult. And they flatly refused to close Nassau Street at all."

"Max Bolt does have the artistic temperament, doesn't he?" said McLeod.

"To an extreme," said George. "But he doesn't look like a murderer."

McLeod was trying to decide if she should talk to Clarence Robbins again, as Sophy had asked. Or should she try to meet the awful Kenneth Coales? But before she could make up her mind which to do first, George put down his half-finished glass of brandy and distracted her completely.

Seven

THE NEXT MORNING McLeod slept a bit late. She woke to find that *The New York Times* had two stories about the murder of Melissa Faircloth, one of them a front-page news story that ran over into a huge obituary in Section B. The other was a "color" story about the incongruity of the murder of a university president at Princeton when the campus looked so beautiful with Japanese magnolias and daffodils in bloom. Neither was written by McLeod's friend Oliver Hunt.

MCLEOD HAD A student conference scheduled at eleven, and as she walked toward the campus, she thought about the murder and worried about Sophy. Who could possibly have a motive? As she neared the campus, she saw television news trucks parked on Nassau Street, along with some of the huge movie company trucks. I thought they were supposed to be gone by now, McLeod said to herself. Poor Jim Macy. How did Bolt manage to stay on?

At her office, she picked up her voice mail messages. Fletcher Prickett wanted her to call him, and the provost asked her to call him as soon as she came in.

What could the provost want? It had to be more important than Fletcher Prickett.

When she called the provost back, his secretary put her through immediately. "Ms. Dulaney, could you possibly come over here?" asked Kenneth Coales. "I have a great favor to ask you." His voice was smooth and gracious.

"Of course," said McLeod. "But I have a student conference at eleven."

"This won't take long," he said. "The trustees are meeting at eleven, so I, too, have to be free before then. I'd appreciate your making the effort—I only ask it because we're in such straits here right now."

"I understand. I'll be right there."

Well, she thought. I'll get to meet Kenneth Coales.

The provost's office was in Nassau Hall, not far from the president's suite. Coales's secretary leaped up from her desk and said, "The provost is waiting for you, Ms. Dulaney."

Coales came to the door of his private office to usher her in. "Thank you for coming," he said. "Sit down." He pulled a fat upholstered chair a little to one side, waved her into it, and sat down in a chair just like it. He was a tall, very good-looking man with a thin face, thin nose, and large clear eyes. He wore very Princetonian drill trousers, a tweed sport coat, and a dark tie, and he smiled at McLeod with what they both thought was great charm.

"First let me say how proud we are to have you teaching nonfiction writing at Princeton again this year. It's quite a coup to have you here."

"Good heavens," said McLeod. "I'm the one who's proud. I love teaching here. Who wouldn't?"

"Well, it's an honor to meet you at last." He pulled himself upright and smiled at her again. "I'm afraid I have the most tremendous favor to ask you, Ms. Dulaney."

"What is it?" she asked him. She had learned long ago not to agree to any favor without knowing what it was. "I'm ready to do almost anything for Princeton."

"Good. Good. Could you possibly move in to Lowrie House for a while? I know it's slightly farther from campus than your apartment, but the university will furnish you a driver if you like. You see, we think poor Sophy Robbins should stay there and not in the dormitory, but she can't stay alone. Her aunt from Texas will come for the funeral, but that can't be scheduled until the body is released by the police. Bruce and Martha Cowan have stayed there two nights, but they have two young children, and it's hard for them to be away from home. Sophy herself asked for you. I told her I'd talk to you." He looked at McLeod expectantly. "I hope you can do this—for Sophy and for us."

"Of course I can and I will," said McLeod. "Sophy is my student, and I'll be happy to stay with her for a while. I'm flattered that she—and you—asked me."

"Wonderful!" said Coales. "Do you need help moving in?"

"Not at all," said McLeod. "I'll just take some clothes and my laptop."

"You won't have any household duties, you understand. Mrs. Linley is the housekeeper and cook. And she has a staff. I hope you'll enjoy—well, maybe not enjoy, under the circumstances. But I hope you won't find it too onerous. And it will be a tremendous relief to all of us to have you there at this difficult time."

"I'm glad I can help," said McLeod.

"Good. I'll call Sophy and tell her you'll be there this afternoon. Is that all right?"

"Certainly," said McLeod.

They both stood up, shook hands, and parted.

After she met with her student, McLeod went off to swim laps at Dillon Gym, where the cream-tiled walls were trimmed with orange and black tiles and ornamented with the crest of each of the Ivy League schools. On the way to pick up a sandwich at the U-Store, she saw that crowds of movie people were working in the courtyard in front of Little Hall, the curious zig-zag-shaped dormitory where Fitzgerald had once lived. Fitzgerald referred to it as "the Gothic snake of Little," and architectural historians doted on its Flemish gables and Tudor chimney stacks.

Tents for the movie stars were set up in the courtyard, and cables wound across the grass. A crowd that included students and townspeople gawked from one side of the courtyard, and more students hung out the windows of Little to see as much as they could. McLeod caught her second glimpse of Billy Masters when he emerged from a tent and walked across the courtyard. When he looked up and saw the students watching from the windows, he gave them the finger. No smiles and tossing hair this time, she thought, as he disappeared into an entry of Little.

Off to one side stood Jim Macy, looking as unhappy as a man could look.

"What's the matter, Jim?" McLeod asked.

"They're not supposed to be filming anywhere," said Macy. "Bolt is supposed to be out of here. He was supposed to leave after spring break was over, and not come back until after Commencement when the students were gone. I told you it would be hard to get him off campus after one week. We're thinking of naming him *persona non grata* and having the campus police eject him and his crew. But everybody is so busy with the murder, nobody has time to fool around with a movie company."

"I hear he talked to the president when you wouldn't give him what he wanted."

"He did, but he couldn't get anywhere with Melissa Faircloth. She is, or was, even more opposed to movie companies on campus than we are. We know what a public relations bonus *A Beautiful Mind* and *IQ* were. We think it's worth some trouble to us, but not this much.

Melissa was all for refusing permission to film at all, even this summer. She thought they might interfere with all the meetings and conferences we have now in the summer."

That was very interesting, McLeod thought. The murder of the president had been a break for Max Bolt. McLeod thought what a diverting murder suspect Max Bolt would be. But he wouldn't have had a key to Nassau Hall, and she doubted that Melissa Faircloth would have let him into her office at night.

McLeod switched her attention back to Macy in time to wish him good day with reasonably good manners, but curiosity about moviemaking—and perhaps the chance of a better look at the divine Billy Masters—drove her over to the door through which the star had gone. A watchdog of a man held a hand up to her.

"I want to see Mr. Bolt," she said.

"Nobody can see Mr. Bolt. Besides, you probably want to see Billy Masters. All you ladies want to see Billy Masters."

"No," said McLeod, "I want to see Max Bolt." She dug out Bolt's card. "He gave me this and told me I could come see him anytime." This was a slight exaggeration; in fact, McLeod feared that lightning would strike her dead for telling such a whopper.

But it worked. The man waved her inside. McLeod carefully put Bolt's card, which she now realized was very valuable, in the zippered compartment of her purse. She found Bolt in his baseball cap and jeans, along with a horde of electricians, cameramen, makeup people, and other enablers in the sitting room of a student suite.

The modern furnishings—computers, CD players, television—had vanished, and the sofas and chairs were all from the pre–World War I era. Pictures on the wall hung from cords reaching from the top corners of the frames to a hook on a picture molding along the ceiling.

"Amory Blaine is talking with his friends about what eating club he'll join," Bolt was saying. "This is a serious and important question to Amory. It matters, matters a lot, whether he makes Cottage or has to go into Quadrangle, the literary eating club. So the lighting has to enhance the scene, heighten the seriousness of the crisis. Don't just light it flatly. This is drama, dammit." He turned around and started out the door, and saw McLeod.

"You again," he said. He smiled when he said it, but she thought it took an effort for him to produce that smile. He took her arm and led her to the entry and the stairway. "I'm glad to see you again. Any more insights about the movie?"

"Oh, yes, one thing I thought of while I was watching the setup outside in the courtyard. You know, those skylights in the roof of Little—they are very modern."

"I thought of that," said Bolt. "There's one wing of Little that doesn't have the skylights, so we use that when we need an exterior shot of the roof. You really shouldn't be here, you know. It would infuriate Masters."

"I understand," she said. "I want to talk to you sometime."

"I'm glad to talk to you. But I get to work at seven in the morning and I'm not through until midnight," Bolt said. "This is a busy time. I tell you what. Come for breakfast at my house in the morning. Six o'clock." He pulled out another card and scribbled on it. "This is the address. See you then, okay?"

"Okay," said McLeod meekly, and left. She went to Micawber to buy a copy of *The Warden* to take to read at Lowrie House. Having finished *The Way We Live Now,* she had decided to reread Trollope's Barchester novels and would of course start with the first one. She got a sandwich and a bottle of juice for lunch and took them home so she could get ready to move to Lowrie House.

Before she packed, she e-mailed George about her new lodging. He replied almost immediately that he knew about it, and he thought she was wonderful to do it. She was rather relieved when George said he had to work late and get to bed immediately after that. He was exhausted, he said, and he'd see her sometime soon, he didn't know when.

"Fine. I have to get to bed early myself," she e-mailed back. She hoped it would be all right to desert Lowrie House at five-thirty in the morning. She packed some clothes, two books, and at the last minute remembered her knitting. She had done precious little on Harry's sweater, mostly because George had taken up so much of her time so pleasantly. Maybe at Lowrie House she would make progress on it.

SOPHY GREETED HER happily when she finally got to Lowrie House that afternoon and took her upstairs to one of the guest rooms, which appeared palatial to McLeod, with its big four-poster bed, walk-in closet with dressing room, and bath. The walls were painted apricot and the fabric in the curtains and bed covers was a paler shade of peach. "I love it," she said.

"I know," said Sophy. "Mine is a lot like it. I invited some of my friends for dinner. I hope that's all right."

"Sure. That's good. They're students, right? Do they like to come to Lowrie House?"

"They like the food. It's better than the eating club. But it's kind of dull for them here, I guess, and I'm not very good company right now."

"At a time like this, friends don't expect you to be bubbling over," McLeod said.

"I guess not. Let's go downstairs. Would you like a cup of tea? Or a drink? Come meet Mrs. Linley and then you can tell her what you'd like. She's nice."

"Wait just a minute, let me get my knitting. I met Mrs. Linley on Monday when I came over the first time," McLeod said as she followed Sophy downstairs, where the smell of flowers was overpowering. The drawing room and sitting room were packed with arrangements of roses, peonies, tulips, anemones, even orchids. They went down the main hall to the kitchen, where Mrs. Linley sat at a desk in the corner. She wore another starched white uniform, matched by stiff, short gray hair, and a stiff face, until she saw Sophy and smiled.

"You remember McLeod, don't you?" Sophy said. "She teaches my writing class and she's going to stay here for a while."

"I heard," said Mrs. Linley. "Good to have you aboard. Sophy, I'm going to make some French fries for you and your friends for dinner. I'll have little steaks and asparagus and a green salad. Is that all right?"

"It sounds lovely, Mrs. Linley."

"Would you like some tea, Ms. Dulaney?" asked Mrs. Linley.

"Or a glass of wine?" said Sophy.

"Tea would be lovely. Do you like tea, Sophy?"

"It's all right, but I'm not crazy about it. I may have a soda."

Mrs. Linley said that Eileen would bring the drinks in. McLeod and Sophy went down the hall to the library, which was not as full of flowers as the other downstairs rooms. It was another splendid room, painted dark brown, with bookshelves on three walls. A young woman in jeans, apparently Eileen, appeared with a tray that held a teapot, cup and saucer, Sophy's Coke and a glass of ice, and a plate of small sandwiches.

"How are things going for you?" McLeod asked Sophy after they had tasted their drinks and tried a sandwich.

"It's hard," said Sophy. "It's not just that my mom died, but that she was murdered and stuffed in a closet. I can't seem to believe it. Now if it had been my dad, I wouldn't have been so shocked. Everybody has always said he would come to a bad end. But my mother was a model for so many people, so successful, so dignified. I just don't understand it."

McLeod agreed that it was unfathomable. Her heart ached for Sophy. How old was she—nineteen? twenty? And apparently all alone in the world, except for an aunt in Texas who couldn't be bothered to come to Princeton when her only sister died until the funeral was scheduled. What would happen to Sophy now? Of course, there was her father—but what good was he?

McLeod got out her knitting.

"What are you making?" asked Sophy.

"It's a sweater for my son, Harry. It's going very slowly, though."

They talked, and McLeod tried to think of comforting things to say, but felt sadly inadequate.

"And I don't know what the police are doing," Sophy said. "Do you know?"

"Haven't you talked to them?"

"Lieutenant Perry talked to me, but he wouldn't tell me much. He and some other policemen went through all my mom's things."

"Did you suggest people for them to talk to?" asked McLeod.

"I did. Lieutenant Perry wrote down their names—but he didn't seem very interested."

"That's just his way," said McLeod, with a confidence she did not really feel. "Sophy, are you lonesome here?"

"It's weird to be here without Mom, but lots of people come by. The policeman at the door checks with me on the intercom, and if I know them, he lets them in. Kenneth Coales came. And the Cowans just left this morning—they've been here since Sunday. Everybody in the Economics Department was here today, I think, and a lot of my mom's former graduate students. They adored Mom so I feel like I have to see them. And my friends from the university come, and old friends in town, too. I grew up in Princeton and went to high school here and so I know a lot of people. Everybody has been really nice. Some of them bring food and they send flowers. But none of the food is as good as that pound cake you brought. And you're right. Ice cream does slide down when nothing else does."

"You're great, Sophy," McLeod said, and meant it. Sophy was brave.

"But you know, I feel so up in the air. Martha Cowan said I'd have a sense of closure after the funeral. But I have no idea when the funeral will be. They have to release the body. We're going to have a small, private funeral, and the university is planning a humongous memorial service for later. I guess after they know who did it. I don't know. I'm afraid. You know, thinking about how there's a murderer out there."

"You have guards, you know, Sophy. I think you're very safe here."

"I guess so. But I know I'm getting behind in all my classes. But I can't possibly go to class right now." Sophy began to cry.

"Of course you can't. It will work out, Sophy. I know that sounds fatuous, but it will. It is hard, to have a death and not to have a funeral," said McLeod. "Martha Cowan's right about that. This dreadful time will pass, and you can have the funeral and they'll find the murderer. And life will go on. I'm not being heartless. It's just the way life is. You'll always remember this with anguish, but life does go on."

Sophy continued to sob, her head down on a pillow on the sofa. McLeod helplessly rubbed her shoulder. It was probably good for Sophy to weep, she thought.

The intercom buzzed, and Sophy sat up and reached for the phone. "Send them in," she said. "It's the kids from school," she said to McLeod. McLeod handed her a Kleenex and she wiped her eyes and stood up. "Onward and upward," she said.

"Attagirl," said McLeod.

She stood up, ready to greet the students. "Would you rather have them to yourself? I can eat in the kitchen, or take a tray upstairs."

"Of course not. It'll be great to have you here. You know one of them. He's in your class—Joel Rabinowski."

"Fine, but I am going to bed early, so I'll leave you right after dinner. I have a breakfast appointment at six o'clock in the morning. You'll be all right here for a while by yourself tomorrow morning?"

"I won't even be up," said Sophy.

McLeod had wine with her dinner and enjoyed the three visiting students, who seemed extraordinarily fond of Sophy. She fell into bed, exhausted. What a day.

Eight

WHEN MCLEOD'S ALARM rang at five o'clock the next morning, she shut it off, got up, took a shower in her luxurious bathroom, dressed, and went to Max Bolt's big house on Hibben Road. She was early, but Bolt answered her ring.

"You came," he said. "I wasn't sure you'd make it this early."

"Of course I came," said McLeod.

"Come in and have some breakfast," he said. He had obviously just showered and shaved—his long blond hair was clean and damp and he had not yet put on his baseball cap.

She followed him to the kitchen and sat down at the table when he waved at it. "I've made coffee," he said. "Here's some orange juice. Would you like cereal or toast? You don't want an egg, do you?"

"No, thanks. I'd just like some toast and juice and coffee." McLeod really preferred tea to coffee, but under the circumstances, she didn't want to ask for tea.

"Good," he said. "This is a good bread. I get it from the Witherspoon Bread Company. A man picks up some for me and some for Masters and some for Temple Jones every day." He hacked at a loaf of walnut raisin bread and put four fat slices into a toaster on the counter. While they toasted, he poured two big glasses of orange juice and gave one to McLeod.

"This is a very nice house," said McLeod, looking around the sunny blue and white tiled kitchen.

"It is," said Bolt. "I was lucky. I didn't want to stay at the Nassau Inn or the Hyatt Regency. Billy Masters got an apartment for himself and his bodyguard, and Temple and her husband and child have a house."

"You've settled in, haven't you?"

"Well, we'll either finish now or have to come back in June. So we all will just keep the real estate."

He buttered the toast, put two slices on each of two plates, poured the coffee, and sat down. "Have you any more helpful insights into Fitzgerald's Princeton experience?"

"I don't think so," said McLeod. "I want to know more about making movies."

"Everybody in Princeton wants to know more about making movies," Bolt said wearily. "We have to spend millions on guards to keep townspeople away. When we shoot on University Place or Nassau Street, I know it will be even worse than it is on the campus."

"Do you have much to film on University Place besides the rooming house where Fitzgerald and Amory Blaine lived their freshman year?"

"I want to film the scene from *This Side of Paradise* where the seniors march singing up University Place at night, led by the football captain."

"That will be great," said McLeod. "Is the Borough being more cooperative than the university?"

"Nobody is being cooperative," said Bolt. "Nobody.

The Borough is going to let us close University Place for a very short time. I told them we had to cover the paved surface with sand because it was just a dirt road in Fitzgerald's time. They said if I didn't remove all the sand, they would fine me. I said, 'Fine me? I'm paying you a top fee to use the street.' They said, 'Well, pay a fine, double the fee, however you want to put it.' "

"Nassau Street has changed a whole lot since Fitzgerald's time, hasn't it?"

"It sure has. We're not going to even try to do much there."

"But you're still working on campus," said McLeod. "I thought you had to leave when spring break was over." Bolt looked at her and said nothing. "How did you manage that?" asked McLeod.

"We just hung in there. Last week they were threatening us with all sorts of drastic consequences if we didn't get out. But Monday and yesterday, naturally, they were too busy with their own crisis. So we're just going to keep on and get as much done as we can."

"That's pretty gutsy of you," said McLeod.

"It takes guts to make a movie," said Bolt.

"I admire your nerve," said McLeod, who was not above a little flattery. "I guess this is a trivial question. How did you persuade students to let you tear up their room and turn it into a replica of a 1913 dormitory?"

"That was easy. We paid the four people in that suite. And told them that later they could be extras in the movie. They were happy to crash temporarily with friends."

"What happened to all the modern furnishings?"

"We stored them in a truck. The kids didn't want anything but some clothes and their laptops and their CDs."

"Students are great, aren't they?"

"Everybody's great, if you pay them enough money," said Bolt. "Except I have to say we're paying the university every day we're on campus, and it doesn't seem to make much difference."

"Was Melissa Faircloth the chief obstruction?"

"She certainly was. I thought Macy was just being stubborn on his own. But he wasn't. Melissa Faircloth hated movie makers on the campus."

"Did you talk to her more than once?"

"I did. Nothing seemed to move her. She said her only concern was Princeton and its students, but she was actually harming Princeton. This movie will be great for Princeton—publicity they couldn't buy."

"In some ways I don't think they seek publicity," said McLeod. "They already have ten applicants for every place in the freshman class." She drank some coffee. "So you are actually better off since Melissa Faircloth was murdered?"

Bolt stared at her. "You could say that, I suppose. But you needn't think I murdered the president of Princeton so I could get on with a movie."

"Did you think about it?"

"Of course I didn't."

"When did you last see Melissa Faircloth?"

"I don't know. A week ago. Or more. The papers say she was missing for over a week before they found her body. Before you found her body. I forget you're personally involved. Why are you asking me when I saw her? What are you, an aging Nancy Drew?"

"What a low blow," said McLeod. "I'm just curious. I believe in asking questions. It's my journalistic training."

"Well, don't ask too many questions. You're not writing anything about me, are you?"

"No, I'm not. I told you, I'm just curious. And also Melissa's daughter is in my writing class. In fact, I'm actually staying with her now at Lowrie House and she is very anxious to find out more about the murder."

"Listen, Sherlock, leave it to the police," said Bolt. "I've got to go. Can I give you a lift?"

"No, thanks, I drove. And thanks for the breakfast. And the talk. I know I ask a lot of questions, but I can't help it."

"Don't ask so many questions," he said. "It could be very dangerous."

"One last thing. I gather Billy Masters is difficult to work with."

"There are worse people to work with than Billy Masters. And he's a good actor. But he doesn't like strangers on the set, and you have to kind of watch him. He likes the ladies. And the ladies like him."

"He has a bodyguard?"

"That works two ways," said Bolt, and it was clear McLeod would get no more out of him.

BACK AT LOWRIE House by shortly after seven, McLeod found not only *The New York Times* and the Trenton *Times,* but *The Philadelphia Inquirer, The Washington Post,* and the *Daily Princetonian,* the student newspaper, on the chest of drawers in the hall.

She took them with her to the kitchen, intending to make herself a pot of tea. But Mrs. Linley was already there and insisted on making the tea for her. McLeod settled down at a corner of the dining room table to read the papers and drink her tea.

In the Trenton paper she read about the autopsy of Melissa Faircloth and learned, to her horror, that the medical examiner said that Melissa had probably been raped as well as murdered. Someone had "attempted sexual intercourse" shortly before death and there had obviously been a struggle. "Bruises and contusions" were found on her body and her clothes were "in disarray." In spite of her shock, McLeod could not help thinking that this meant the murderer was a man. Half the human race could be eliminated as suspects, though the field was still wide.

When she picked up the *Prince*, she read that a woman maintenance worker had reported being raped last night in the courtyard in front of Little Hall. She said her attacker was a white man, older than a student, in T-shirt and jeans, and he had jumped her while she was collecting trash. He had gagged her, yanked down her sweatpants and raped her quickly, then run off before anyone else appeared. She was furious, and there were angry quotes from executives of her union.

The *Prince,* a paper that McLeod regarded as quite enterprising, got reaction from all sorts of people, including the provost ("This kind of behavior is not acceptable on the Princeton campus"), the director of Public Safety ("It's an isolated incident"), and a spokesperson for the English Department ("Another example of the abuse of the male hegemony").

Two rapes, McLeod thought. The president and a nameless worker. Was there any connection?

She heard the intercom buzz, and Mrs. Linley came in to say, "George Bridges wants to see you."

"Oh, good," said McLeod. "Tell him to come in. Can I make him some coffee?"

"I have coffee ready," said Mrs. Linley reprovingly. "And I can offer him some breakfast."

McLeod went to let George in, kissed him, and led him back to the kitchen, where Mrs. Linley was pouring a cup of coffee for him and smiled at him brightly. "Would you like some pancakes, Mr. Bridges?" Mrs. Linley asked. "A waffle? Bacon, sausage, eggs?"

"Mrs. Linley, it all sounds wonderful. I'd adore some of your pancakes if you're sure it's not too much trouble."

"No trouble, Mr. Bridges," she said. "No trouble."

"I'm going to take my coffee into the dining room," he said. "I want to talk to McLeod a minute."

"Certainly. I'll bring your pancakes in no time, and Ms. Dulaney, I made a fresh pot of tea. I'll bring it now." She brought a tray into the dining room, whipped out another place mat, and laid it on the table. McLeod sat down at the end of the long table, and George sat next to her on the side.

"How do you like your new digs?" George asked.

"They're fine," said McLeod. "Couldn't be more deluxe. But I feel sorry for Sophy."

"It's too bad," George said. "But she's a strong woman,

like her mother. She'll pull through. And it's good she has you with her, McLeod."

"She's brave. Three friends of hers came over and had dinner with us last night, and that was good for her. I went to bed right after dinner. I think they watched television afterwards. There's a huge-screen TV in the family room. What did you do yesterday? What did the police do?"

"The trustees met yesterday, and they did not name an acting president. They decided it was simply too soon, that they had to wait until after the funeral. And the funeral can't be"—here McLeod joined him in a choral completion of the sentence—"until after the body is released."

"Who do you think they'll name?" McLeod asked him.

"I suppose they'll name Ken Coales. Melissa didn't leave a truck letter."

"What's a truck letter?"

"A letter saying who she thought should be named acting president if she got hit by a truck. Other presidents have always left a truck letter, but she's just been president nine months. I guess she never got around to it."

"If she had written a truck letter, she wouldn't have named Ken Coales, would she?"

"Definitely not, but since she didn't . . ." His voice trailed off.

Mrs. Linley appeared with two plates and a platter of pancakes. "I thought you might want one or two, Ms. Dulaney," she said.

"Do call me McLeod."

"And I'm Lily. Mr. Bridges, I'll have hot pancakes in the kitchen when you're ready for more."

"Thanks, Lily," said McLeod. George was too busy eating to speak. He had put butter and syrup on his pancakes in record time.

"Did you hear about the autopsy?" George asked after he had slowed down.

"About the sex? Maybe rape? It was in the Trenton *Times.*"

"That's right. People will say this means the murderer was somebody not connected with the university."

"Nobody at Princeton would rape anybody? Is that what you mean? Are you serious?" asked McLeod.

"Of course not."

"I can't joke about it," said McLeod. "The rape will make it so much harder for Sophy."

"You're right," said George. "Of course. But I was thinking about what the Old Tigers will say."

"George, who do the police suspect?"

"There aren't any suspects that I know of," said George. "They said they found four million fingerprints in Melissa's office. They're trying to talk to everybody who has a key to the offices, but then they remember that she could have let anybody in that back door, so I don't know. It's an open field, I guess."

"Didn't anybody see anything or hear anything?"

"Not that I know of," said George.

"I can't help thinking about it, and of course, Sophy longs to have it cleared up."

"The university would like to see it cleared up. The longer this goes on, the worse it will be for us. I'm going to get some more coffee." George stood up, but Mrs. Linley, who was psychic or had been listening, appeared with a silver coffeepot and poured him a fresh cup.

"More pancakes?" she asked him.

"No, thanks; those were great, but they were enough."

"Who does have keys to the president's office, George?" McLeod asked him.

"Not too many people, when you get down to it. Melissa had a set of keys to the outside and inside doors. And I do, too. I don't know who else does. Not many people have keys to Nassau Hall. The provost and the vice presidents do, but I don't think they have keys to the president's suite. Oh, the provost probably does. He has everything."

"What about the two other assistants in the president's office?"

"They have keys to the main door of the suite to use when the building's open. Several people in the office have those," George said.

"What do those assistants do?"

"One is chiefly a writer, and the other one is a kind of gofer for the president. They're both alumni, and they both left the office at five o'clock on that Monday and went home to their spouses. They both, I believe, have solid alibis."

"So, you and Ken Coales are the only ones who could get back in the office after Nassau Hall was locked? Could anybody have stayed after you and the two assistants left, and killed her later?"

"One of the secretaries, you mean? I don't think so."

"Who would Melissa have opened the door for?"

"That's the question. She might have opened the door for anybody. Probably not just anybody who knocked—but if they knew how to call her after five o'clock, anybody might have asked to come by and see her."

"Is there any way an unauthorized person could have gotten hold of a key?" asked McLeod.

"I can't think of any way. I really can't."

"Could that back door have been left unlocked?" asked McLeod.

"I don't think so," said George. "I've thought about it a million times and wished I had checked it before I left that Monday."

"Don't feel guilty!" McLeod said. "It locked automatically whenever it shut, didn't it?"

"It was supposed to," said George.

Sophy came in, dressed in jeans and a sweatshirt.

"Good morning!" she said. "You're back already, McLeod? Hello, George."

The intercom buzzed, and they waited while Mrs. Linley answered it in the kitchen. She poked her head around the door and said, "Sophy, your father is outside and wants to see you."

"All right," said Sophy.

"I've got to leave," said George. "I have to get to the office."

"And I'll leave you with your father," said McLeod. She got up.

"Oh, no, McLeod. You stay. I want you to talk to him. I really do. Please."

"Of course, Sophy, I'll do whatever you want," McLeod said. She sat down again.

"Sophy, would you like some breakfast?" asked Mrs. Linley. "I can do eggs and sausage. I have more pancake batter."

"Thanks, Mrs. Linley. I can't turn down your pancakes."

McLeod turned to say good-bye to George, but he was already out the door.

Nine

CLARENCE ROBBINS CAME into the dining room wearing his shabby trench coat, and held out his arms. "Baby!" he said to Sophy. "My baby."

"Hello, Daddy," said Sophy. She walked over and kissed her father on the cheek.

"And hello, Ms. Um-er. You're Sophy's writing teacher? Is that right?"

"Yes, I'm McLeod Dulaney. Nice to see you again, Mr. Robbins."

"Sophy, I know you need me now. After what happened to your mother. So I came over."

"Did you just find out about it, Daddy?"

Today was Wednesday, McLeod noted to herself. Melissa had been found Sunday night, and the murder was common knowledge by Monday morning. Robbins had taken his time.

"Nobody told me about it. I didn't know about it until I read it in the paper Monday morning," said Clarence.

"And then to tell you the truth, I was in shock. Shock for two days. But I came over this morning. I went to your dorm first, and they sent me here. Pyne, is it? Funny name."

"That's right, Daddy," said Sophy.

"Anyway I couldn't get in the dorm, but one of your buddies came out and he said you were here so I came over. I brought my stuff. I can stay. I thought you might need me."

"Well, McLeod is staying with me."

"I am your own father."

"I know you are, Daddy, and it was sweet of you to come over."

Mrs. Linley appeared with a plate of pancakes and sausage for Sophy, orange juice, a glass of milk, and a pot of coffee.

"Thanks, Mrs. Linley. It looks lovely," said Sophy. She began to eat. McLeod reflected that a lot of people had eaten breakfast with her that morning.

Clarence looked at the food hungrily. "Oh, Mrs. Linley, is it? I'll just have a few of those pancakes and maybe a sausage." He took off his trench coat, threw it over a chair, and sat down. He wore the same shabby clothes he had worn to lunch five days ago. They looked no cleaner.

"Yes, Mr. Robbins."

Lily Linley returned with a plate for Clarence and a cup and saucer. As soon as Sophy had finished her food, she got up. "I'll just leave you two to talk," she said.

"But I wanted to talk to you," said Clarence. He looked up at his daughter, his shoe polish eyes plaintive.

"I want you to talk to McLeod," said Sophy. "I have to go upstairs. I'll be back down in a little while." She left.

"Young people!" said Clarence. "Youth is wasted on young people."

"I think Sophy is pretty special."

"Oh, she is. But did you see how she treated me? Here I've come over to be with her and she didn't even act glad to see me."

McLeod sipped her fourteenth cup of tea of the morning and said, "I'm sure she's glad to see you. Girls always adore their fathers. Have you seen much of Sophy since the divorce?"

"Not at all, really. Almost never. Melissa wanted to cut me out of the picture. And I was always so busy with various projects, trying to earn my living in a very competitive world—and hard as I worked, I'm not sure I've ever found my niche."

McLeod, like all good interviewers (and interrogators), knew enough to keep quiet when someone like Clarence Robbins was talking. Chances were he'd just rattle on to fill the silences and she would learn more that way than by firing questions at him.

Sure enough, Robbins went on. "And I got tangled up in a couple of very bad marriages, although my true love has always been Melissa. The first was a girl from Springfield, my hometown. I ran into her in New York and first thing you know, she wanted to get married. She wasn't even pregnant. But I'm easy. We got married and went back to Springfield. It didn't last long, and she took up with another man, a real good-looking guy, an architect. They still live in Springfield. And then a few years later, I met this girl in San Antonio—I do seem to have a weakness for Texas gals—and we got married. We moved around, out to the West Coast, up to Seattle, and back to New Orleans. That marriage fell apart, too. I have had the worst luck with marriages and other relationships."

He paused to leer at McLeod when he said "other relationships," and then went on. "I should have hung on to Melissa, through thick or thin. She was a terrific woman. Terrific."

"Do you have any other children?"

"Two others," he said. "I don't see much of them either. I've had bad luck with my kids, as well as my marriages. Sophy has always been the special one."

"And you've seen more of her than the others?"

"What? I saw as much of her as I could, you see.

Melissa meant so much to me, I knew Sophy would be wonderful. But I guess I really haven't seen much of any of my children. Would you pass the coffeepot down here?"

"How old are your other children?"

"I'm not sure," said Clarence. "It's hard to keep up with their ages."

"They do change every year," said McLeod. "Ages, I mean."

"That's right," said Robbins, without a flicker of a smile. "They both live with their mothers. I guess the girl is twelve or fourteen and the boy six or eight."

"How long have you lived in Austin?" she asked him.

"About a year this time. I've been there before."

"And what kind of work is it you do?"

"This and that. I've had bad luck with jobs, too. I don't really like to work for the other fellow, so I'm always trying to make it on my own, some little business or other. Right now I'm selling Thunderbirds on the Internet."

"Internet businesses are fascinating," said McLeod. "They're pretty chancy, aren't they?"

"No more than any other business, it seems to me," said Clarence. "The trouble is, I don't have a computer right now, so I have to do most of my business in cybercafés. And do you know there's not a cybercafé in Princeton? So I guess it's all going to rack and ruin."

"There used to be a cybercafé here," said McLeod. "I remember."

"Well, it's gone. Once I went to the public library but that was very unsatisfactory. I had to stand up to use the computer."

Robbins drank coffee and looked around the dining room.

"Have you talked to the police?" McLeod asked him.

"Have I talked to the police?" said Clarence. "Have I ever! They came to see me on Monday and I went down to Borough Hall yesterday. I never answered so many questions in my life."

"I'm sure you were a help," said McLeod.

"I guess I was, in my way," said Clarence modestly, wiping his mouth. "I'll just get my things. I left them outside with the guard."

"Mr. Robbins, I'm not sure it would be appropriate for you to move into Lowrie House," McLeod said.

"What do you mean 'appropriate'? Wouldn't it be appropriate for a father to be with his daughter in a time of grief?"

"As I said, I'm not sure," said McLeod. "You see, the university asked me to come and stay here with Sophy. I know they think she should be here, but whether they think Melissa's ex-husband should be here or not, I don't know. Actually, I guess it's up to Sophy."

"I'm positive Sophy wants me here," Clarence said. "I'll just get my things."

Mrs. Linley appeared with a man from the florist, bearing new arrangements of flowers, which he carried around while Mrs. Linley looked for places to put them.

McLeod hurried upstairs and knocked on Sophy's door.

"Come in," said Sophy. She was lying on a chaise lounge, not reading, just lying there. Sun streamed in the east windows.

"This is a beautiful room," said McLeod. It was larger than her room, and decorated in a bluish green.

"I think so, too. It's just the way it was when Mother moved in. I haven't changed anything. Did you talk to my father?"

"We talked a little. Sophy, he's gone to get his things. Is it all right with you if he stays here?"

"I guess so," Sophy said. "He *is* my father."

"Are you close to him?" asked McLeod. "Forgive me for asking, but I don't quite understand him."

"I don't understand him at all. I don't know him at all. But I have to say I've always wanted to know him. When I was younger, I used to daydream about him. I would fantasize that he would come to rescue me from John Witherspoon Middle School and then Princeton High. I know he drove Mom crazy. But I never saw him. If he came to see

Mom, which he did every now and then when she was teaching, she'd send him away. She never let me go off alone with him, never let him into the house, really."

"Did he want to see you?"

"I used to imagine that he did," said Sophy. "But now I doubt it. And he is kind of weird, isn't he?"

"But you don't mind if he stays here?"

"I mind, but I mind everything that's happening right now. What's one more thing? And as I say, he *is* my father."

"Okay. It's up to you, I'd say. I guess Mrs. Linley will take care of him."

"I'll go back down. I did want you to talk to him. Did you learn anything from him?"

"Learn about what?" McLeod temporized. What she had learned was that Clarence Robbins was an extremely self-centered man who did not seem to know the ages or even the names of his other two children and had not managed to see anything at all of Sophy, although he claimed to regard her as "special." He had also repeated his statement that he was still in love with her mother. She did not want to tell Sophy any of this, however.

"Do you think he knows anything about what happened to my mother?"

"I have no idea, Sophy. But the police questioned him extensively—Monday and yesterday. So if he knows anything, I imagine the police know it, too. Do *you* think he knows anything?"

Sophy said nothing. She got up and said, "Well, let's go get him." McLeod trailed her down the big stairway and saw that Clarence Robbins was looking around the drawing room. "Come on, Daddy, I'll show you your room."

Clarence smiled and followed his daughter up the stairs. McLeod could hear him at the door to his room say, "Well, well. Pretty nice . . ." and his voice trailed off.

In the dining room, Eileen was clearing the table. McLeod went into the kitchen. "Sophy's father has moved in. Sophy put him in one of the guest rooms," she told Mrs. Linley.

"Well," said Mrs. Linley. "And Ms. Faircloth's sister is coming, isn't she? We'll soon have a full house."

"That's the way it is when somebody dies," McLeod said.

"I know. I'm not complaining. I don't know Mr. Robbins, but I guess he'll be a help to Sophy."

"Maybe so," said McLeod, who rather doubted it. But as Sophy kept saying, he *was* her father.

Clarence and Sophy came into the kitchen, Clarence looking for more coffee. Mrs. Linley said that Eileen would bring it into the library, if that was all right.

"That's fine. I love it," said Clarence. "This is a wonderful way to live, Sophy."

"Come with us, McLeod," said Sophy.

McLeod trailed them. As soon as they were sitting down, Clarence asked his daughter if there was a computer in the house that he could use. "I need to check on my business," he said.

"Sure," she said. "There's a laptop you can use. I'll get it. Where do you want it?"

At that point, Mrs. Linley came in to say that George Bridges wanted to talk to McLeod on the telephone.

"Thanks, I'll come in the kitchen."

"I just called to tell you the police are going to release Melissa's body," George said. "So the provost wants to talk to Sophy about the funeral."

"I want to ask you something first," McLeod said, and told him about Clarence Robbins.

"I don't know what Ken Coales will think, but it seems to be a *fait accompli.* And you're right; it's up to Sophy."

"Thanks." They said goodbye and hung up.

When the phone rang again, it was Ken Coales. "I want to talk to Sophy—and to you. I think George told you the police have released the body and we can now plan the funeral. Is it all right if I come now? Will you ask her?"

"Of course it's all right," Sophy said when McLeod

asked her. "Oh, that's good that they've released the body, isn't it? That means we can have the funeral."

They waited in the library until Kenneth Coales arrived, announced on the intercom as usual by the guard, and met at the door by McLeod, who led him to join the others.

Coales looked at Clarence inquiringly. McLeod waited in vain for Sophy to introduce them, then did it herself. Robbins got up and shook hands with Coales and began to act like a host. "Sit down, Mr. Coales, is it?"

"Yes, Kenneth Coales." He decided to ignore Robbins and spoke to Sophy. "Did Ms. Dulaney tell you that the police have released your mother's body? So we can plan the funeral now. I believe you had already decided it would be small and private. Is that right?"

"Small and private for the president of an Ivy League university? What kind of claptrap is that?" asked Clarence Robbins.

"It's all right, Daddy. This will be just for family and close friends. It will be fine."

"And we will have a much larger memorial service after things have settled down," said Coales.

"After the murder is solved," said Sophy. "It's what we want to do."

Robbins did not look happy. "It just seems like a bum's rush, and for such a fine woman," he said. McLeod wondered if he wanted to play a starring role at a huge service.

Coales stared at him silently, the whites of his eyes looking enormous. He could quell anyone with that look, thought McLeod. "Do you think Saturday will be all right?" Coales asked Sophy. "Can your aunt get here by then? Is there any other family that we need to consult?"

"The cousins. I'll call them. Or Martha will. I'll call my aunt right now." She picked up an address book on the desk, looked up a name, punched in a telephone number, and began to talk. While Sophy was on the phone, McLeod looked at Coales's handsome angular face. She had been so bemused by him yesterday in his office that she had forgotten that he was a potential suspect. Could Kenneth

Coales be the murderer? He had keys to the building. Everybody seemed to know that Melissa Faircloth had planned to fire him, and he did not want to lose his job. Would he kill to keep his job?

"Aunt Claudia said they could be here by Saturday," Sophy said when she had hung up. "They'll come Friday. She'll call back and let us know their flight number and arrival time. She offered to call the cousins for me and I was very grateful."

"Now I know we decided earlier that the service would be in the choir of the chapel, didn't we?" asked Coales. "You're sure you don't want it in a secular setting? The Faculty Room, perhaps?"

"No, I know Mom told that interviewer she was an atheist, but that was just a reaction to her strict upbringing. She sent me to Sunday school. She said all children should have some religious education, so if they rejected it, they'd at least know what they were rejecting. I know she would want a decent funeral, with good music. She loved the chapel."

Coales agreed, and made the call to the Dean of Religious Life immediately. Glancing at Sophy for concurrence, he set the funeral for eleven on Saturday morning. After Coales hung up, he and Sophy continued to discuss details of the service, and Coales made notes. The dean would preside over the brief service, and eulogies would be saved for the memorial service to be held later.

When Coales had left, promising to handle all the details of the service, Mrs. Linley came in to tell them that lunch would be ready in an hour. Would it be just the three of them? They looked at each other and Sophy said that she thought that was all.

"Baby doll, can your daddy get a drink in this spacious house?" asked Clarence.

Mrs. Linley heard him and turned back. "Of course you can, Mr. Robbins. What would you like?"

Both Sophy and McLeod frowned at her, but Mrs. Linley repeated her question.

"I'll have a martini," said Clarence. "If it's not too much trouble."

"Not at all."

Sophy excused herself, saying she would be upstairs.

When his martini arrived, Clarence took a big gulp and said that this was a mighty fine kind of life to lead. "It is a great life," he repeated, and then asked McLeod how long she had been staying there.

"I just came yesterday," said McLeod.

"Pretty nice for you, I'd say."

"Very nice," said McLeod.

"Tell me, McLeod, what do you know about Melissa's will?" Robbins said.

"Me? I don't know anything about her will. Nothing."

"Well, since you seem to be such a close family friend, I thought you might know."

Did this awful man think Melissa Faircloth might have left him some money?

"I would think she left anything she had to Sophy, wouldn't you?" she said.

"I'm sure she had quite a stash. She was an economist and she knew how to invest. She was always tight with a dollar. Never seemed willing to help me out when I needed it, I'll tell you. So I expect there's quite a tidy sum. And if she left it to Sophy, Sophy needs a guardian, or trustee, doesn't she?"

"I think you should talk to Melissa's lawyer," said McLeod.

"And who might that be?" asked Clarence.

"I have no idea," said McLeod.

"NOW, BABY DOLL, how old are you exactly? I forget," Clarence said to Sophy when they were eating clam chowder at lunch. Mrs. Linley had asked him if he wanted wine with lunch and brought in a bottle of white. He was drinking it up as fast as he could.

"I'm twenty. I'll be twenty-one next month."

"Oh," said Clarence, "so you don't need a guardian much longer."

"I don't need a guardian at all. I'm over eighteen."

"What are you going to do with yourself? Who are you going to live with?"

"I don't know," said Sophy. "I've got a lot of thinking to do."

"I can take over some of that thinking for you, you know."

"Thanks."

"I could move to Princeton, get a little house. Better yet, what happened to Melissa's house? She didn't sell it, did she?"

"No, she rented it furnished to a visiting professor, who's here for the year."

"We could live there, you and me."

"Daddy, I'm a junior in college. I live in the dormitory."

Clarence finished his soup, and poured himself another glass of wine.

Eileen removed the soup dishes and brought in plates of ham salad. Clarence smiled a satisfied smile. "This is the life," he said. "Tell you what, baby doll, you can spend the summer with me in Austin. That would be great. I could get a little house—"

"I'm going to spend the summer on a dig," said Sophy.

"A what?"

"An archaeological dig, an excavation on Cyprus."

"That's very exciting, baby doll. I can't believe you're such a big girl. You've grown up so fast. I can't believe it."

"You better believe it," said Sophy.

Mrs. Linley came in to tell Sophy that the guard had buzzed and said Martha Cowan was outside. "Oh, good," said Sophy. Martha bustled in, kissed Sophy on the cheek, and sat down at the table with them. She seemed surprised to see Clarence Robbins, and introduced herself.

"Oh, yes, good to see you again," Clarence said.

Clarence was the only one who wanted dessert, and McLeod, who had decided that she had to get out of

Lowrie House for a while or go mad, asked to be excused. "I think I'd better go check in at my office," she said. "I do have to teach a class tomorrow. You'll be here, won't you, Martha?" McLeod indicated Clarence with a turn of her head and a rolling of her eyes.

"Yes, I'll be here," Martha said, nodding as though she got the message.

McLeod went upstairs for her book bag, got her coat out of the closet downstairs, and set off to walk to the campus. It was a real relief, she thought, to be out of Lowrie House.

Ten

WHEN MCLEOD REACHED the campus, the movie trucks and trailers reminded her that Max Bolt was still taking advantage of everyone's concern with the death of the president.

In her office, McLeod picked up her voice mail messages—there was another one from Fletcher Prickett—and answered her e-mails. She had forgotten she had scheduled a conference with Joel Rabinowski for Wednesday afternoon, and heaved a sigh of relief that she had come into the office. She called some of the people who had left phone messages, Fletcher Prickett among them.

"I'm sorry I couldn't call sooner, but I've been very busy," she said and told him about staying at Lowrie House.

"That's very nice of you, my dear, to help that poor child," said Prickett. "I wonder if I could take you to lunch at the Nassau Club tomorrow?"

"Can we do it next week?" asked McLeod. "My class

meets tomorrow at one-thirty, so that makes it hard. And Sophy Robbins might need me."

"Certainly, my dear. How about Monday? I believe in doing pleasant things as soon as possible."

"I think Monday will be fine. I'll call you if something comes up, may I?"

"Certainly, my dear."

Why on earth did Fletcher Prickett want to have lunch with her? McLeod wondered.

When Joel came in, he asked about Sophy. "She's doing fine, I think," said McLeod.

"I'll try to get over this afternoon or tonight," Joel said.

They talked about the assignment the class was currently working on—to interview someone from a different ethnic group about a problem the person had. "I talked to this Guatemalan woman, but her English was so poor, I had to go back with an interpreter, a friend of mine who's majoring in Spanish," Joel said.

"How did you find her in the first place?" asked McLeod.

"I see these short brown women on the streets and I have always wondered about them. Another friend of mine volunteers for this group that works with Guatemalans in Princeton and he took me to meet her. His Spanish wasn't good enough to interpret, so I went back to see her. It's harder to interview people through an interpreter."

"You know, I've never done it," said McLeod. "You see, the teacher learns from the students . . ."

The conference proceeded, with Joel confirming McLeod's conviction that Princeton students were the brightest and most enterprising young people on earth.

AFTER JOEL HAD left, she made a few notes for her class the next day. John Mackintosh, an old friend of hers who used to work in Tallahassee and was now with *Newsweek*, was coming out to talk to the students. That made preparation easier.

Then McLeod called George Bridges, who sounded glad to hear from her. "When can I see you? I'm not sure I like this duenna role you're playing," he said.

"It's not for long," she said. "The funeral is Saturday, and I'm sure Sophy will want to go back to the dormitory as soon as she can. I know she's worried about missing more classes than she has to. Tell me something. When did Clarence Robbins see Melissa Faircloth?"

"I'll have to check back," said George. After a minute, he was back on the line. "It was last Monday."

"The last day Melissa was in the office? Melissa disappeared after she saw him."

"Well, not right after she saw him. Melissa worked him in for a few minutes that morning."

"Did they have an argument?"

"Not that I know of," said George. "He wasn't in there long. She may have been a little upset after he left, but she had iron control."

"Thanks. George, come to dinner tonight at Lowrie House. I'm sure it will be all right. I'll tell Sophy and Mrs. Linley and let you know if by chance it's not."

"Fine," said George. "See you about six. We're getting organized around here and I can get away by then."

GEORGE ARRIVED AT Lowrie House promptly at six. McLeod took him to the kitchen, where they picked up drinks, and led the way to the library. "Dinner's at seven," Mrs. Linley told them.

"This is a nice life, isn't it?" said George, looking around the room.

It was the same thing that Clarence Robbins had said, but the way George said it, it didn't sound as revolting. "Princeton presidents live well," she said.

"Where's Sophy?" asked George.

"She came back from a long run with a friend of hers and went upstairs to take a shower. She's not down yet," said McLeod. "And Clarence is still upstairs, napping,

Mrs. Linley said when I got back from the university. He'll be down for dinner, since he's always ready for a meal—and a drink. Or else he's working on the computer Sophy took him. You know, he sells Thunderbirds on the Internet, but he hasn't had a computer in some time and there's no cybercafé here. So he has neglected his business."

"Some business! At least I'll get to talk to you alone for a while. Do you know that I'm a murder suspect?"

"What?"

"I am. Your friend Nick Perry has been grilling me. You see, I have a key to the offices and no alibi."

"But you went to the dentist."

"I left the office for the dentist at six. He took me that late as a special accommodation. I was finished there about seven-thirty. The police say Melissa was murdered sometime between six o'clock Monday night when I left the office and the time I got back there on Tuesday morning."

"And you were at home alone after you got back from the dentist?"

"Where else would I be after a root canal?"

"Do they think you went back and killed Melissa Faircloth? You liked her. Everybody knows you liked her."

Eileen appeared with a plate of miniature quiches—a specialty of Mrs. Linley's for cocktail parties—and they each took one and munched on it until Eileen was out of hearing.

"Everyone doesn't know I liked her. They know I *said* I liked her. That's what Perry said."

"Good heavens!" said McLeod.

"But there's more. Somebody told the police that they called me at home that night and there was no answer."

"Who was it?"

"Perry said he was not at liberty to disclose that information, but he said it was a reliable witness," said George.

"Did you let the phone ring? Or disconnect it?"

"It didn't ring, McLeod."

"What does Perry think your motive was?"

"He says means and opportunity are important. He says they'll find a motive if there is one."

"This is terrible!"

"It is indeed terrible. And it's scary. I keep thinking of all those innocent men on Death Row. I could be railroaded."

"They're saved, some of them, by DNA. Melissa was raped. Can't they test your DNA?" asked McLeod.

"Oh, they took a sample all right, but it takes forever to get the results. Four or five weeks. They have to send it to the State Police laboratory in West Trenton. Meanwhile, I guess I'm under suspicion."

"I should think they could do it more quickly than that," said McLeod.

"They did say something about asking them to 'expedite' it."

"This is the most ridiculous thing I ever heard. I know who the murderer is and it's not you. I'm going to call Nick Perry."

"Who is it?" asked George.

"Clarence Robbins," said McLeod.

"Why do you say it's Robbins?"

"He's got every motive in the world. Unrequited love, for one thing. He says over and over that Melissa Faircloth was his true love, the only woman he ever loved. But she would not have one thing to do with him, would scarcely see him. Two, he's jealous of her achievement. He's a no-good bum, who has no job, and his ex-wife, who threw him out, is a superachiever, a world-class economist, and the first woman president of an Ivy League college. And for a third motive, there's money. He thinks Melissa left her money to Sophy and he can be the trustee and handle the money."

"That's quite a lot of motive," said George.

"Right," said McLeod. "Any one of them would be more motive than you have."

"How do you know all this?"

"He told me," said McLeod. "He told me most of it

today, but some of it last Friday when we had lunch. He was even asking me who Melissa's lawyer was. He wants to talk to him and find out what Melissa did with her money."

"Cowboy Tarleton is her lawyer," said George.

"Well, I told him to ask Sophy," said McLeod. "And you know, you said Clarence saw Melissa Faircloth that Monday, the last day she was in the office."

"Would he have come back that night?" asked George. "He didn't have a key to the office. I'm the suspect with the key, remember. How could he get in?"

"He could have knocked on the door to the private office."

"I don't think she would have let him in," said George. "And all she had to do was call the campus police to get rid of him. They would have been there in seconds."

"But I don't think she called for help. Everybody says she faced up to challenges. Anyway, I'm going to call Nick Perry and talk to him. This is ridiculous."

Clarence Robbins appeared in the room. "Drinkies time?" he asked. "How are you, George? And Ms. Uhmm?" He gave McLeod a long stare with his shoe polish eyes, making her shiver. But he looked cleaner and his long wavy hair shone. "Why didn't you call me for a drinky poo?" he went on. "How do you get hold of Mrs. Thingamagummy? Is there a bell to ring?" He took one of the quiches off the plate. "I love this life. I could get used to it."

"I'll get a drink for you," said McLeod. "What would you like?"

Clarence asked for a scotch on the rocks, and as McLeod left, she heard him asking George if he knew who Melissa's lawyer was.

DINNER WAS MADE bearable by George and the Cowan family, children and all. Mrs. Linley had outdone herself in her efforts to please the children: fried chicken and mashed potatoes for them, *coq au vin* for the grown-ups. The Cowans in general and the ebullient children in particular drowned out Clarence's incessant talk about his Internet business. After dinner and coffee in the drawing room, McLeod walked with George to his car.

"I'm going to call Nick Perry tonight," she told him. "I want to tell him about Clarence."

"I hope it takes his mind off me," said George. He left her with only a quick, preoccupied kiss.

The downstairs was empty when she came back in the house, but she heard voices upstairs. She started climbing the steps—they seemed steeper than before—and had just reached the second floor when she remembered her book bag was downstairs. She wanted to read *The Warden* before she went to sleep. She turned to head back down, and paused. Should she call Nick Perry before she went down? No, she decided, she'd go get her book bag. She might be put on hold, and it would be nice to have *The Warden* handy. She had just put her foot on the first tread when she tumbled down the stairs with terrible momentum, stopped as she sprawled on the landing halfway down, then slid to the bottom of the stairs and the bottom of a pit.

Eleven

WHEN MCLEOD CAME back to consciousness, a uniformed paramedic from the Rescue Squad was wiping her forehead. She saw the cloth he was using and it was very bloody.

"We're just going to put you on this stretcher and get you to the ambulance and then to the emergency room," he said.

McLeod saw Sophy and the Cowans. "George?" she asked.

"He's gone. Remember? He left. But we just called him," Martha Cowan said. "He'll meet us at the ER."

WHEN GEORGE CAME into the emergency room cubicle where they had put her, Sophy said, "I'll leave you with George. Martha is in the waiting room and I'll go sit with her until we know how you are."

"Somebody pushed me," McLeod said to George. "I felt it, a thud on my back."

"Don't worry about it right now," said George.

"It was Clarence, don't you think?"

George shook his head, puzzled.

Nurses buzzed in and out. An ER doctor came in and examined her for injuries. "Your right knee is banged up, but we'll x-ray it. I think it will be okay. You will have some colorful bruises." He sewed up the gash on her forehead. After a CT scan showed no internal damage to her head, the doctor said she could go home. "You won't be alone, will you?"

"No, I won't be alone," she said. She didn't tell him that she would be in the house with a man she was sure was a murderer. She got dressed and found it hard to walk—her knee hurt.

WHEN GEORGE TOOK McLeod back to Lowrie House, it was almost midnight. "It's late and I'm tired," McLeod said.

"I'll bet you're tired. You need to rest. I'll help you get upstairs."

Sophy, who was lying on the sofa in the drawing room, got up when they came in. "We're waiting for you. I'm so glad to see you. Are you all right?"

Martha Cowan, who had been sitting in a big chair, got up, too. "Yes, are you all right?" she said.

McLeod limped in. "My knee hurts, and my head hurts, but I'm fine, thank heavens. I have a class tomorrow."

Everybody deplored the idea that McLeod would even think of trying to teach, but McLeod, who knew how unusual it was for a teacher to cancel a class at Princeton, insisted that she would go to class. "John Mackintosh from *Newsweek* is coming, so I won't have to do much. Where's Mr. Robbins?"

"He went to bed," said Sophy. "I'm sure he's asleep."

Sophy and George insisted on going upstairs with her.

She thanked them, and once upstairs sent them away, undressed, and got into a hot bath. It helped.

THE NEXT MORNING, Thursday, her knee seemed no worse, but no better. She got dressed and started downstairs, but before she put her foot on the first step, she looked around to make sure there was nobody behind her. She went down, moving carefully and putting both feet on each tread because her knee hurt. She held tightly to the bannister and glanced behind her at least twice. She got the papers from the front hall and sat down at the dining table, finding it wonderfully luxurious to order her breakfast from the magically appearing Mrs. Linley.

"Orange juice, toast, and tea," she said.

"You look peaked," said Mrs. Linley.

"I guess I am." And she told her about her fall.

"I would have sent Eileen up with a tray, or brought it myself," said Mrs. Linley. "I think you need more for breakfast than just toast. Wouldn't you like a nice egg and some bacon? Oatmeal? Pancakes? A waffle?"

McLeod said a waffle and bacon would be lovely, and opened the papers. There was nothing new about the murders in the papers. The Trenton *Times* interviewed Nick Perry at length about the fitness of the Borough Police to carry on the investigation. "The prosecutor's office has offered help if we need it, but so far we're doing everything that could be done," Perry said.

No, they had not found the murder weapon. No, they had no suspects in custody. They were proceeding carefully, interviewing a great many people, and would keep up the good work.

The *Daily Princetonian* was also restive about progress on the murder case, but even more disturbed that there had been an attempted rape on campus the night before, the second "incident" of that nature in two days. An editorial demanded that police, while continuing at full speed to investigate the murder, should not fail through neglect to apprehend what was apparently a serial rapist.

The attempted rape had taken place in Prospect Garden, according to the victim, who was on her way from the E-Quad to her room in Brown Hall. She said she had been attacked from behind and thrown to the ground, but she was a member of the field hockey team and had fiercely defended herself and escaped, leaving her attacker writhing in a flower bed full of tulips.

McLeod was digesting the day's news and drinking tea when George arrived to check on her. Mrs. Linley happily volunteered to make him pancakes and sausage, and George assured her he had hoped she would do just that and had, in fact, not bothered to eat at home because he knew she would be such a good provider.

"If you insist on going to your class today, I'm going to arrange for you to park on campus for a while," George told McLeod. "You can pick up a permit at the main kiosk by Stanhope Hall. I don't want you hobbling around with a rapist at large."

"I must say I never would have thought of that myself," McLeod said. "I have always assumed any part of the campus was safe any time of day."

"Obviously, it's not," said George, more gruffly than she would have expected.

"Why are you so cross?" asked McLeod. "It's not like you, Mr. Congeniality."

"Would you be congenial if you thought the police were going to arrest you for the murder of your boss?"

"I see what you mean, and I still haven't called Nick Perry." She got up and limped to the kitchen to use the phone in there. At police headquarters, they said Lieutenant Perry had not come in yet but they took her name and the Lowrie House number.

After he had eaten a vast quantity of pancakes and sausage, George left for the office, rubbing his stomach. "The condemned man ate a hearty breakfast," he said.

"Don't worry, you'll beat the rap," said McLeod. "Forgive me for not seeing you out. I'll just sit here and drink tea."

McLeod wanted to go upstairs to avoid Clarence Robbins, but she also wanted to be available for Sophy. Finally, she went back to the kitchen and told Mrs. Linley she was going upstairs but she was expecting a phone call.

"Oh, that policeman you called? I'll put it through to the extension in your bedroom, if he calls back."

"Thanks, and tell Sophy if she wants me, I'm there. I think I'll just lie low until it's time for me to go meet the man who's going to talk to my class this afternoon."

"I understand," said Mrs. Linley. "I won't say anything to Mr. Robbins."

"You're very perspicacious," McLeod said. "Thanks." She limped to the stairs and climbed them slowly. She noticed a bolt on her door which she had not seen before and fastened it securely. She lay down and was sound asleep when the phone woke her. It was Nick Perry.

"You wanted to talk to me," he said. McLeod realized that Nick Perry had no time to waste on the amenities. She plunged in.

"You're barking up the wrong tree with George Bridges," she said.

"What am I supposed to be doing with George Bridges?"

"He says you suspect him of the murder of Melissa Faircloth," McLeod said.

"The guilty fleeth where no man pursueth," said Perry.

"He doesn't fleeth. He feels you've unjustly—well, not accused him, but suspected him. Let me tell you that George is the soul of integrity," said McLeod. "I'm sure of it. And he's incapable of murder, I'd say."

"How long have you known him?" asked Perry.

"Two months," said McLeod, after adding the weeks.

"Just two months?" said Perry.

"Well, you can get to know a person awfully well in two months. And besides, I know who the real murderer is. I'm pretty sure I do."

Perry said nothing. Perry knew as much about questioning people as she did, McLeod thought. If you don't say anything, people will keep on talking. So she talked. "It's Clarence Robbins," she said. Perry was still silent, so she went on.

"He has three motives. One is unrequited love. He swears he's never loved anybody but Melissa, that she was his one true passion. Two, is jealousy. He is really jealous of her accomplishment—he's a bum who can't hold a job or earn a living really, and his ex-wife was a superachiever. He resented it. And three, he needs money, desperately. And while Melissa probably didn't leave him any money, she surely left Sophy everything she had, and he thinks he can get his hands on it because he thinks he'll be responsible for Sophy now."

Again, Perry was quiet. So was McLeod. I can do this as well as he can, she thought.

Perry spoke first. "How do you know all this?"

"He's told me himself. Told me most of it yesterday. You know, he has pretty much moved into Lowrie House, where I'm staying now. But he told me some of it last Friday when we had lunch. When he gets a drink in him, he starts talking about himself and tells everything. He's a big bore, and totally selfish besides."

"We talked to Clarence Robbins, and what he said was not as revealing, shall we say, as what he said to you," said Perry.

"People always tell me things," said McLeod. "I think it's because of my white hair."

"Do they think you're motherly?"

"I guess so, although I'd hate to be Clarence Robbins's mother. I think he tried to kill me last night."

"What?" Perry didn't try to outwait her this time.

"Somebody pushed me down the stairs and I hit my head and my knee and the Rescue Squad took me to the emergency room. I'm sure it was Clarence Robbins. Who else could it be? I think he did it because he heard me tell

George I was going to call you and tell you all this. He did it before I could call you last night."

Perry was silent again, but not for long. "If you want to file charges because you think he pushed you down the stairs . . ."

"I don't think I want to do that," said McLeod. "Aren't you interested in what I'm telling you?"

"I'm always interested in what you tell me," said Perry. "You've always been very helpful. And I will take what you said very seriously. We have to weigh what you've told me with everything else we've learned."

"What have you learned?" McLeod asked quickly.

"This and that," said Perry.

"Did you find the weapon?"

"You know I can't talk to you about an ongoing investigation," said Perry. "Let me warn you about one thing." McLeod felt a surge of hope—he was going to warn her to be careful of Clarence Robbins and that meant he believed her. But no, that wasn't it, for Perry went on: "Don't take any action on your own. If something needs to be done, we'll do it. And keep in touch. Thanks very much for calling."

He was gone.

MCLEOD GOT READY to meet John Mackintosh and limped to the top of the stairs, where again she looked around her carefully before she hobbled downstairs. Sophy was sitting at the dining table, where everybody seemed to gather to wait for the next event.

"I wish you could come with me, Sophy," she said. "I'm off to meet John Mackintosh from *Newsweek* and take him to Prospect for lunch and then he's going to speak to the class. You'd like him."

"I'm sure I would," said Sophy. "Why don't you bring him here for lunch instead of Prospect? At least, that way I'll get to meet him. I'll tell Mrs. Linley."

"That's a great idea," said McLeod, and left.

Lunch was fine. Mrs. Linley produced lamb chops and couscous without raising an eyebrow. Clarence, who didn't drink as much as usual, fixed his gaze on John and explained exactly what was wrong with the American news media.

"That's a brilliant analysis," said John. "The only thing is you don't have the least idea what you're talking about." He smiled, but the smile did not entirely cancel the sting of his remark. "But then neither do I half the time, so that's all right."

McLeod took John off to class and asked him, once they were in the car, what he thought of Clarence. "He's all right. He's the ex-husband of the murdered president? And the father of that nice daughter? He looks familiar to me somehow."

McLeod got her new parking decal from the kiosk, and they drove around to Joseph Henry House, where her class was held.

"What are all those trucks and trailers?" asked John.

"Max Bolt is making a movie of *This Side of Paradise* and you know most of the novel takes place at Princeton. They've told him he can't work while classes are in session, but he keeps right on. You have to admire his stubbornness."

When she had parked right next to Joseph Henry House, she said, "This is luxury. I should have a banged-up knee all the time."

"How did you hurt your knee?" asked John.

"I fell downstairs, but I think Clarence Robbins pushed me."

"Really?" asked John. "I'm going to see what I can find out about Clarence Robbins. I'll let you know."

Class went well; John was so interesting when he talked about interviewing people in the arts and the theater that the students stayed after five o'clock, a very unusual occurrence.

When George came to dinner, he reported that he had heard nothing from the police. "Nothing personally, I mean," he said. "They were still in the office poking around, but they didn't seem to suspect me of anything but having an incomprehensible filing system."

"You must have imagined that they suspected you. What are they looking for in the files?"

"Anything and everything in Melissa's past. And of course, she's only been there since September. They're trying to find her old files from her office in the Economics Department."

"They searched here too, Sophy said," McLeod told him.

The Cowan family came to dinner again. Mrs. Linley really was a saint, McLeod decided. After dinner when George and the Cowans had left, McLeod told Sophy that she thought she would leave the next day when Sophy's aunt arrived. "It would free up a bedroom, and I don't want to intrude on the family," McLeod said.

"Oh, no," said Sophy. "Please stay until I go back to the dorm on Sunday. It's so wonderful to have you here, and I want you to meet my aunt Claudia."

"Of course, I'll stay if you want me to," said McLeod, who really did not want to stay in the house with Clarence Robbins any longer. "But is there room for the cousins and me, too?"

"My aunt and uncle can have the fourth bedroom on the second floor and there are three on the third floor. There's plenty of room. You'll like my uncle. His name is Barefoot. It's not a nickname, it's his given name. His father was Barefoot, and he and Claudia have a son named Barefoot."

McLeod limped upstairs and went to her room with relief. She looked in the closets, the bathroom, the dressing room, and under the bed before she bolted the door and went to bed.

FRIDAY WAS HELLISH for McLeod. She stayed at Lowrie House all day and lay down most of the time because of her knee, which seemed to be no better. She felt guilty because she wasn't downstairs with Sophy, but she wanted to avoid Clarence.

Claudia and Barefoot Harris arrived right after lunch. They were both tall and thin. Claudia hugged her niece and greeted McLeod with caution. Barefoot said he needed some exercise, and Sophy volunteered to take him for a run.

McLeod and Claudia had a cup of tea in the drawing room.

"Well, this is something, this house," said Claudia. "My big sister did very well for herself, didn't she?"

"Have you seen much of Melissa over the years?"

"Not really. We never were close. She was older than I was, and smarter, and she went off to the University of Texas and really never came back. As long as our mother was alive, she'd come home to Abilene from time to time, but she hasn't been back since. Our parents were fundamentalist Christians and they had high moral standards. They disapproved of sex before marriage and disapproved of divorce. They were very hard on her. My mother felt like Melissa's wild life killed our father."

"But she didn't refuse to see Melissa?"

"Oh, no. And she was interested in Sophy. Her first grandchild. So Melissa would come back to see her, until Mother died."

"And you kept in touch with her after that?"

"I stayed in touch with her but I didn't see much of her. I'm more like our parents—I don't approve of sex before marriage and I don't approve of divorce. But I believe in family, and I always admired my big sister. So I kept in touch, even though we didn't agree on anything. Barefoot and I are very conservative, and Melissa was never conservative. She's always been a liberal." Claudia hesitated, clearly about to say something even worse about her sister than "liberal." "She even worked for *The Texas Observer* when she was at the university," Claudia added in a hushed voice.

"What's that?"

"It's this left-wing journal that's a disgrace to Texas. Texas is a conservative state, and it's good enough for me." Claudia paused. "In a way, I'm sorry I didn't see more of her. I guess I had a sister I never knew. Would you look at all the flowers in this room!"

"They keep coming," said McLeod. "Every day more come." She felt a strong wave of pity for Melissa Faircloth. Divorced from her husband, separated from family, isolated from friends by the demands of her important job, she had led essentially a lonely life. And now she led no life at all.

"Who do you suppose could have killed her?" Claudia asked. "That's what I keep wondering. College presidents don't get murdered all the time, do they?"

"I don't think it's an occupational hazard," said McLeod. "I wonder who could have killed her, too. I guess we all do. Nobody seems to have a clue. Literally. Is there anything back in Texas that would lead to her murder?"

"Nothing," said Claudia. "She left Texas so long ago, well, Abilene anyway."

"That's what Clarence said."

"Clarence?" said Claudia.

"Clarence Robbins, her ex-husband," said McLeod.

"Oh, him. She never spoke about him to me," said Claudia. "Except to say marrying him was the biggest mistake she ever made. She said if she had had any sense, she would never have told him she was pregnant, just gone on and had the baby as a single mom from the beginning. But she couldn't do it, not after the way we were brought up. It's my opinion you make your bed, you lie in it. But at least divorce is better than abortion."

They had no more chance to talk alone. The cousins, two tall pale middle-aged women, arrived; Sophy and Barefoot returned from their run; and Clarence Robbins appeared.

Sophy hugged her cousins and introduced her father to all the Texans. Then she took the cousins upstairs.

McLeod, deciding she should go back to her own apartment to get some clean underwear and pick up a black outfit to wear to the funeral, followed them. When she had her car keys, she sought Sophy and found her in her own room.

"Sophy, do you have anything black to wear to the funeral?"

"I do," she said. "I'm glad you mentioned it. I have a nice black dress. And it's here, not at the dorm. Isn't that lucky? Thanks."

McLeod went out in the hall, looked around, and limped carefully down the stairs.

Twelve

ON SATURDAY MORNING, Sophy came downstairs dressed for the funeral in a long-sleeved black dress. From the waist up, it was severely suitable for a funeral. Although its skirt was minuscule, Sophy looked almost demure, with her black tights and black shoes and her black hair in a bun. She also looked beautiful.

McLeod, still limping because of her knee, rode in the car with Sophy to the chapel, since Sophy insisted. The crowd was bigger than McLeod had expected for a "private" funeral—Sophy, of course, and her Texas relations, Clarence, all of Melissa's staff, the university trustees, all the members of the president's cabinet, and most of the faculty of the Economics Department, all with spouses of course, and a small contingent of Sophy's classmates. The crowd overflowed the choir and spread into the nave, where a scattering of strangers also sat. Whether they had heard about the funeral or were simply attracted by the crowd arriving at the chapel, McLeod could not tell.

She looked around the great Gothic chapel in awe. It was the largest gothic chapel on an American college campus and was a most impressive space. McLeod was glad she was in the choir, which seemed cosier than the vast reaches of the nave.

After the brief service, everyone adjourned to Lowrie House for a buffet lunch. Mrs. Linley and her staff had outdone themselves.

"Funeral baked meats!" said Clarence. His face had been composed into a mask of grief all morning but it now broke apart in his joy at the food and drink. "It's a sad occasion, but a mighty fine meal, isn't it?" He turned down the sherry that everyone else was sedately drinking and mixed himself a martini.

Kenneth Coales spent most of his time with the trustees, smiling and deferring or, as McLeod put it to herself, fawning. She began to downscale her opinion of Kenneth Coales, and moved faster in that direction when Sophy whispered, "I told Kenneth Coales I didn't want the trustees at the funeral! It was supposed to be private, and family."

"I guess he felt they had to be here. He must have thought it was important," McLeod fibbed consolingly.

"Important to him," said Sophy, and glided away.

McLeod, whose knee was feeling better, was disappointed when George said he had to leave. "I wish we could have dinner together," he said, "but the trustees are meeting as soon as we leave here. I'll be tied up 'til God knows when."

"That's all right," said McLeod. "In that case, I may stay here. It depends on Sophy and when her relatives leave."

When McLeod spoke to her, Sophy again begged her to stay. "Claudia and Barefoot are going to leave later this afternoon. But Mom's lawyer wants to talk to them before they go, and talk to me too. Couldn't you stay for that? The cousins are going to stay until tomorrow. They want to look around Princeton."

"Of course, I'll stick around if you need me," said McLeod.

WHEN EVERYBODY BUT the Cowans and the family had finally left, Cowboy Tarleton, Melissa's lawyer, asked for a few moments with them. The cousins were excused, but Sophy insisted that McLeod stay, and McLeod, whose curiosity was sharpened to the breaking point, was happy to oblige. She sat down with Claudia, Barefoot, Martha, Bruce, Sophy, and Clarence. McLeod reflected that at no other Princeton meeting were men named Barefoot and Cowboy likely to have been present. At least Cowboy was a nickname.

Cowboy did not keep them long. Melissa Faircloth, to put it briefly, had left everything she had in trust for Sophy Robbins. The trustees, Martha and Bruce Cowan, would turn the money over to Sophy when she was thirty.

"She can't do that!" said Clarence. "I'm Sophy's own natural father. I should be her trustee."

"I'm afraid she can do that," said Tarleton. "She did."

"I'll take it to court!" said Clarence.

"You have every right to go into Chancery Court and ask, as the natural father, to be named trustee," said Tarleton. "But I don't think you'll get anywhere, under the circumstances." He turned to Claudia and Barefoot. "I thought you'd better be here as the next of kin. Melissa didn't name you trustees because you live so far away."

"I understand," said Claudia. "I wish we didn't have to go, but we do. Sophy, you're going back to the dormitory tomorrow? What will you do with all your things in this house?"

"She can store stuff at our house," said Martha Cowan. "And Melissa's house still has some space in the attic. I'll talk to the professor and his wife who are renting it."

"If there's anything you want to ship to us in Abilene . . ." said Claudia. "Somebody said you were going to work on an excavation this summer. Can you come out to see us before that, or maybe after?"

"We'll talk about it," said Sophy. "Thanks."

"Nice to have met you," said Tarleton to the Harrises. He nodded at the Cowans. "I'll talk to you next week. And you take care," he said to Sophy, giving her a hug.

"What about me?" asked Clarence.

"Yes?" said Tarleton.

"Did Melissa mention me in her will at all?"

"No, she didn't," said Tarleton.

Clarence's big brown eyes looked dull.

"I'm on my way," said Tarleton, and left.

The university had provided a car and driver to take the Harrises to Newark Airport, and Sophy unexpectedly said she'd ride up with them. "We can have a little visit that way," she said. "McLeod, it's five o'clock now, and I won't be back before eight. Mrs. Linley has gone, I'm afraid."

"We can eat leftovers," said McLeod. "Is it all right if I invite my friend Stephanie King over?"

"Sure. And leftovers will be fine. See you."

The Cowans left, too. Clarence sat in a big chair, looking disconsolate.

"Clarence, I'm going out. I'll be back before Sophy gets back." She was determined not to be in Lowrie House alone with Clarence.

"Do you think I could have a little drink?" asked Clarence.

"It's up to you," said McLeod, and left.

Although she would have liked to change out of her funeral garb, she had not wanted to go upstairs while she was alone in the house with Clarence. She drove to her apartment and called Stephanie King. Stephanie was one of the friends she had made while she was on her previous tour of duty at Princeton. The manager of the English Department, handling scheduling, budgets, and the day-to-day business of the department, she had always been extremely helpful to McLeod. Furthermore, Stephanie seemed to know everything about Princeton and everybody there, and liked a good gossip as well as anybody McLeod had ever known.

Stephanie was at home and was glad to come to dinner.

STEPHANIE AND MCLEOD both arrived at Lowrie House about six-thirty. McLeod had changed out of her funeral attire and put on jeans at home. She now had no qualms about wearing jeans at Lowrie House. Stephanie, for once, was not wearing a power suit, but had on khaki pants and a huge thick sweater.

"Let me make sure there are enough leftovers for our supper," said McLeod. Rummaging around, she found cold ham and turkey and beef, noodles, and spinach casserole. "I'll throw together a salad," she said, and opened a bottle of wine. She took the bottle, two glasses and a plate of Mrs. Linley's miniature quiches into the library. "I'm sorry you're seeing us without staff tonight," said McLeod. "Life has been sad, but normal life around here is very grand."

"Good," said Stephanie. "Tell me about it? How is Sophy? She's a nice kid, isn't she?"

"Very nice. Right now, she's gone to Newark Airport with her aunt and uncle from Texas. She's wonderful. But I'll be glad to get back to my own place, let me tell you. There are two middle-aged cousins staying here, but they're going to Lawrenceville to a friend's for dinner. So it will be you and me and Sophy—and I guess Sophy's father. He's staying here."

"Melissa's ex-husband? The mystery man. What's he like?"

"He's awful," said McLeod. "I'm kind of scared of him. I'm glad you're here with me. I don't like to be in the house alone with him. But now tell me what you know about Kenneth Coales."

"Nobody really likes Kenneth Coales," said Stephanie. "Ever since he became provost, he's been everyone's *bête noire*. And he gets more bêtish, or *plus noire,* as time goes by."

"What does he do that's so horrible?"

"What doesn't he do?" asked Stephanie. "He hates the humanities, for one thing. Or at least he must, given the way he treats English and art—we can hardly get the money to get our copy machines repaired. He doesn't keep his promises; he agrees to a thing on Wednesday and on Thursday he's 'rethought it,' and says 'upon reflection' he's changed his mind. And he's rude in meetings. He says the most awful things, calls people fools and morons—that's just not done at Princeton."

"It's certainly not done anywhere, if you're decent. I must say he was very suave and polite to me."

"He can be the perfect gentleman when he wants to," said Stephanie. "When he wants something from you."

"He's good-looking," said McLeod, "except for those very odd whites of his eyes. They're so big and transparent they make him look like Skilling or whatever that man's name was—you know, from Enron. But that's not something to hold against a man."

"I guess not," said Stephanie. "But there's lots more to hold against him. Everybody knew that Melissa was going to fire him. And he can't bear the thought of leaving Princeton."

"Why couldn't he stay here and teach molecular biology again?"

"They wouldn't have him back. He's been awful to everybody, even in his old department—they say he was evening up old scores."

"And he doesn't want to leave Princeton? Is he one of those Old Nassau nuts? Or does his wife refuse to move or what?"

"Oh, no, neither one. I don't think his wife would mind moving. She's a terribly dowdy woman—she's a potter, and she always seems to be stained with clay, but it doesn't bother her. No, Ken has been having an affair for years with a woman who works in the Spanish and Portuguese

Languages Department. She's Spanish, a really sultry Latin type. He's besotted with her. He can move his wife, but he can't take his lady friend with him, and he can't bear to leave her. That's why he didn't just gracefully resign when Melissa came in."

"Well, couldn't he leave his wife and marry the lady friend?" McLeod asked.

"No, no, she's married. And they say she won't divorce her husband. I don't think she cares as much about Ken as Ken cares about her."

"It's kind of romantic," said McLeod. "I hate to tell you what Melissa's sister, the fundamentalist Christian from Texas, would say about the situation."

"Tell me about her. What is she like?"

"Let me pour us some more wine," said McLeod, and did. Full glass in hand, she went on. "She's, like I said, a fundamentalist Christian, with very strict ideas about right and wrong. She didn't approve of Melissa but she admired her and she's interested in Sophy. And Sophy likes her Aunt Claudia and her uncle, whose name is Barefoot."

"Barefoot? Is that true? Well, Sophy must like them if she's ridden up to Newark Airport with them," said Stephanie.

"It's drinky time, is it? You should have called me." McLeod had mercifully forgotten about Clarence Robbins for a few minutes, but here he was.

McLeod introduced Stephanie to Clarence, and Clarence said he didn't want wine, he wanted a real drink. McLeod again said she'd fix it. "Scotch on the rocks?"

"That's right," he said.

"Have you been resting?" McLeod asked him when she limped back with his drink.

"I took a little nap," he said. "The past week has been exhausting." He gulped down all his scotch. "Exhausting." He held out his glass to McLeod and looked at her appealingly with his brown eyes.

"I'll get you another drink," said Stephanie. "McLeod

limps around more than she should. Is the scotch out where I can get it, McLeod?"

"Yes, it is. Thank you so much, Stephanie. But I've got to get up and get supper ready," McLeod said.

"I'll help," said Stephanie, "but let me get the drink now."

Clarence thanked her when she brought his drink back and asked where Mrs. Ummmm was.

"She's off," said McLeod. "She's been working like a beaver all this week. She needed time off. She said she'd be back tomorrow—to see us all off."

"See who off?" said Clarence.

"All of us," said McLeod.

"Well, I wasn't planning on going anywhere," said Clarence. "As a matter of fact, the police don't want me to leave town. I guess I'm being a real help to them."

"Sophy plans to move back to the dormitory tomorrow. She's already worried about the classes she's missed," McLeod said. "I think we should all leave tomorrow."

IT WAS AT this moment that Sophy got home. "Hello, everybody. Were you talking about me?"

"Yes, I was just saying you were moving back to campus tomorrow—and that Mrs. Linley would probably be glad to see us all go," said McLeod. She introduced Sophy to Stephanie, and then got up and started toward the kitchen. Stephanie followed her, and Sophy trailed after them.

As McLeod began to get out the leftovers, Sophy said, "McLeod, I think I'll take a sandwich up to my room. Is that all right? I'm really wiped out. You all will excuse me, won't you?"

"Certainly," McLeod said, and Stephanie chimed in her assent. "You must be exhausted," Stephanie said.

"Are you sure you want to go back to the dormitory tomorrow?" McLeod asked.

"Yes, I'm sure. I'll sleep late tomorrow and go back

sometime in the afternoon. I want to go to class Monday. I have to get back into the routine sometime."

McLeod hugged her. "You're wonderful, Sophy. I'm so glad you let me stay with you."

"I'm glad you're here," said Sophy. She slapped some ham between two pieces of bread, took a Diet Coke from the refrigerator, and left. As she went out one door of the kitchen and headed upstairs, Clarence came in the door from the dining room.

"Where's everybody? Where's my baby doll?" he asked.

"Sophy took a sandwich upstairs," said McLeod. "Here's a plate. Fill it up from all this stuff left over from lunch. We can take our plates to the dining room, or just eat in here."

"Kitchen's fine with me," said Clarence. "As long as I have booze." He poured scotch over the ice in his glass. "Funeral baked meats," he said again as soon as he sat down. He talked while they ate, talked about his childhood in Springfield, his wonderful old grandmother who had smoked a pipe and his wonderful mother who had been a saint. He told about the time he had almost won the spelling bee, but had missed the word "fierce." "I always have trouble with that 'i before e' business," he said. He talked about swimming in Barton Springs in Austin. "That water is as cold as ice," he said. "It's like the Antarctic Ocean. But man, when you come out of there, you feel like a million dollars. Austin's not a bad place to live. Not bad at all. But Princeton's not bad, either, especially if you live like this. But I guess this is about to end for us, isn't it? I'll just have another little drinky-poo. You ladies want one?"

They refused drinks, and McLeod put on a pot of coffee. She and Stephanie loaded the dishwasher while it brewed. Clarence talked in the background. "Austin is the music capital of the world," he said. "Some people say the noise is awful at night when you walk down the street. They're playing music in every storefront along the sidewalk. You can't help but hear it when you drive down the street. A lady cop goes around measuring decibels and she makes them cut it down if they're too loud. But you still hear it. It's nice. Princeton is almost too quiet, you know. I think baby doll would love Austin. Don't you agree?" Interpreting their silence correctly, he changed the subject, and said to Stephanie, "You've lived here a long time? Can you recommend a good lawyer?"

"What for?" asked Stephanie. "What kind of lawyer?"

"A suing lawyer," said Clarence. "I have a great friend in Austin, best little suer in Texas. But I got to have somebody here."

"Who are you going to sue?" asked Stephanie.

"I'm going into Chancery Court and sue to become Sophy's trustee, trustee for the money her mother left her. Those people, the Cowans, are the trustees now, but I think it's much better for Sophy's father to be the trustee, don't you?"

"Well . . ." said Stephanie. "I don't know."

The intercom buzzed, and it was the guard saying that Lieutenant Nick Perry from the Borough Police was outside to see Mr. Robbins. "Send him in," said McLeod. She turned to Clarence, who was sipping another scotch. "The police are coming to see you."

Thank heavens, she thought. They would surely arrest him. And she could have a good night's sleep with him out of the house.

MCLEOD'S FANTASY DID not come true. Lieutenant Perry and Clarence went into the drawing room, while Stephanie and McLeod waited in the dining room. Perry did not arrest Clarence, who came out of the drawing room, lurching a little as he walked, and went upstairs.

Perry came into the dining room.

"Sit down," said McLeod. "Or we can go where it's more comfortable." She introduced him to Stephanie.

"I remember you," said Stephanie. "You were on campus when McLeod's class got involved in investigating those murders last year."

"You're manager of the English Department, aren't you?" said Perry.

"That's right," said Stephanie.

"Did you know Melissa Faircloth?"

"Everybody who works at the university knew her to some extent. I hadn't had time yet to get to know her well," said Stephanie. "Her schedule was so frantic that I was never alone with her."

"Thanks," said Perry. "I just want to talk to McLeod a minute."

"I'd better go," said Stephanie.

"You don't have to go. Does she, Lieutenant?"

"I think I'd better leave," Stephanie said. "I'll talk to you tomorrow, McLeod. Nice to see you again, Lieutenant."

Perry stood up when she did, and said it had been good to see her again. McLeod saw her to the door, came back to the dining room, and offered Perry a drink or coffee. He accepted coffee and asked McLeod why she was limping.

"That's because I hurt my knee when Clarence Robbins pushed me down the stairs," said McLeod bitterly. "I was hoping you'd arrest him."

"We couldn't arrest him," said Perry. "We told him he was free to leave town. He can go back to Austin. We checked his alibi for that Monday night and it stood up. If he leaves town, you won't be so uneasy about him."

"I don't think he wants to go back to Austin," said McLeod. "He wants to stay here and start filing lawsuits."

"Well, he did indicate that he was in no hurry to leave town. He said he wanted to help find the killer of his beloved wife. They were divorced, weren't they?"

"Yes, they were. Can you tell me who gave him an alibi?"

"A dozen people will swear he was in the Tap Room of the Nassau Inn, drinking steadily from five o'clock in the afternoon until the Tap Room closed at one o'clock in the morning and he passed out. Two waiters took him to his room and took off his shoes and stretched him on his bed. They were afraid he might be really toxic—they talked about calling the Rescue Squad—but they decided he'd sleep it off. They swore he could never have made it over to Nassau Hall, much less had sex with Melissa Faircloth, killed her, and stuffed her body in a closet."

"But he's horrible!" McLeod said.

"We can't arrest everybody who's not nice," said Perry, emphasizing the word "nice" with sarcasm.

"He scares me," said McLeod.

"If he leaves town, he can't hurt you," said Perry. "I thought you'd be pleased."

"I don't think he's going to leave town. I think he's going to figure out a way to stay here. He'd love to stay in this house, but I'm sure the university won't permit it."

Perry stood up. "I'm sorry you're uneasy," he said, "but you can go back to your apartment tomorrow. Sophy's here tonight, and there's a guard outside all night, you know. Keep in touch. Will you?"

"I sure will," said McLeod and walked him to the front door. "Thanks. I'll see you."

Clarence and Sophy were coming down the stairs as she turned. Sophy brought down her dirty plate and said she'd put it in the kitchen.

"Put it in the dishwasher. We didn't turn it on," said McLeod. "Let's surprise Mrs. Linley with a clean kitchen."

"Sure," said Sophy. "And now I'm going back up to bed, you guys. See you, Dad."

"Sophy, I don't know where I'm going to stay," said Clarence. "McLean, I mean McLeod—that's your name, isn't it?—doesn't think I can stay here."

"I don't think either one of us can, Dad. Aren't you going back to Austin? I thought you said the police said you could go."

"Of course I can go back. But I want to help you. And I want to stay here and find a lawyer and file my suit to become your trustee. And I think you should sue the university for negligence, for failure to protect your mother. I bet that lawyer of hers would be happy to sue the university. If you threatened to sue them, I bet the university would be glad to let us stay here for a little while."

"Oh, Dad, I don't want to sue the university."

"It's a golden opportunity. Anyway, I need to stay in Princeton for a few days. And where am I going to stay?"

"I'm afraid you're on your own," said Sophy, and went upstairs.

Thirteen

SOPHY CAME DOWNSTAIRS Sunday morning while McLeod was eating breakfast and reading *The Washington Post*. "You're up early—early for somebody your age, anyway—and I thought you were going to sleep late. How are you today?" McLeod said.

"I'm okay," Sophy said. "I went to bed early last night for a change, and when I woke up, I thought I'd get up. I've got to move a lot of stuff back to the dorm. But I've got to figure out what to do with everything else of mine that's here. I only took what I needed to the dorm. Then I have to do something—I guess—with Mom's things. Her books, her clothes, the pictures and stuff she moved over here. What a nightmare."

Mrs. Linley came bustling in when she heard Sophy downstairs and asked if she wanted pancakes.

"Mrs. Linley, you're a hero to even come in on Sunday. I'd love pancakes."

"I know you'll need me today," said Mrs. Linley. "And

speaking of pancakes, where is George Bridges? I haven't seen him in a day or two."

"I don't know," said McLeod. "He had a trustees meeting after the funeral. I haven't heard from him since."

"Well, if he wants some more of my pancakes, he'd better get himself over here." Mrs. Linley went back to the kitchen.

McLeod turned to Sophy. "You don't have to move everything out of Lowrie House immediately. I'm sure the university will let you take your time. I'll help you any way I can. And you know Martha Cowan will help."

"You're right. I've got to talk to Martha. But I want to talk to you. Who do you think could have killed my mother?"

"Sophy, I've thought about this, of course. Who hasn't?" McLeod hesitated to tell her that she had suspected that Sophy's father had killed her mother, but she decided that she might as well be frank. "I have to say I strongly suspected your father."

"My father!"

Sophy was so taken aback that McLeod regretted having voiced her suspicion. "I'm sorry I told you," she said. "He seemed to be still emotionally involved with her and insisted that she was the love of his life—but she had ditched him. He seemed to be jealous of her professional success. And it seemed to me that he was eager to get his hands on the money your mother left you."

"I see what you mean, but I think Dad's harmless really. He's pretty inept and I don't think he'd hurt a fly—physically, I mean."

"I expect you're right," said McLeod. She did not mention that she was sure someone, probably Clarence, had pushed her down the stairs. "As you know, the police have cleared him and said he could go back to Austin."

"I know. And he doesn't want to go back. He wants to start litigating."

"Don't worry about it, Sophy. It will work out."

"But I do worry. I worry about everything. I worry

about how much money there is. Where am I going to stay when I'm not in a dormitory? Where am I going to put all our stuff? And who killed my mother?"

"Sophy, tomorrow you can get at least a ballpark figure for how much money there will be. And meanwhile, right now, I'll help you make a plan about what to do with your belongings. And let's leave the identity of the murderer to the police."

"I guess you're right about the police," said Sophy, "although I don't have a lot of confidence in them."

McLeod then tackled the problem of possessions. "I still don't think the university will make you clear out everything today, or even this week. But I know you want to get your own things back to the dorm. And I think you should take with you any small things like jewelry that belonged to your mother that you want to keep."

"I'll go through her room right now," said Sophy.

"I'll call Martha Cowan," said McLeod.

McLeod also called Provost Coales at home. She thought it would make Sophy's life simpler if she knew that she did not have to rush to get everything moved out right away.

To her surprise, Ken Coales did not agree with her that Sophy would not have to hurry to move.

"Oh, no, Ms. Dulaney, I think Sophy had better clear everything out of Lowrie House. We want a clean deck."

"But the poor child has classes and a junior paper to write. It will be very hard for her to clear everything of her mother's out of here immediately."

"Sometimes we have to do things that are very difficult," Coales said. "And we grow stronger from the experience. Haven't you found it so?"

"I think it's an outrage," said McLeod. "It's inhumane and uncivilized."

"I think she can manage very well. She's quite capable," said Coales. "I thank you for bringing all this to my attention, Ms. Dulaney. I'll expect to hear that Sophy is out of there, lock, stock, and barrel, very quickly."

"Thank you, Mr. Coales." What a horrible man, she thought. McLeod hung up and called Martha Cowan. Where was George? she wondered.

Clarence came downstairs, ate breakfast prepared by Mrs. Linley, and went upstairs to pack his own suitcase.

By eleven o'clock, McLeod, Sophy, Martha, and Mrs. Linley were in conference around the dining table, each making notes on a yellow legal pad.

Together they worked out a plan of action that involved colored tags to mark everything in the house that had belonged to Melissa or Sophy. The color of each tag would indicate whether it would go into storage, to the Cowans' house, to the attic of Melissa's house, to Sophy's dorm, or to the curb for trash collection.

Mrs. Linley and Sophy together would do the tagging today, and Mrs. Linley would see that everything was packed on Monday and the cartons labeled.

McLeod helped them as much as she could, preparing lunch for everybody. Martha Cowan very kindly stayed to help. Clarence ate lunch and left with his suitcase, saying he would check into the Nassau Inn again. Sophy told him to take the laptop with him and he accepted it gratefully. "I can do business here now," he said, and left.

McLeod helped Sophy pack up to return to campus, and thanked Mrs. Linley sincerely and effusively. She hugged Martha Cowan, and then drove Sophy over to Pyne Hall and helped her carry her belongings up to her room. Then, at last, she was in her own apartment, exhausted again.

George called. "I've been with the police all day," he said. "At the office. Perry wants to know everything, everything. Can I come over? I won't stay long—I'm tired and I know you are."

It was very good to see George, who looked tired and rumpled in an old sweatshirt.

"Do the police still suspect you?" McLeod asked him.

"I think they do, but they ostensibly want to get information from me. Perry and the others asked thousands of questions about the office and the people who came to see

Melissa. Now and then one of them would ask me about my relationship with Melissa. Over and over, I said, employer-employee, and they would ask if I was sure I had never had an affair with her."

"Did you?"

"I did not."

"I'm glad," said McLeod.

"When she was a young assistant professor and I was working for Hamilton—he was two presidents back—we had a few dates. It was strictly platonic. We had very little in common. And she was a hardworking, ambitious single mother. She wanted to get ahead. I'm more laid back. I don't think she ever went out with anybody much. When she was named president, she asked me to stay on and I did. We had no problem slipping into the right relationship—boss and helpful worker. But somebody must have told the police that we were an item or something."

"It will all work out," said McLeod with a confidence she did not altogether feel.

"Oh, I forgot to tell you. We have an acting president," said George. "The trustees went ahead last night and did the inevitable."

"Well, who is it?"

"Kenneth Coales," said George.

"I can't believe it," said McLeod. "The man's a monster."

"You've changed your tune," said George.

McLeod told him about Ken Coales's edict that Sophy had to move everything out of Lowrie House immediately.

"Typical," said George. "Typical. I'll tell you this. I can't work for Kenneth Coales. I'm going to start looking for a new job. If I don't get arrested."

They decided they were too frazzled and tired even to bother with Chinese takeout. McLeod said she could make an omelet and a salad. "That's a staple of English novels," said McLeod. "Somebody whips up an omelet."

"I've got to have more than that. Have you got any bread?" asked George. McLeod got bread out of the freezer and said she would make cheese toast, lots of it. While they were eating, McLeod told George about Clarence Robbins's alibi.

"That's too bad," George said. "It would have been nice to see him put away forever."

When they'd finished eating and had had coffee, George went home early. "I haven't done a crossword puzzle in a week. I'll go home and tackle today's," he said.

MCLEOD WOKE LATE on Monday morning and thought how wonderful it was to be back in her own apartment. She sat down on the sofa with her feet up, prepared for a leisurely breakfast with *The New York Times* and the Trenton *Times*. She read the stories about the appointment of Kenneth Coales as acting president. Then another story in the Trenton paper shocked her so that she sat up, put her feet on the floor, and closed her eyes.

AA QUESTIONED IN PREXY MURDER, said the headline. It was written by Dick Coffey, who covered Princeton University for the Trenton *Times*.

"Under intensive investigation in the murder of Melissa Faircloth, president of Princeton University, is her assistant, George Bridges.

"Many administrators and faculty members at the university have been questioned, but Bridges has undergone the most extensive scrutiny. Borough Police, who are still in charge of the case, refused to confirm that Bridges is a targeted suspect. 'He has been very helpful,' Lt. Nick Perry, chief of detectives, said."

The story went on to recount the many hours George had spent with the police—the reporter knew about a lot of interviews and added a few more for good measure—and speculated about motives George could have.

McLeod was horrified. Poor George. The publicity would be awful for him, she thought, pure torture. When she called him at the office to offer her sympathy, he sounded strained. "It's the worst thing that could have happened," he said. "How could Perry have done this to me?"

"I don't think it was Nick Perry," said McLeod. "Nick Perry never tells anybody anything about a case. It's anomalous that he told me about Clarence Robbins's alibi. Somebody else tipped off the Trenton *Times*. You mark my words."

George had to hang up, so McLeod got dressed and walked to the campus, where she found a copy of the *Prince*. She was happy to see that at least George had escaped publicity in the student newspaper, which instead was focused on the rapes on campus. The *Prince* cried out editorially for action by the police.

In her office, McLeod caught up with the e-mail from her students, scheduled conferences, handled the mail and phone messages. Before she knew it, it was time for her lunch with Fletcher Prickett at the Nassau Club, an appointment she had forgotten all about until she looked at her calendar. It's a good thing I wore this good pink suit, she thought.

The Nassau Club had been founded in the nineteenth century as a place in Princeton where men from the university faculty and men from town could come together. The club still flourished, but it was now all town and no gown, except that the members, most of them alumni of the university, maintained a strong interest in the institution.

McLeod was happy at the chance to see the inside of the clubhouse, a former residence on Mercer Street, acquired when Woodrow Wilson was club president. Fletcher Prickett, waiting for her in one of the parlors off the entrance hall, stood up when she came in.

"Hello, m'dear. I'm so happy to see you. So good of you to come. And you're looking lovely in pink."

They went to the big, airy dining room at the back, and sat down. Fletcher was an attentive host, consulting her about the wine, conferring with her over the menu and making recommendations. The snapper soup, he said, was a specialty of the Nassau Club, so McLeod ordered it and the smoked duck salad.

"Not exactly haute cuisine," said Prickett, "but the food is good here." After the wine was brought and deemed properly chilled, he poured it, a Pouilly-Fuissé. "Now, m'dear, you have to realize I never took a lady professor to lunch before. I wish everybody who's called me an Old Fogey could see me now."

"I'm not a real professor," said McLeod. "I just teach a writing seminar and have the rank of lecturer."

"Nevertheless, m'dear, you teach, you profess, at the university, the best old place of all, and I want everybody here to notice what I'm doing."

"You mean, taking me to lunch is a radical act that will astonish your friends?"

"That's right. I've been very much opposed to what I call the feminization of Princeton," he said to her confidingly, as if it were the greatest of secrets. McLeod briefly tried to imagine bringing Fletcher Prickett and Gertrude Sergeant, the noisiest feminist in the English Department, together for a discussion of gender roles, but shook her head at the thought of the din that would surely ensue at such a meeting.

"It was all male for almost two hundred and fifty years," she said to Fletcher. "Wasn't it about time to bring in some women?"

"But they're bringing in too many women," said Fletcher. "A woman president, a woman dean of the college, a woman dean of admission, a woman dean of the Woodrow Wilson School, a woman dean of the graduate school, a woman vice president for personnel, a woman director of libraries. Where will it all end? Last month I was saying the next thing you know That Woman will name a woman dean of the engineering school. I thought that was impossible. But she did it. She did the unthinkable. I ask you, m'dear, where will it all end?"

"There are still more men than women around the place," McLeod said. She thought they had been through this same discussion last Sunday, and began to feel that she was paying a high price for her duck salad.

"Half of the top twenty-five administrators are women," Prickett said.

"Isn't that about the same proportion of women to men as there is in the student body?"

"They'll have a woman director of athletics, you mark my words, and that will be a disaster."

"The provost is a man and he's been named acting president," said McLeod.

"He's a good man, too, Ken Coales, Class of '65. I'd like to see him named permanent president."

"Why?" asked McLeod.

"He's a *man* and he's an alumnus. He understands this great institution."

"Is that all? Do you mean that any man would be better than Melissa Faircloth?"

"I certainly do. But Ken Coales is a good, tough man. He's not as much a bleeding heart liberal as some of those people over there. He's tough on cheating."

McLeod snorted. "Isn't everybody at Princeton tough on cheating? It seems to me they emphasize the honor code more than any school in America."

"I guess so," admitted Fletcher, "but Ken Coales is strong. He doesn't mind expelling students who cheat. He doesn't believe in second chances. And it's not just cheating that he's firm about. He believes in preserving the canon, doesn't want anything to do with adding all these things like African studies and women's studies and teaching inferior women writers."

"But he's a molecular biologist. What does he know about teaching literature?"

"He's a true conservative," said Fletcher solemnly. "He believes in conserving our heritage, the heritage of the Western world. Everybody seems to forget that Princeton was founded by men to educate men, educate them to be Presbyterian preachers. Of course, the seminary pulled out a long time ago. I know that. But that's our tradition."

"Tell me more about Ken Coales," said McLeod. "He doesn't seem to be very popular. But nobody has a specific complaint."

"I guess they don't like it that he's not namby-pamby," said Fletcher.

"What about his affair?"

"Affair?"

"Yes, the woman who works in Spanish and Portuguese, his lady friend."

Fletcher grinned, apparently in spite of himself, at this, and said he didn't think it was important.

But McLeod thought it was important.

"Why are you so interested in Ken Coales?" Prickett asked her.

"Well, he's acting president," she said. "Maybe I should do an article about him."

"You write as well as teach?" said Fletcher. "What a woman."

"I write more than I teach," said McLeod. "And I also wonder if he killed Melissa Faircloth."

"What?" Prickett was obviously startled. "Impossible," he said. "Impossible." He looked troubled. "What makes you say that, m'dear?"

"Well, somebody killed her, and Coales wanted to be president."

"Ken Coales didn't kill That Woman," said Prickett. "It was some prowler. Or another woman. Or one of these people that lend 'diversity' to Princeton, as they say. The place is nothing but a freak show nowadays, with all this diversity. When I was a student here, we were all gentlemen, and we all wore suits and ties. No, no, the murder couldn't have been done by an upright alumnus like Ken Coales."

McLeod repeated that it had to be somebody with a key to Nassau Hall.

Prickett laughed out loud. "This is all very funny," he said. "All this would never have happened if Princeton had not turned its back on its Presbyterian heritage. A woman president seems to encourage a moral climate that's simply intolerable."

"Good heavens, women can be puritanical, too."

"I see what you mean, but I'm thinking of these rapes on campus. If women weren't there, roaming around at night all over the campus, then there wouldn't be anyone to rape, now would there?"

McLeod thought of and discarded several tart replies such as: "They'd be reduced to raping men." She even thought of the feminists' stock observations about rape being a symbol of the hegemony of men. But instead she asked, "Do you have any children, Mr. Prickett?"

"Call me Fletcher, or Fletch, m'dear," he said. "No, Mrs. Prickett and I were never blessed with children. And now that she's passed away, I'm all alone."

It was a pity he had no children, McLeod thought. Many an Old Tiger, she had been told, had been bitterly opposed to coeducation at Princeton until his own daughter, or granddaughter, was admitted.

"Do you have children?" Fletcher asked her.

"That question means I get to talk about them a minute," said McLeod. "I have a son who's going to get his Ph.D. at Yale any minute, and daughter who's a reporter on the Charlotte, North Carolina, newspaper."

"And your husband?"

"He died twenty years ago," said McLeod.

"I'm sorry, m'dear."

When she'd finished her duck, Prickett asked her if she wanted dessert. She said she thought not. "Just coffee," she said.

"I'm going to have ice cream. I have a sweet tooth, and I do like ice cream," he said.

McLeod drank her coffee and looked at the other people in the Nassau Club's dining room. They certainly comprised an older, quieter group than she had yet seen at Princeton. And duller, she decided, duller by far than she had seen.

Fletcher offered after lunch to drop her off at home or

on the campus, but she said she needed the walk. In fact, her knee began to hurt as she walked home. Fletcher Prickett was courtly, all right, almost like one of those old-time Southern gentlemen you hear about. Was courtliness always a cover-up for misogyny? she wondered. She liked him, in a way—he had been very attentive and flattering to her—but there was definitely an unpleasant edge to him. Why did he object so much to women in leadership roles at Princeton? Was it something to do with his mother? Probably. Every bad quality in a person was always Mama's fault, it seemed. Poor Harry and Rosie—what pain and anger had she caused them? Her uneasy thoughts kept turning back to Fletcher Prickett—was there enough venom down there in his innards to propel him to murder a woman who dared to become president of his beloved Princeton?

As she walked, McLeod tried to focus instead on the beauty of Princeton in the spring, with the ornamental pear trees the Borough had planted on Nassau and Witherspoon streets in full bloom. Cherry trees danced like ballerinas along University Place and on Washington Road. The magnolias on the plaza of the Woodrow Wilson School were past their prime, but crabapple and redbud trees were just coming into bloom. Spring was more spectacular up here than it was in Tallahassee, she thought, and then reproved herself for disloyalty. Was anything prettier than the azaleas, the camellias, the wisteria, and the dogwood at home? But they were all gone by now. Spring came earlier down there and was gone much more quickly. When she finally limped into her apartment, she sat down on the sofa and put her foot up to rest her knee.

Then she thought of George, and limped into the bedroom to call him at the office. "I'm sorry, Mr. Bridges is not here," said the secretary who picked up the call.

"This is McLeod Dulaney. Can you tell me when he will be back?"

"Oh, McLeod, this is Maureen. I'm afraid he won't be back."

"What?"

"You'd better talk to him, McLeod. I'm sure he's at home."

McLeod hung up, too stunned to thank Maureen. Quickly, she dialed George at home.

"What's going on?" she asked him. "Are you sick?"

"I've been suspended," he said. "I'm on administrative leave."

"Why have you been suspended?"

"Because of the publicity," he said. "Because it reflects badly on the office of the president of Princeton University. Because Ken Coales is a shit, that's why. If he was going to be the permanent president, I certainly wasn't going to stay. But I hate being kicked out like this."

"I should think so," said McLeod. "It's dreadful."

"It is. I agree."

"Come over here. I'll cook you a fine dinner."

"I have a better idea. Let me call the Ryland Inn and see if they can squeeze two of us in tonight."

"Hadn't you better—isn't this the time to economize?"

"Oh, I'm suspended with pay," said George. "I don't think Ken dared suspend me without pay. Anyway, I'll call you right back."

McLeod sat by the phone. The Ryland Inn was miles away, but it was by all accounts the best restaurant in New Jersey. It was out in the country and in summer grew all its own herbs and vegetables. The food was said to be superb.

"I got us a table," said George when he called back. "But we have to be there for the early seating, at six. Can you be ready by five-fifteen?"

"I'm ready now," said McLeod. "I had lunch at the Nassau Club today with Fletcher Prickett, and I wore my best pink suit. But, you know, I think I'll take a quick shower and change. This is very exciting, going to the Ryland Inn."

When George picked her up, McLeod wore the good black dress she had worn to the funeral. It seemed elegant enough for the Ryland Inn and mournful enough for the circumstances. On the drive up, McLeod asked George if he had seen the police during the day.

"Of course. Nick Perry came by the office this morning to talk to me and started quizzing me again. Who had keys? Who had a grudge against Melissa? Where was I that Monday night? Why didn't I answer the phone, if I was at home? The same old, same old. When he finally left, Coales sent for me. Didn't even call me, just sent Maureen to tell me to come to his office. I went in and he said this was very difficult for him but he felt that it was in the best interests of the university that I leave. He said it would be a suspension, 'until this mess is cleared up.' I asked if I should clean out my desk, and he said that he was sorry, but he thought it was better if I did. So I packed up all my belongings and Maureen helped me carry the cartons to my car. That was it."

"This is the most horrible story I've ever heard. How many years have you been there?"

"I've worked there ever since I graduated in 1972. All my adult life."

"Well, one consolation should be that it's a chance to think about doing something else for a change."

"I knew it was time I did something else. But I thought I'd help Melissa get started and maybe train somebody else while I found the ideal job. Now I don't know what I'll do. Day trading? This is all so demeaning—to be suspected of murdering my boss, whom I *liked*, to have the newspapers print that I'm a suspect, and then for the university to suspend me."

"It doesn't sound like Princeton," said McLeod.

"It's very un-Princetonian," said George. "But then murder is un-Princetonian. Very un-Princetonian."

"But you didn't do the murder."

"I'm suspected. It's un-Princetonian to be a suspect."

When they got to the Ryland Inn, they had time to walk around, inspecting the herb garden before they checked in with the maître'd. He led them to their table, a tiny table for two tucked back into a corner.

"We're lucky to get in at all," said George, "but I'm sorry we're not by a window overlooking the garden."

"Never mind," said McLeod. "I'm delighted to be here."

They took a long time ordering, and George spent even longer with the sommelier. They had both ordered seafood, but they both liked red wine. The sommelier suggested an Alsace red that was good with either red meat or fish, and they were delighted. It went very well indeed with their wild mushroom and red pepper soup, their salad of fresh baby greens from the garden, and their soft shell crabs. They drank the last of the second bottle with their apple tartin for dessert.

BY AN UNSPOKEN agreement they did not talk about the murder. The food they were eating seemed to be the safest topic, and inexhaustible.

Fourteen

MCLEOD AND GEORGE were quiet on the way home from the Ryland Inn. McLeod was thinking about Kenneth Coales. He was an evil man, she decided. Melissa had been about to fire him when she was killed. Nobody likes to be fired, but firing would have been a disaster for Kenneth Coales. While an academic of his stature could always find another job, Ken Coales really wanted to stay in Princeton. He liked being provost. And there was his girlfriend. Not only was he possibly the murderer, but McLeod thought Coales was the one who had tipped off the Trenton *Times* about George's being questioned so much. And he could easily be the one who told Nick Perry that he had tried to call George the night of the murder and got no answer.

Yes, Kenneth Coales was somebody she really wanted to find out more about. But how?

When George asked her what she was going to do the next day, she almost told him, "Get on the trail of Kenneth Coales," but recovered in time to omit that part of her agenda. "I'm going to spend a lot of time, no doubt, recovering from the hangover I'm going to have."

"There's that," said George gloomily. When they got to her apartment, she invited him in for coffee. George came, but said, when she headed for the kitchen, "Don't bother with coffee. Come here."

He kissed her with such ardor that she decided it was her Christian duty to help him through this bad patch in any way that she could and led him off to her bed.

They did have hangovers the next day, which vast quantities of cold orange juice and black coffee (for George) and tea (for McLeod) failed to assuage. They read the papers and were pleased to note that there was no follow-up story in the Trenton *Times* or *The New York Times* about George's being interviewed extensively.

"What are you going to do today?" asked McLeod.

"I don't know. I don't think it's the proper time to talk to a head hunter about a new job. I guess I'll just sit around and read Trollope for a while, wait until the murder is solved. And you?"

"It's Tuesday. I'm going swimming. I haven't been swimming for a week. Swimming always helps a hangover. I think I have a student conference sometime today. And I need to concentrate on planning Thursday's class. I've neglected the class this past week. And I want to talk to Sophy and find out how she's doing." She rattled on about everything she intended to do, except the most important thing: investigating Kenneth Coales.

"I'll go home and clean up my apartment," said George. "And I may play some golf."

As McLeod walked to campus, she wondered how to proceed. I wish my head were clearer, she thought. She could go down to the Lewis Thomas Laboratory—the students called it the "Purina Building" because the distinguished architect who had designed the exterior had come up with a design of bricks laid in a checkerboard fashion—and talk to people in the Molecular Biology Department about Kenneth Coales. Should she try to talk to Coales's girlfriend? Or his wife? Maybe the wife would be easiest. If she had a grievance, maybe she would pour out all the dirt on her husband.

That would be best, she thought, to seek out the wife. First, she would go to her office to check the mail, e-mail, and voice mail; then swim, eat lunch, and try to see Mrs. Coales.

In her office, she looked at the *Daily Princetonian,* and noted that it had a brief story about George being interviewed, but then listed a great many other people from the university who had also been interviewed more than once. "Good for Nick Perry," McLeod said to herself. "I bet he pointed that out to the *Prince.*"

From her office she called Stephanie King, that perpetual fount of information, to ask her more about Mrs. Coales.

"Caroline?" said Stephanie. "She's a saint. Like I told you, she throws pots. That's really all she cares about. I guess she had to find something to do since Ken has been such a ladies' man. Her children are grown and she devotes herself to ceramics. And she's good. She has shows all over, and she's sold a piece to the Museum of Modern Art, I think. You'd like her."

So McLeod called Caroline Coales and asked if she could come by and see her that afternoon.

"What is this about?" asked Mrs. Coales. "Are you selling something?"

"Oh, no," said McLeod. "I'm working on an article about your husband, since he's acting president." Why didn't I do this sooner, wondered McLeod. Charlie Campbell would be glad to have a story by a staff reporter about the acting president of Princeton for the *Star of Florida.* Wouldn't he? She had sent him a story about Melissa Faircloth's inauguration and he had been very pleased. Anyway, it was a good excuse to get people to talk. "And I wanted to talk to you, of course," she said to Mrs. Coales.

They set a time, and McLeod went swimming, ate a salad at the student center, and headed for home to get her car, since the Coaleses lived out in Griggstown.

As she reached Nassau Street, she ran into Fletcher Prickett, who seemed inordinately glad to see her. "Hello, m'dear," he said, clasping her hand warmly. "My favorite lady professor. And by the way, I saw in the paper this morning that That Woman hired four more women just before she left. Can you believe it? The place is definitely going to be without men. I hear they've taken all the urinals out of Nassau Hall." He laughed loudly at his own joke.

McLeod laughed, too. You had to laugh, she thought, at such rampant sexism. It was so grotesque it was funny. Fletcher was a diversion from criminal detection. "That's a pretty tie," she said. "I like the little gold leaves."

"That's my Ivy Club tie," Fletcher said. McLeod remembered *This Side of Paradise*, where the Fitzgerald/Blaine figure describes Ivy as the eating club for the "detached and breathlessly aristocratic." Cottage, which Fitzgerald joined himself, he said, was a "mélange of brilliant adventurers and well-dressed philanderers." Fletcher was fingering his tie, which was green with little gold ivy leafs on it, with obvious pride. "I wear it sometimes when I come to events on campus."

"And what brings you to campus today?"

"I'm here nearly every day," said Fletcher. "I love this place to death, you know. It's the breath of life to me. But I came today to see the exhibition in Graphic Arts in the library. It's tigers."

"It's what?"

"Tigers." When McLeod still seemed puzzled, he shouted: "Tigers! You know, Princeton tigers."

"Oh," said McLeod, imagining a gallery full of stuffed tigers.

"The curator of Graphic Arts—fine fellow he is, but I suppose he'll be replaced by a member of your fair sex soon—has gathered up a lot of examples of the tiger in art. It opens officially on Sunday, but I'm here for a sneak preview. I lent my painting by—oh, what's his name? Anyway, it's a beautiful painting six feet tall and eight feet long. Can you come along with me to take a look at it, dear lady?"

"I wish I could, Mr. Prickett, but I'm on my way to an appointment."

"Oh, you ladies are always so engaged," said Prickett. "But you must call me Fletcher, m'dear. And we must schedule another delightful lunch."

"Wonderful," said McLeod and walked on home, thinking it was odd that Fletcher couldn't remember the name of the artist who had painted his tiger—all that mattered to him was that it was a tiger.

WHEN MCLEOD DROVE out Canal Road and found the Coaleses' house, she loved it. It was an old house overlooking the Delaware and Raritan Canal. The surrounding woods were lace-trimmed with dogwood blossoms and wild roses. Mrs. Coales answered the front door, and led McLeod out to her studio in a smaller building behind the house, and then offered her coffee.

McLeod accepted—she preferred tea, but it seemed cozier to go ahead and have some coffee with Caroline Coales. Anything that would make the interview go more easily. The studio apparently consisted of two rooms. The room they were in was lined with shelves holding handmade pitchers and vases and bowls. A desk with a chair stood by the window looking out over the woods. The kiln and the potter's wheel must have been in the other room.

Mrs. Coales was thin and rangy and redheaded, rumpled-looking in old clay-stained dungarees and sweater. If Bruce and Martha Cowan had seemed like two rosy baked apples, Caroline Coales was a carrot, just dug up.

"This is such a charming building," said McLeod. "All this afternoon sun pouring in. What was it originally?"

"I don't know," said Caroline. "Who knows? A chicken house or workshop of some kind. But it's one reason I wanted to buy the house. The other room, where I work, gets lots of sun, too."

Taking this as an invitation, McLeod walked over and glanced through the door into the other room, which held, as she expected, a potter's wheel and a kiln.

"It's so warm in here," said McLeod.

"The kiln heats it up," said Caroline. "And I have a heater, too, for times when the kiln's not running. But you wanted to talk about my husband."

"Tell me about yourself first," McLeod said, having learned, when interviewing A about B, to ask A first about herself before getting down to business and asking about B.

"There's not much to tell," said Caroline. "I'm just a faculty wife who throws pots."

"But I understand you're a very good potter. . . ."

"I am good," said Caroline, "but I'm not as good as I'd like to be."

"From what I see," said McLeod, looking around at the ceramics on the shelves, "you've very good indeed. I love the soft glazes, especially that pale green with the overglaze of yellow. Do you sell from your studio here?"

"Sometimes I do, but I have a gallery in Lambertville and one in New York that takes a few pieces."

"How long have you been potting?" asked McLeod.

"For years," said Caroline. "I got interested when I was in college."

"And you kept it up?"

"After I graduated, I worked in a department store—isn't that what all art majors do? Then I married Kenneth, and I worked to help him finish graduate school at Stony Brook and then I had a baby. You know the story." McLeod did know the story, and had long ago decided that wives who worked to support their husbands through graduate school were saints who were usually repaid with complete disloyalty by the ungrateful husbands.

"When did you get back into potting?"

"After the children got bigger."

"Was that before you moved to Princeton? You came here in 1980?" McLeod had done her homework.

"Yes, I had gone back to potting before we left Stony Brook. I shared a studio with three other potters there."

"Did you buy this place as soon as you moved to Princeton?"

"No, Kenneth wanted to live in one of those grand faculty houses on Fitzrandolph, so we did, but there was no place there for me to work. I looked for houses out from town with a place to put a kiln and found this one. Kenneth agreed. I think he decided that it might be a good idea to have me out in the country."

"Why was that?"

"Oh, various reasons. Anyway we moved out here and I fixed up this building and really got down to work."

"Has your husband ever done any ceramics?"

"Oh, no. He's a molecular biologist. He's into theory. I don't think he'd get his hands dirty with clay. He says that he could do art if he wanted to, that if you can do science, you can do anything."

McLeod gaped. "Did he really say that?"

"Oh, yes. And he believes it."

McLeod thought this over. "Do you agree?"

"No," said Caroline Coales. "I don't. I think some people can do science and do art but not many. Lots of scientists don't know the difference between a painting and a sculpture."

"Are you interested in science?"

"I'm interested in the science of baking clay, but that's about it. I garden, so I guess I'm interested in botany."

McLeod changed direction. "How many children do you have?" she asked.

"Two. A girl and a boy."

"Where are they now?" Interviewing Caroline Coales was like pulling teeth, McLeod thought. Wasn't she going to volunteer anything?

"Our son is in Washington. He's at a think tank, a rather conservative one, actually, and doing well. Our daughter is married and has five children. She lives not too far away—

in Hopewell, so that's nice. I get to see a lot of her and the children."

"Five children? In this day and age? That's wonderful. Does your son have any children?"

"He and his partner have adopted one," said Caroline Coales frostily.

"So I can say the acting president has six grandchildren?"

"Kenneth doesn't acknowledge our son's child."

"Do you?" asked McLeod.

"Of course. He's my son, isn't he?"

"But your husband enjoys your daughter's children?"

Caroline Coales looked at McLeod coldly. "My husband enjoys his work and his—" she said, and stopped. She continued in a determinedly brighter tone. "He really is a workaholic, and he cares a great deal about Princeton."

McLeod could feel Caroline Coales's unhappiness, which chilled her, in spite of the sunshine and warmth in the studio. Poor woman. Her husband had apparently been delighted to get her out into the country. Why? Because of his girlfriend? She was sure that Caroline had meant to say that her husband enjoyed his work and his mistress, but had decided to protect him. Why didn't she divorce the man? Her children were grown. She could surely support herself, or live on whatever she could get out of Coales. She decided to keep going. "Will you move into Lowrie House?"

"No."

"Why not?"

"In the first place, the acting president doesn't live in Lowrie House," said Caroline Coales. She stopped.

"And in the second place?"

Caroline looked at her. "McLeod, would you like a drink? Let's go in the house, shall we?"

"That would be great," said McLeod, and followed Caroline back to the house. Caroline led her to a glass-walled room filled with plants.

"It's lovely," said McLeod. "It looks like a conservatory in an English novel."

"That's precisely the effect I was after when we built this addition," said Caroline. "Maybe we should have tea instead of a drink. What will it be—tea or sherry?"

"I think I'll have tea," said McLeod. "I have to drive back to town. But you have a drink if you like."

"Are you sure? Sit down and I'll be right back." McLeod hardly had time to gaze at the potted palms and ficus trees before Caroline reappeared with a tea tray on which stood a lone, but rather large, glass of sherry. She poured McLeod's tea, offered her cream and sugar and tiny watercress sandwiches. "It grows in a brook back in the back," said Caroline when McLeod exclaimed over the cress. "That's the first of the season's cress." She sat down with her sherry and caressed the glass with her hands before she sipped from it.

"You were about to tell me the second reason why you'd never move into Lowrie House," prompted McLeod.

"I was, wasn't I? Don't put this in the paper, but you know Kenneth is dying to be named president, I mean permanent president. He has wanted it for years. He fought to get the appointment as provost. Provost was second best, but second best is pretty good if you think about it. Still he had hopes of being promoted to president when Edgar resigned. But the trustees went mad—at least Kenneth thought they were deranged—and hired a woman. He didn't like Melissa Faircloth. He hated Melissa Faircloth, as a matter of fact, but he decided to stay on. He had some job offers, but he decided to stick it out at Princeton. Then he found out Melissa Faircloth didn't like him either and wanted him to leave. He was shocked."

"Why didn't he just resign? And go somewhere else?"

Caroline Coales was quiet for a few minutes before she answered. "You are the nicest person I've talked to in years, and I'm telling you things I haven't told my best friends. Kenneth didn't want to leave Princeton. He tells everybody he wants to stay because he loves Princeton, but that's not it at all. He loves a woman named Rosita Sanchez. He's obsessed with her. And she won't divorce her husband and marry him, and he won't leave Princeton without her. I told him it might be better if he didn't take the acting presidency. He could still be a candidate for the permanent job, and if he didn't get it, at least he'd still be provost."

"He can go back to teaching molecular biology, can't he?" asked McLeod, trying to remember what Stephanie had told her about Kenneth Coales. Then another aspect of the situation struck her. "You mean you and your husband discuss all this—I mean Rosita and everything. And you advise him on his problems?"

"Oh, yes. I'm his friend and advisor, he says."

McLeod mutely held out her cup for a refill. "The situation doesn't upset you?"

"Not any longer," said Caroline. "It used to. When I first found out, I tried to get Kenneth to a marriage counselor, and then I said I'd divorce him. He said I'd never move out because of the kiln. I guess he was right. He said he'd never move out either. Don't ask me why. And I just didn't care anymore. In a way I was tired of him, tired of his ambition, tired of his attitude toward our son because he's gay, tired of his affair with Rosita. But it just bored me. I realized I had created my own little life—the children, grandchildren, pots, reading, gardening, the few friends I have left. I didn't really need Kenneth. But he needs me. At least he needs the appearance of a marriage to be president, even acting president, I guess. And besides, Rosita's husband, I understand, is insanely jealous of her. I'm some protection for poor Kenneth."

How could she say "poor Kenneth"! And why on earth would Caroline bother to protect Ken Coales? But McLeod reflected that nobody ever understands other people's marriages anyway. Caroline certainly appeared to be the classic enabler.

Caroline was finally volunteering information. "And I

have more money this way," she said. "I can help the children more, especially my daughter. They don't have much money, and if we split up and had two households, I wouldn't have much either. I can tell you think I'm crazy, but it just seems to be best for everybody this way."

Again McLeod changed tactics. "What were you and Ken doing on the night that Melissa Faircloth was murdered?" she asked.

"What night was that?" asked Caroline. She got up and went to get the bottle of Harvey's Bristol Cream and refilled her glass. "I guess I haven't kept up with it. I hardly ever read the papers anymore. I told you I live in my own little world."

"It was Monday night," said McLeod, naming the date.

"I don't have any idea," said Caroline. "Let me finish this sherry and I'll get my diary. It's upstairs."

It was some time before Caroline brought her diary—and a fresh glass of sherry—into the conservatory and sat down. "Let's see," she said. "You know, I don't keep much of a diary. I just note down what I did and what Kenneth did, if I have any idea what he did. I don't know why I bother. But it's interesting to look back over the old diaries and see what we did on, say, Easter Sunday ten years ago."

She flipped through the pages of the diary. "Here it is. I was at home. I watched 'Masterpiece Theatre.' It was *The Way We Live Now.* Kenneth wasn't here. He had said he would be—and I was ready to cook him a steak, but he didn't show up until midnight. I don't know why I write things like that down."

"It's good to have a record," said McLeod. "And he was home after that? I mean after he came home at midnight?"

"Oh, yes."

McLeod felt enormous pity and great admiration for this woman. "Look, I've stayed too long and taken up too much of your time. I must go."

Caroline Coales rose with her. "You will protect me, won't you? Don't quote me on all that stuff about Kenneth."

"I won't. I promise," said McLeod. "I want to talk to your husband, too. He's the one who's acting president. But it was good to talk to you. And personally, I'm very glad I got to meet you."

"Me, too," said Caroline.

ON THE DRIVE back to Princeton, McLeod reflected on the interview. It always amazed her—the things people told her. But Caroline Coales was marvelous, in her own way. No wonder nobody seemed to like Kenneth Coales. How on earth could you like him? She thought about George, a suspect in a murder case, but a model of probity and so funny and dear. Kenneth Coales is behind all George's troubles, she said to herself. He's the one who told the police he tried to call George and nobody answered. I bet he told the police George had an affair with Melissa. And now he's gotten rid of George at the office. I've got to talk to Nick Perry again, but first I have to talk to the devil himself.

Fifteen

MCLEOD DROVE STRAIGHT home from Griggstown and called the president's office. Kenneth Coales couldn't have been nicer when he found out she wanted to interview him for "a story about being acting president."

"Would you like to come out to our house?" he asked. "See where I live?" He was obviously reveling in the prospect of an article about him.

"No, the office will be fine," said McLeod, not telling him that she had seen his house and met his wife. Caroline would tell him later, she was sure.

"When would you like to come?" he asked her.

"Tomorrow?" she said tentatively.

"Fine." Coales said he had a full calendar but that he would put her up front, ahead of all his other appointments, if she didn't mind coming in at seven-thirty.

"I'd love to come at seven-thirty," she said.

"I'm still in my old office," he reminded her. "The president's office is still off-limits to some extent."

McLeod hung up and called George at home. "What did you do with your newfound leisure?" she asked him.

"I worked on my résumé," he said. "You should see it. It's beautiful. It's a work of art. I may frame it. And then I played golf. I picked up a partner at the Princeton Country Club—that's the public course in case you didn't know. The exclusive one is Springdale. Wouldn't you know the public course in Princeton would be named the Country Club? Anyway, my partner and I joined another pair to make a foursome. They were great. Two of them had been laid off and one took early retirement. We exchanged all these hard-luck stories. They're my new best friends."

"A support group," said McLeod.

"That's right. Then I came home and went grocery shopping. You're invited to dinner tonight."

"I accept. Can I bring anything?"

"I've got it all. See you about six."

"Wait a minute. Did the police bother you today?"

"Didn't hear a peep out of them."

"What about newspapers? Were they on your back about being questioned?"

"I got a couple of calls this morning but I said I had no comment and they left me alone. Then I was gone to play golf. If they called, they didn't leave messages."

"Oh, good, maybe it will all die down," said McLeod.

"Maybe, but the damage has been done."

"I'll see you at six. Can't wait."

"Same here."

AT DINNER, SHE reported on her visit with Caroline Coales. "Kenneth Coales really is a horrible man," she said. "He's wildly ambitious. He doesn't want to leave town to get another job because he's madly in love with the woman in Spanish and Portuguese. He hated Melissa Faircloth. He won't have anything to do with his son, who's gay. Their marriage is a shambles. Caroline knows all about the mistress, but she aids and abets him as far as I can tell. He's a real shit. I hate to be driven to using language like that, but that's what he is. She worked to help him get through graduate school, too."

"I knew he was awful," agreed George. "I couldn't work for him. Now I'm not working at all."

"You're just on leave, paid leave."

"I'm going to be jobless, though. I'm going to resign. I can't work for Ken Coales."

"He may not last long. The trustees may get busy and find a president in a snap, like that." McLeod snapped her fingers. "It took me forever when I was a little girl in Atlanta to learn to snap my fingers."

"You do it very well," said George. "But presidential searches are long and drawn out, let me tell you."

"Maybe you can stay on leave with pay until they find somebody and then it will be somebody you love, who loves you, and everything will be hunky-dory."

George sighed. "That's not the way life works," he said. "Who knows how long I am going to be under suspicion of murder?"

"Well, if Kenneth Coales did the murder and they catch him, then you'll be cleared," McLeod said. "It's that simple. And Kenneth Coales will definitely be gone. And anybody else in their right mind will want you back in the president's office. Don't you think so?"

"I don't know, McLeod. I don't know. I'm not sure of anything. I've lost my self-confidence."

"Don't do that. All we have to do is prove Kenneth Coales did the murder. That should be simple enough," said McLeod.

"So you think Coales murdered Melissa?"

"I do," said McLeod.

"Last week you thought Clarence Robbins was the murderer," said George.

"That was last week. Sometimes it takes a while to get things straight."

"So Coales is the suspect *du jour*?"

"*De la semaine,* I guess," said McLeod, determined not

to lose patience. "I don't change my suspicions every day, just every week."

THE NEXT MORNING McLeod got up at six and showered, ate breakfast, drank her tea, and drove to campus. She reached the provost's office at seven-twenty-five and found the door to the outer office open, and the door to Coales's office also open. He appeared immediately, smiling more broadly than she had ever seen before.

"You're a real early bird, aren't you? Come in," he said.

He really likes publicity, McLeod thought. He wasn't this friendly even when he was asking me to move into Lowrie House. "Good morning," she said, producing as good a smile as she could manage for a man she had grown to detest beyond belief.

"We'll sit here," said Coales, leading her over to a pair of armchairs by the window. McLeod sat down. "Will you have some coffee?" said Coales, still standing. "My secretary isn't here, as you can see, but we've all learned to make coffee for ourselves since the women's movement has become so powerful."

"I should hope so," said McLeod tartly. "No, thanks. I'm fine."

"Good." Coales sat down in the other armchair and looked at her expectantly.

As usual, McLeod began with noncombative questions. Where did he grow up? (Montclair.) Was he interested in science in elementary school? (Yes.) High school? (Yes.)

What did he major in at Princeton?

"Biology. I thought I was going to be a doctor. And the department had not split, as it has since, into ecology and evolutionary biology on the one hand and molecular biology on the other."

"And why didn't you go on to medical school?"

"I realized I was better at experimental work than—" He stopped.

"Than what?" McLeod prompted him.

"Than a lot of other people were," Coales went on. "That sounds vain, I know, but it's true. And I figured that other people practice medicine and get along with people. I wanted to work in a lab."

"And you did?"

"Oh, yes, and then molecular biology came along. I knew that was my destiny. The very basic modules of life, nuclei and cells and the transmission of genetic information, and then DNA and how to manipulate it."

"And ecology and evolutionary biology is the old-fashioned biology?" asked McLeod.

"That's right—botany and physiology and animal behavior and evolution. That's not bad, but I like the harder stuff."

McLeod always felt inadequate interviewing scientists about their work—she could handle writers, politicians, preachers, but not scientists. She decided to move on to other topics.

"Didn't you hate to give up science for administration when you became provost?"

"In a way, I suppose I did, Ms. Dulaney, but I wanted to do anything I could to help Princeton. Princeton changed my life. I went to public school, and Princeton opened up another world to me. And Princeton has a way of making you want to give back. Not just take, but give back. Do you understand what I'm trying to say?"

"Of course," said McLeod, who was thinking, What a phony he is.

"And I thought if I could be of service to Princeton, then it behooved me to give up my scientific work for the time being. Although, you understand, I still have an office in the Lewis Thomas Lab building, and in fact, I still teach a seminar in morphogenesis from time to time."

"What is morphogenesis?" asked McLeod.

"It's the formation of the structure of an organism," said Coales.

"I see," said McLeod, who didn't see at all. "Is that an undergraduate course?"

"Yes, it is. Princeton emphasizes undergraduate teaching above everything else, you know."

"I know," said McLeod. "Nobody ever misses an opportunity to tell me. And do you miss the science?"

"Of course I miss the science, but I feel that I'm useful in Nassau Hall, and I enjoy the experience of being among the leaders of this great institution."

"But now it will be some time before you can get back to science, won't it?"

"That's right. But again I feel that I'm being of service."

"When the trustees name a new president, will you go back to being provost?"

"The provost serves at the pleasure of the president," said Coales. "It will depend entirely on the person they name."

"Is there a chance that they'll name you?"

"I suppose there's always a chance," said Coales, smiling ruefully, "but I would say that chance is very small."

"Let's say you're not named president," said McLeod, "and that the new president for some unknown reason doesn't want you as the provost. Will you go back to the Molecular Biology Department?"

"I'll cross that bridge when I come to it, Ms. Dulaney."

"You were provost under Edgar Battle. And then provost for Melissa Faircloth. Was it a big change to have a woman boss?"

"I liked to think I worked with, not for, Edgar Battle and Melissa Faircloth. It was a change, of course, but a change because they were two different people, not necessarily because they were two different genders."

"I see," said McLeod, who was thinking that she would never interview another academic scientist as long as she lived. "I'm asking this because I know my editor will want to know. How does it affect you when your boss, or the person you work with, is murdered? Were you a suspect? Are you a suspect?"

"A suspect? Good God, no," Coales was truly upset, but seemed to pull himself together. "I was a suspect, I suppose, in the sense that everyone who knew the murdered person is a suspect until proven innocent."

"Have you been proven innocent?" she asked him. Coales did not answer. "Do you have an alibi that proves you innocent?"

"Yes, I have an alibi. I was at home with my wife."

"She says you weren't."

"What is going on?" Coales was clearly angry. "She told me you were out there asking questions, but she thought it was just the wife-of-the-successful-man feature. What were you talking about to her?"

"We just talked about what it's like to be the wife of the successful man, as you say. But I did happen to ask about that Monday night, and she said you weren't at home."

"Bitch," said Coales. He stood up.

It was unclear to McLeod whether he was calling her or his wife a bitch. She stood up too. "I'm sorry," she said. "Look, this is not worth getting angry about. Caroline was sure, and I'm sure, that you were with someone else who can vouch for your presence. Right?"

Coales was recovering. "I apologize for my language. Yes, of course, I was in a meeting. I shouldn't have told you I was at home with my wife. That was silly, wasn't it? I just thought it sounded like a good husband and family man. I want to appear friendly in this article. Where will it appear, by the way?"

"The *Star of Florida*," said McLeod. "That's Florida's oldest newspaper."

"Oh, really?" Coales was obviously disappointed, but he was calming down. She risked sitting down again.

"Tell me about what you do in your spare time," she said.

"Spare time?" asked Coales, genuinely puzzled. He, too, sat down.

"It's a question interviewers always ask. We want to present the whole picture of a man, or woman. Do you fish? Listen to music? Paint? Travel?"

"I listen to music." Coales appeared to be relieved to have an answer.

"What kind of music?"

"All kinds."

"No favorites?"

"You know—Bach, Beethoven, that kind of thing," said Coales vaguely.

McLeod, giving up on the music and spare time activities, asked him about his grandchildren. "Oh, yes, we have five grandchildren."

"Do you spend a lot of time with them—they live fairly near, I understand? Do you have pictures of them?"

"Pictures? No, I don't."

McLeod gave in to an impulse. What did she have to lose?

"This may seem off the subject, but I wonder if you think there's a plot to implicate George Bridges in the murder of Melissa Faircloth? Somebody told the police that he didn't answer his phone that night and George says he was at home with a bad tooth and the phone didn't ring. And somebody gave all that information to the Trenton *Times* about the police questioning him." She pounced. "Was it you, Mr. Coales?"

"Is this a question for this *Florida Star* or whatever it is?"

"I just wondered."

"Why on earth would I do things like that? George is a valuable assistant. Why would I want to implicate him?"

"And if you were in a meeting that Monday night, why did you call George?"

"I think this interview is ranging too far afield, Ms. Dulaney. These questions are quite inappropriate for an interview for a Florida newspaper—no matter how distinguished a small paper it might be."

"These are things that have puzzled me," said McLeod. "That's all." She returned to more conventional questions. "Tell me if you have any goals to accomplish as acting president," she said.

"I have one goal: to guard this institution and turn it over to the permanent president in the best possible condition. Princeton, as I've said, means a great deal to me—and I hope I mean something to it."

"I'm sure you do," said McLeod. She rose this time before he did, thanked him for the interview, and left.

Sixteen

MCLEOD WAS IN her office by eight-thirty, raging about Kenneth Coales. What a pious poseur he was. He must have been with his Rosita Sanchez on the night Melissa was murdered. He must have told the police where he was. Was the girlfriend a good alibi? Would she back him up? In court—where her husband would learn about it? How did she and Ken manage to get together anyway? As busy as he was—and as married as she was? No wonder he had no spare time. He had said he listened to music—what humbug! "Bach, Beethoven, that kind of thing." And he was the most conceited man she'd ever met—saying he was "better at research than other people" and "if you could do science, you could do anything."

McLeod was driven as never before to unmask the murderer of Melissa Faircloth. It wasn't just a disinterested desire for justice, although she liked to think she was strong on that score, too, but the real motivation was the need to clear George Bridges. It was so absurd that he was under suspicion. It was horrible that the newspaper had printed a story about his being questioned, and it was monstrous that that evil Kenneth Coales had dared to suspend him. Coales was, she was sure, the real murderer.

Was this a good time for another little talk with Nick Perry? Maybe so. But first, she had to type up her notes on the interviews with Caroline and Ken Coales. She would indeed write a story about the acting president of Princeton and his wife.

And before she did that, she would read the papers. There was nothing new on the murder investigation. The *Daily Princetonian*, however, had a story about yet another rape on campus, and this time the victim was a student. The young woman had been walking along Shapiro Walk from the engineering quad to her dormitory at 3 A.M. when a man jumped at her from behind and raped her. She said he was white and, she thought, older than a student.

Why did young women walk alone in dark places at three o'clock in the morning? McLeod asked herself. The *Prince* trumpeted that the university was going to have to do more to protect its students. Perhaps locks and keys were the answer, an editorial mused. Residential colleges at Yale were walled and the gates locked at all times. Would Princeton have to do the same thing? the *Prince* asked.

How horrible, thought McLeod. But she did not want to be distracted from the search for the murderer. She wanted to talk to Nick Perry, but first, she must check on Sophy.

Sophy didn't answer the phone in her room, so McLeod sent her an e-mail to say she was sorry she hadn't seen her, but would look forward to seeing her in class the next day.

Then she called Nick Perry. She wanted to talk to him about the provost, and she wanted to thank him—if, indeed, he was the one who had told the *Prince* about people besides George whom the police had interviewed extensively. Perry told her that they had just made an arrest.

"You have? Who?"

"Billy Masters."

"Billy Masters, the movie star?"

"Yep."

"But why would he kill Melissa Faircloth?"

"What? Oh, he didn't kill Melissa Faircloth. We arrested him for the rapes on the Princeton campus."

"You're kidding."

"I don't kid about things like this."

McLeod was speechless.

"I thought you'd like a scoop," Nick said.

"Thanks, Nick. It won't be a scoop long. All the wires will have it, and my paper in Florida wouldn't be all that interested in paying for my own version." The truth was that she found the story distasteful. "You'll be telling everybody, right?"

"The chief will be holding a press conference soon in that temporary press room in Alexander Hall," he said. "He hopes that this story will hold the attention of the media crowd long enough to keep them quiet about the lack of progress on the Faircloth case. But the important thing for you to remember is that you had an exclusive for ten minutes."

"I'll remember it, Nick," said McLeod. "How did you catch him?"

"The last victim said she thought it was Billy Masters. I guess he got careless about covering his face. The girls couldn't believe it really was Billy Masters, and neither could we. But we talked to him, and everything he said raised questions. Then DNA clinched it—they expedited the analysis. We just got the report today. The chief and I went over and picked him up. They were actually shooting a scene with him in it. The producer-director guy was mad, let me tell you."

"Max Bolt?" said McLeod. "I bet he was. I was on campus all morning. When did you make the arrest? Where was I?"

"Not long ago. I just got back."

"Well, I guess I'll go over to the press conference, even if I don't write a story. Thanks, Nick."

• • •

AT THE PRESS conference in Alexander Hall, Princeton Chief of Police John Ives handed out brief press releases, and formally announced the arrest of Billy Masters of Los Angeles, California, for two rapes on the Princeton University campus. Sean O'Mally, the Director of Public Safety for the university, stood beside him. In answer to questions, the chief said that Masters had been taken to the Princeton Borough lockup and been arraigned before the Borough judge. The judge, because of the seriousness of the charges, had refused to grant bail. Master was accordingly transported to the county jail. Chief Ives refused to answer questions about the evidence.

Masters's lawyer, Cowboy Tarleton, said that he would go to the superior court judge and ask for bail there. "It's insane that a man of Mr. Masters's stature is being held without bail. He's not going to run away."

Max Bolt was there, and spoke emotionally to the press, first saying that Billy Masters absolutely must not remain in jail, that he wouldn't run anywhere, that he had a movie to finish. He added that Billy Masters was a sick man and needed help, not condemnation and persecution from the criminal justice system. Masters was a great artist and deserved every consideration.

"You mean that a movie star should get special treatment?" asked Dick Coffey from the Trenton *Times*.

Bolt looked startled. That was exactly what he meant, but he couldn't say so. He refused to answer more questions.

The reporters turned back to the chief and began to question him. He, too, refused to answer more questions, but reporters began to shout questions at him. "Did Billy Masters rape Melissa Faircloth?" The chief looked startled at that one, but said, "No." "Are you still working on the murder investigation?" asked one.

"What do you mean, 'Are we still working on that?' " he said. "Of course we're still working on it. We're devoting a hundred percent of our resources to that investigation."

"What percentage of your resources did the rape investigation take?"

"The Public Safety Office at the university was invaluable in that regard." He added that there was nothing new at the moment, but that reporters would certainly be kept informed of progress, as information could be made public. But that was all he had to say today, he said.

As everybody began to leave, McLeod hurried to catch Max Bolt. "How will this affect your movie?" she asked him.

"It pretty well brings it to a grinding halt," said Bolt. "How can I get anywhere without Masters?"

"Don't you think Cowboy Tarleton will be able to get him out on bail in Superior Court?" she asked.

"Maybe. I hope so. But you know what worries me? Not that he'll run away if he gets out, but that he'll do it again," said Bolt.

"Good heavens!" said McLeod. "Did you know about these proclivities of Billy Masters?"

"I did. Everybody did. That's why he had body guards. The guards weren't hired to protect him, but to protect the nubile young women of Princeton University. They were supposed to keep him from this kind of activity, but they failed miserably. I think the one that was on at night was always drunk. Don't print any of this. Please. He is sick, you know."

"He must be," said McLeod. "Why else would he take women by force, when he's the idol of millions and could have almost anybody he wanted?"

"A good point," said Max.

"What will happen next?"

"I don't know," said Bolt. "The studio is flying in lawyers. I suppose this is just another snag in this accursed movie's progress," said Bolt. "I've got to go. See you."

"See you," said McLeod, looking around for Dick Coffey. She wanted to ask him a question. It was still the murder that concerned her most, much as the capture of the rapist was a welcome relief.

Coffey was leaving, and she ran after him, catching him in the courtyard in front of Alexander Hall.

"Dick, my name is McLeod Dulaney. I've met you. I'm teaching a writing course here, but I'm really a newspaper reporter."

"I remember you," Coffey said. He was tall and thin and good-looking with a nice smile. He was very, very young.

"I wanted to talk to you a minute," she said. "You know that story you had in Monday's paper about George Bridges?"

Coffey nodded.

"Would you tell me where you got that information about him being questioned?"

"I can't reveal my sources," he said primly.

"Come on. I want to know if it was the police, or somebody else. It seems to me someone is out to try to frame George."

"Somebody else is trying to help George. The *Prince* had a story—"

"I saw that, too," said McLeod. "Still, I think somebody is trying to get George in trouble. And I want to know who it is. I think whoever told you about George being questioned may be the murderer."

"Really?" Coffey blanched.

"Isn't it logical? Somebody who wanted to divert attention from himself."

"Maybe so, but I just can't tell you," he said. "You know how it is. I promised the source anonymity."

"I understand," said McLeod. "Just tell me if I'm right. I won't betray him as your source. I just want to *know.* I think it was"—she lowered her voice—"Kenneth Coales?"

"I can't tell you," said Dick, miserable and no longer prim.

"Well, thanks anyway," said McLeod. "I'm impressed with your rectitude."

"Keep in touch," said Coffey.

"Sure," she said, and started back to her office. Now she had to ask Nick to reveal who had told him that George had not answered his phone that Monday night. Well, she could ask Nick, but he probably wouldn't tell her. Still, she had a good idea that it was Kenneth Coales's work, too, all part of a diabolical scheme to incriminate George.

In the office, she delayed calling Nick again and finally typed up her notes. By the time she'd finished that chore, it was noon, and time for a swim, she decided. She strolled down to Dillon Gym, glad it was somewhat warmer today, glad her knee was getting well, and glad she could go swimming. Swimming, as a friend of hers had remarked, was the only sport that was both relaxing and stimulating.

In the locker room, while she undressed, she admired once more the tall Gothic windows that filled the place with light. She put on her suit, weighed herself—shuddering at the figure on which the scale marker finally rested—and carrying towel, cap, and goggles, walked down the five flights of stairs—forty-two steps in all—she had counted them—to the pool. It wasn't crowded, and she dived into the medium-fast lane and began to swim.

Most swimmers in the pool at Dillon Gym were courteous, but McLeod had noticed that a few were sometimes not too good at sharing a lane and tended to flail wildly and hit other swimmers with their arms. Alas, today, she had one of those flailers in the lane with her, a man who kept hitting her. He was faster than she was and he passed her often, whopping her each time. It was almost as though he were doing it on purpose.

Finally, feeling somewhat bruised, McLeod ducked under the barrier and moved into the slow lane. Somehow she wasn't enjoying the delights of Dillon Pool as much as she usually did. Even the orange and black tiles seemed merely garish, not warmly sentimental, and the shields of the Ivy League schools looked pretentious, not warm and clubbable. She felt cold and decided to cut her swim short. When she climbed the ladder to get out, the man who had flailed away at her was getting out of the medium lane, pulling himself up over the edge of the pool. Showing off his muscles, McLeod thought, just because he doesn't have to use the ladder. And then she realized the man was Kenneth Coales.

She hurried out of the pool area and up the stairs. She reached forward to push the swinging door open, but Coales had caught up with her and held it for her, his expression full of mock courtesy.

"I didn't know you were a swimmer," she said. She was very conscious of his strength and stared helplessly at his chest, which seemed to be very hairy.

"I should have mentioned it as one of my recreations, but I didn't. You can add it to your article, can't you?" Coales was not smiling.

"I normally love swimming, but today I had a neighbor who wasn't very good at staying in his own lane," said McLeod, and she was not smiling either.

A man, dripping water, flapping his flip-flops, came up the stairs and started toward them from the landing below where they stood. When Coales looked back at the flopping sound, McLeod seized the moment to duck into the gym corridor and then into the women's locker room.

Showering and shampooing and then getting dressed, she thought about Coales, more certain than ever that he was indeed the one who had tipped off Dick Coffey about George being questioned. Why would he do that if he weren't guilty himself? She wished she had kept her temper and said something charming; now the two of them had as much as admitted they were enemies.

On the way out of Dillon Gym, she was pleased to encounter Fletcher Prickett, looking rosy and dapper in a sport coat instead of his usual dark suit.

"How are you, m'dear?" he said, clasping her hand in both of his.

"Fine, and you? I see you believe in exercise."

"Oh, yes, I have to keep fit. And I like the fitness room here. It's not as convenient as the health club at the shopping center, but I love any excuse to come on campus. Although, you know, m'dear, I still can't get used to women in Dillon Gym."

"Oh, I guess when it was all-male, everybody went around without any clothes on," said McLeod.

"That's right," said Fletcher. "Still asking your little questions?" He raised his white eyebrows until they looked like the edges of basketball hoops.

"Still asking my little questions," she said.

"Maybe you should take a holiday from asking questions," said Fletcher. "So tiresome."

"Everybody seems to agree with you," said McLeod. "But I'm curious by nature. I can't help it. And my friend George is under suspicion, so I want to find the real murderer."

"'It is of fundamental importance,'" Fletcher quoted, "'that justice should not only be done, but should manifestly and undoubtedly be seen to be done.'"

"That's exactly right," said McLeod, who went away thinking what a nice old pet Fletcher Prickett was, in spite of his sexism.

MCLEOD WENT FROM the gym to the informal restaurant in the basement of Prospect House for a quick lunch and chewed over Kenneth Coales's guilt and George Bridges's innocence along with her bowl of miscellany from the salad bar, including bean sprouts, asparagus, beets, and half a hard-boiled egg. The scale had spoken. And I'm listening to it, McLeod said to herself.

After she'd finished a student conference early that afternoon, she walked over to Borough Hall, hoping to see Nick Perry. She had to wait thirty minutes, which she didn't mind since she had brought a book. She had finished *The Warden* and was now reading *Barchester Towers*, and had by a miracle remembered to bring it with her.

"Thanks again for telling me about the Billy Masters arrest," she said when she finally got in to see Nick Perry. "I went to the press conference. The chief did a good job."

"He always does," said Nick loyally.

"I know you said you hoped the press would be diverted long enough to get off your neck, but somehow I don't think they'll lose sight of the murder of the president of Princeton University. In fact, I, for one, have a new suspect," she said.

"Who is it this time? What about Clarence Robbins? Incidentally, he did go back to Austin."

"Are you sure?"

"Yes. He talked to two lawyers here, and they both told him he didn't have a chance in hell of winning a suit in chancery to get to be a trustee for his daughter, so he went home. Rode the Greyhound bus out of Trenton. He came down and told us he was leaving, and we actually took him to Trenton and put him on the bus. We asked him to check in with the Austin Police and he said he would. That was yesterday afternoon. He should get there sometime today."

"At least I don't have to worry about him anymore," said McLeod. "And I can well imagine that by the time of the murder, he would have been too drunk to get himself to Nassau Hall, much less do all those other things after he got there."

"Good of you to concede that much," said Nick.

"But why did he push me down the stairs?"

"Are you sure he did?"

"There wasn't anybody else who could have done it."

"It might be—if he did push you down the stairs—that although he wasn't guilty of murder, he was tired of you asking questions and raising suspicions. You could have filed charges against him. You should be more careful on stairs. And you shouldn't ask so many questions."

"I can't help asking questions," wailed McLeod. "And as for filing charges against Clarence Robbins, it would have looked awful. The papers would have printed it. And

I was staying at Lowrie House to chaperone his daughter. I couldn't have done that, Nick."

"Well, what is it now? Not that I'm not glad to see you. Just wondering."

"I really think Kenneth Coales killed Melissa."

"The provost?"

"Yes, the provost." And McLeod enthusiastically went over the case against Coales. Melissa was going to fire him and Coales did not want to leave town. In desperation he killed her. Since the murder, Coales had tried to implicate George. He had tipped off Dick Coffey—"

"Are you sure about that?" interrupted Nick.

"As sure as I can be. Coffey wouldn't tell me, of course, even though I asked him. And isn't he the one who told you that George didn't answer his phone that Monday night?"

"Everybody tells you to quit asking questions, and everybody can't be wrong," said Perry. "McLeod, I think you're a little bit off-base on this one. Not totally—because even I know what a bastard Coales can be."

"I know it! Did I tell you about how he made Sophy Robbins move out of Lowrie House, move out completely, the day after her mother's funeral?"

"I didn't know about that."

"Did you know about his girlfriend in the Spanish Department? And that's why he didn't want to leave town? Not just 'didn't want' to leave town—couldn't face the possibility of being fired and having to leave town? Did you know his wife told me he was not at home that Monday night? She looked it up in her diary. Did you know he has disowned his son because he's gay?"

"I've talked to enough people at the university to know he's bad news. But that doesn't mean he's a murderer," said Perry. "Go easy, McLeod. And Kenneth Coales has been the provost of Princeton University, the second in command, and now he's acting president. We can't arrest him unless we have incontrovertible evidence. You understand that, don't you?"

"I'm just trying to help you get the incontrovertible evidence."

"Go easy, McLeod."

"I know George didn't do it," said McLeod. "And it drives me insane with fury that somebody is trying to nail him for it."

"Okay, okay. Relax. You tend to George. We'll find the murderer. I'm confident. Don't worry. Do you understand me?"

"I guess so," said McLeod. "Don't the police always want the amateurs to back off? No matter what the amateurs tell them."

"Don't I always listen to you?"

"You do, Nick. I'm sorry. I'm just upset about George."

"Look, the investigation is ongoing. It may be somebody you don't like; it may be somebody you like. Go home and look after George."

McLeod looked at Nick speculatively. "Are you telling me George Bridges might be a murderer? I know he's not. I'd bank money on that. He's true blue, all the way. Can't you tell me how the investigation is going? You must have a good idea by now who did it. Tell me."

"We haven't arrested George, you know. But that's all I can tell you."

"Okay, I'll go home and look after George." She left, knowing he meant it.

Seventeen

MCLEOD WALKED HOME, brooding about Coales and George and Clarence Robbins. George was good and Coales and Robbins were bad and it was George who was accused of a crime and put on administrative leave. It didn't make sense.

When she got home, she checked her voice mail for messages and her laptop for e-mail. A few e-mails from students, but nothing from George. She called him.

"Did you have a good day?" she asked him when he answered.

"Oh, a wonderful day," he said.

"What did you do?"

"I went to Firestone Library—I haven't been named *persona non grata*, just put on administrative leave, so I guess it's all right for me to be on campus. Anyway, I looked in recent issues of the *Chronicle of Higher Education* to see what administrative jobs have been advertised."

"See anything good?"

"Nothing like I had here."

"George, you're not out of a job here. As soon as they arrest somebody for Melissa's murder, you'll be back in Nassau Hall."

"When will that be? Besides, I don't want to work for Ken Coales."

"George, he's not president. He's just acting president. There will be somebody else."

"When? By the time they get somebody else, I will have killed myself—or Ken Coales."

"Don't joke about murder," said McLeod.

"I know," said George. "My phone is probably tapped."

"I doubt that," said McLeod.

"You're quite the Little Mary Sunshine, aren't you?"

McLeod ignored the gibe. "Did you play golf again?" she asked.

"I did not."

George was very grumpy, McLeod thought. "What about supper?" she asked.

"I did not cook your supper, if that's what you mean," George said with unaccustomed ferocity. "I'm not yet reduced, I hope, to total domestic servitude."

"George, don't be cross. I didn't mean to imply you should have cooked my supper. I'll be glad to cook, if you'd like to come over here. Or maybe you'd rather be alone. Whatever you want is okay with me."

"That means you don't want to eat with me, doesn't it? I'm an unproductive member of society and you want nothing to do with me."

"Not at all. Give me an hour or two and I'll go to the grocery store and turn out something delicious for us to eat. Are you in the mood for seafood? What about scallops? Steak? Hamburger?"

"Whatever," said George. "I'm sorry I'm such a sorehead. I'm not used to a life of leisure."

"Play like you're on vacation," said McLeod. "Relax. Enjoy it."

"I can't do that," said George.

Well, try to keep a civil tongue in your head, McLeod thought, but did not say. She went to Nassau Street Seafood and bought big sea scallops. Across the street at Wild Oats she bought rice and tomatoes. Scallops creole was easier than shrimp creole and better besides. With a big salad, that should do nicely.

George arrived with a bottle of Veuve Cliquot, which they drank while McLeod finished up the dinner. She could tell that he was trying manfully to be his old self but was unsuccessful. At first he picked at the scallops creole, but at last ate heartily, then sulked because he said he had overeaten.

When she brought out the chocolate cake from Chez Alice, he began to relax a little, but with coffee, his mood worsened.

McLeod told him about her interview with Coales, the chief's press conference on the Billy Masters arrest, and Dick Coffey's refusal to tell her who had tipped him off about George's being questioned. "But I'm sure it was Coales," she said.

"Quite the busy little bee, aren't you?" said George.

"I'm trying," she said, determined not to lose her temper with George. "I honestly don't think Nick Perry believes you killed Melissa."

"Why doesn't he tell the press?"

"You know he never tells anybody anything. I'm still amazed he came by Lowrie House and told me Clarence Robbins had an alibi. I wonder if Clarence got to Austin yet?"

"When did he leave?"

"Yesterday."

"Then he must be there by now."

"Busses are slow," said McLeod.

"You never rode one in your life," said George. "How do you know?"

"I certainly have ridden the bus," she said. "Lots. When I was young and giddy. I used to ride it from Atlanta to

Athens and to Macon and to Savannah once. We didn't have trains."

"I beg your pardon," said George. But he said it nastily.

McLeod did not encourage him to stay, but told him she was tired and had to get ready for her class the next day. He left without helping her clear the table. The world's nicest man had become the orneriest.

MCLEOD HAD NO visiting writer scheduled for class the next day, and she chatted with the students as they came in. She was glad to see Sophy Robbins, looking somewhat subdued and pale, but present. At least she was functioning, thought McLeod.

They were talking about characterization. The students were working on articles about a professor, their most important assignment of the semester.

"Years ago I had a writing teacher in college who talked about using a person's salient points in characterizing," said McLeod. "I had never heard the word 'salient' before that, and I've never forgotten it. It's a concept that's useful to have in mind when you're writing about people."

They talked for a while about the salient points of people in literature. Madame Bovary, for instance, "Oversexed?" suggested Joel Rabinowski. Robinson Crusoe? Elizabeth Bennett in *Pride and Prejudice?* This went on for some time, before they got around to talking about salient characteristics in the professors they were interviewing.

"Now, you don't say, Professor So-and-so's salient characteristic is a love of detail. You show it by giving examples of his insistence on memorizing," said McLeod. "It's an interesting concept to use in your own mind, anyway."

It was a fairly good session, McLeod thought. Not spectacular, but adequate. When Sophy paused on her way out, McLeod told her she was glad to see her. "How's it going?" she asked.

"Oh, all right," said Sophy.

"How's your classwork? Are you far behind?"

"It's not too bad," said Sophy. "At least I'm enjoying the piece I'm doing for you."

"You're writing about one of your professors in art history, aren't you?"

"That's right. Bud Trippett, the archaeologist. It's fun. I'd like to write about archaeology instead of doing it, maybe. But the schoolwork is okay."

"And you got your stuff moved out of Lowrie House?" McLeod asked. "After that bastard of a provost laid down the law."

"Ssssh," said Sophy. "Don't speak of him like that. He has great power, you know. Yes, I did get moved. Martha Cowan was wonderful, just wonderful."

"Good. Is there anything I can do for you at this point?"

"Not a thing," said Sophy.

"Let me know if there is," said McLeod. "Have you heard from your father?"

"Oh, no," said Sophy. "He left town yesterday and I think with Dad it's out of sight, out of mind. At least that's the way it's always been."

"He doesn't know what he's missing," said McLeod, patting Sophy's shoulder.

"How are the police doing? Are they making any progress on finding out who killed my mother?" Sophy asked.

"I'm sure they are," said McLeod. "I have faith in Nick Perry."

"I think you ought to conduct your own investigation," said Sophy. "I really do."

"Don't worry, Sophy," said McLeod. "Your mother's killer will be brought to justice."

Sophy smiled at her. "I hope you're right," she said, and left.

McLeod went home and thought about Clarence Robbins—his salient characteristic was pure selfishness, she thought. And Ken Coales. His salient characteristic was nastiness, preternatural nastiness.

George didn't call her and she didn't call him. Let him stew in his own bad mood, she thought. But what more could she do about proving Coales committed the murder? She simply must get George off the hook so he would be his merry old self again. She went to bed early and read *Dr. Thorne*, the third of Trollope's Barsetshire series. What heaven it was, she thought, to be in Barsetshire, along with Dr. Thorne and his niece, all the Greshams, and Miss Dunstable, not to mention the perennials who appeared off and on throughout the series—Archbishop Grantly and Mrs. Proudie, Dr. Arabin and Mr. Slope. No murderers there.

WHEN MCLEOD WOKE up Friday morning, the murder was very much on her mind again. It occurred to her that she should talk to Rosita Sanchez. Why not? She was supposed to be doing a story on Coales, the man, the acting president. Why not all facets of his life? The mistress should provide some interesting insights. No, that was crazy, she thought. No woman would consent to be interviewed as the mistress of a man who was the subject of the interview. What excuse could she use to talk to the woman and find out if Coales had been with her on that Monday night?

First she called Stephanie, faithful Stephanie, and checked on Rosita Sanchez. "Do you have any idea how I could get her to talk to me?" she asked Stephanie.

"Let me see. Let me think. What is Rosita interested in—besides Kenneth Coales, that is?" There was a long pause while Stephanie pondered this. "She likes clothes."

"You mean I should call her up and tell her I want to come talk to her about her clothes?"

"You could say you wanted to do a story about her clothes," said Stephanie. When McLeod snorted derisively, she hastily said, "Wait a minute. Let me call her friend, Wanda. No, I can't do that. What would I tell Wanda was my reason for wanting to know what Rosita is interested in?"

"Tell her it's a matter of life or death," said McLeod. "And it is. I want to find out who killed Melissa. I have to find out who killed Melissa because George is a suspect and it's ruining his disposition to be on leave because he's a suspect."

"Hmmm," said Stephanie. "Okay. I'll call you right back."

She did call right back. "Wanda says Rosita wants to be a writer. So you could talk to her about writing—right?"

"You mean I should call her up and say, 'I hear you want to be a writer. I teach writing. Can I help you?' "

"Can't you do that?"

"I don't see how I can. What has she written? Do you know?"

"She writes fiction," said Stephanie, "I think."

"I don't know anything about writing fiction," said McLeod.

"Wing it," said Stephanie.

"Okay, I will," said McLeod. "Thanks, Stephanie."

She called Romance Languages and asked to speak to Rosita Sanchez. When she came on the phone, McLeod was ready. "Ms. Sanchez, I'm McLeod Dulaney. I'm teaching a nonfiction writing class this semester. I'm interested in writing a novel and I don't know anything about writing fiction. I've always done nonfiction. A mutual friend of ours tells me that you write fiction. I wonder if I could take you to lunch and pick your brains."

"I don't know enough to be any help to you," Sanchez said. "I haven't published anything but a few short stories."

"That's more than I've done," said McLeod. "How about today? Lahiere's?"

"Lahiere's? I can't resist that."

• • •

WHEN SHE MET Rosita Sanchez, McLeod, to her surprise, liked her immediately. She indeed had a sultry Latina look with her blond hair and dark skin and eyes and a remarkably good figure, shown to perfection in the tight short skirt she wore with a sweater of some silky yarn that fit like a glove. It soon became plain that she was also a very bright woman. McLeod conceded that she must take her hat off to Kenneth Coales. He had a nice, talented wife, and an attractive, likable mistress. What had he done to deserve them?

Rosita ordered soup and salad and a glass of wine. McLeod ordered the same meager lunch, without the wine.

"You're very good at writing yourself, I understand," said Rosita. "Why do you want to write fiction?"

"Doesn't everybody want to write a novel?" asked McLeod. "Isn't it the highest art?" She felt a little uneasy since Sanchez had taken the initiative in the interview. Usually she set the pace herself.

"Maybe so," said Rosita. "I don't know how to help you, though."

"I'm sure you can help me . . ." McLeod began. Rosita Sanchez eyed her with what looked suspiciously like amusement.

"I think you want help," Rosita said, "but not for writing fiction. You are writing a story about my friend Ken Coales, and you want information about him. And I gather you are also asking a great many questions about the big murder. I know I can help you with that."

"You're very open," said McLeod.

"Open? *Abierto*?"

"Just open. You like to get things out in the open, up front. You're frank. I like that."

"Oh, yes. I like to get things out into the daylight. What do you want to ask me about the murder?"

Black bean soup arrived, and McLeod waited until the waiter had left.

"First, were you with Ken Coales the night of Melissa's murder?" asked McLeod.

"Yes, I was with him the entire evening."

"Where were you?"

"We were in a little restaurant in Lambertville, and the proprietor will confirm that we were there together from six o'clock until ten. We had a leisurely dinner and, I'm afraid, a good many drinks."

So that was Ken Coales's meeting on that Monday night, thought McLeod. "And then what?" asked McLeod.

"It took about forty-five minutes to drive to Princeton. And then we went to Ken's office in Nassau Hall."

"What?!" McLeod was startled.

"Yes. Unfortunately, we have to sneak around. I am married and so is Ken. It is not a perfect world, but he has a very comfortable sofa in his office. We were there for about an hour."

"Until eleven forty-five?"

"Around eleven forty-five," said Sanchez.

"And then what?"

"Ken drove me to my car and I drove home."

This all fit in with what Caroline Coales had told her, McLeod thought.

The busboy removed the soup plates, and the waiter brought their Caesar salads.

"Did you hear anything while you were in Nassau Hall?" McLeod asked.

"Hear Melissa Faircloth quarreling with someone? No, I'm afraid not. We weren't listening anyway."

"Did you know she was still in her office?"

"No, I didn't. Was she?"

This was all very interesting. No wonder the police were having a hard time finding the murderer. Everybody—except George—had a perfect alibi. "She was there, dead or alive," McLeod said to Rosita. "Have you told the police this?"

"Many times. Now I've answered all your questions, although I don't know why I should. Tell me why you're asking these things. You can't put this in the paper."

"No, I won't put any of this in my story about Ken

Coales," McLeod said. "The police seem to suspect my friend George Bridges of the murder, and I want to find out who really killed Melissa Faircloth so I can clear George."

"So you want to clear your boyfriend and put the blame on somebody else? On my boyfriend?"

"Not necessarily," said McLeod. "I want to find the person who did the murder, the perpetrator, as they say on television, and clear George. But I don't know how to proceed, except to ask questions, and then ask the next question. If I talk to everyone, maybe somebody will tell me something that will lead to the real killer."

"Very plausible," said Rosita. "I guess."

"I'm very curious by nature," said McLeod. "What did you tell your husband about that night?" She thought for a minute that Rosita was going to balk at this impudent question, but no, she answered it.

"I told him I was at the office, working on a short story. That's what I always tell him."

"He wouldn't check up on you?"

"He didn't, this time, at least."

"He sounds very tolerant."

"He is," said Rosita.

"You don't have children?"

"Oh, no. That would be a different story, wouldn't it?"

"Somebody said that Kenneth Coales wouldn't leave Princeton because you wouldn't leave your husband and go with him."

"That's ridiculous. I'd leave if Ken asked me to. But he's not going to do that. He likes the setup. A wife who's presentable and not too demanding, a lover who's eager to please and doesn't ask too much of him, either. Why should he leave?"

"But you'd really leave if he asked you?" said McLeod.

They had finished their salads and they both ordered espressos.

"I'd leave in a minute," said Rosita.

"Your husband?"

"He's nothing to me. I'm nothing to him. It's a marriage of convenience. I've got a green card and that's what I wanted. It's only a matter of time until we divorce."

"I thought he was insanely jealous," said McLeod.

"Not at all," said Rosita.

"I appreciate your frankness. Where are you from, originally?"

"Ecuador," said Rosita.

They began to talk about Spanish and Latin American writers—at least Rosita talked about them and McLeod racked her brains for intelligent questions to ask about Gabriel García Márquez and Carlos Fuentes. "Márquez, for one thing, is a master of the opening sentence," said Rosita. "How's this? 'The scent of bitter almonds always reminded him of unrequited love'?"

"Sounds like Proust."

"It's from *Love in the Time of Cholera*," said Rosita. "Wait a minute, *One Hundred Years of Solitude* is even better. It begins, 'Many years later as he faced the firing squad Colonel Aureliano Buendía was to remember that afternoon when his father took him to discover ice.' Isn't that lovely?"

"It is," said McLeod. "I must read him."

Before they parted, McLeod asked Rosita for the name of the Lambertville restaurant where they had had dinner that Monday night.

"It was the Rabbit Hutch," said Rosita.

I've always wanted to go to Lambertville, McLeod said to herself on the way home.

Lambertville was a little town on the Delaware River, about forty-five minutes from Princeton. McLeod knew that much. When she got home from Lahiere's, she looked at a New Jersey road map and figured the best way to get there from Princeton was to go through Hopewell.

It was a beautiful drive for a nice spring day, and though it was still a bit chilly for McLeod, she loved swooping up and down the hills, especially going down the last steep hill before she reached Lambertville. The town was full of

Victorian houses, antique shops, art galleries, and restaurants, nestled against the Delaware and Raritan Canal, which ran parallel to the Delaware River there. She stopped at a gas station and had her tank filled. One of the many nice things about New Jersey was the absence of self-service filling stations. It was luxury to sit in the car while somebody else filled the tank, but this time she got out of the car to look up the address of the Rabbit Hutch in the Lambertville telephone book inside the station. It was on Front Street.

McLeod asked directions and was told it was right by the river bridge.

She found it easily enough and was happy to see that the Rabbit Hutch had a few parking spaces beside it. Inside, the lunch crowd was gone, and the dinner customers had not yet arrived. She found the proprietor, a jolly-looking man with a red beard and a beer belly, sitting at a table by a window overlooking the river drinking a beer.

McLeod introduced herself. The man smiled. "Clint McCarty," he said. "Glad to see you. What can I do for you?"

"I just want to ask you some questions," McLeod replied.

"Sit down," said Clint. "Have a beer—on the house."

"No, thanks. It's about a week ago Monday night. Was a couple from Princeton here? Kenneth Coales and Rosita Sanchez? He's dark haired, good-looking, tall, and she's gorgeous, really. Latina, with a marvelous figure. Blond with dark eyes."

"Funny you should ask me. Are you a private eye? The Princeton Police have been here. And I'll tell you what I told them. I didn't know their names, but the police showed me their pictures. They were here for several hours. We don't have huge crowds on Monday nights and I remember them."

"Did either one of them leave and come back?"

"No. The police asked me about that. They were here

the whole time. Eating and drinking and talking, talking, talking."

"They make an attractive couple, don't they?" asked McLeod.

"Yeah, I guess so. They're not married. I know that."

"How do you know?"

"I can just tell when people are up to something."

"You must be a pretty astute judge of character," said McLeod. To herself, she wondered: Why am I wasting time buttering up this man? But she asked him if the couple had been there before that Monday night.

"Don't remember them from before. But I remembered them this time, because when they left, they stopped on the way out to speak to me. Told me they had enjoyed their dinner, and the man said to me, 'We've stayed the whole evening, I hope you didn't need the table.' And now all these questions. It makes you think, doesn't it? What is it they're supposed to have done?"

"Well, the police are investigating the murder of the president of Princeton University, Melissa Faircloth. They've questioned them both."

"Oh, that murder. I do remember reading about it. That's something, isn't it? Sure you won't have a beer?"

"I'm sure. But let me leave you my card. If you think of anything else, call me," said McLeod.

"I will," said Clint McCarty, staring at the card as though he wanted to memorize what it said.

McLeod left the Rabbit Hutch, drove over the Delaware Bridge to get a glimpse of New Hope, the Bucks County, Pennsylvania, town everybody talked about. It looked to be full of tourists—and tourist traps. She liked Lambertville better, she decided. She drove back to Princeton by another route, driving to I-95 on the Pennsylvania side of the river, and then home. What a wonderful landscape, she thought, but she spent most of her time brooding about what McCarty had told her. She didn't know what to make of the information that Ken had made sure the proprietor knew that he and his girlfriend were there all evening. Was he trying to establish an alibi in advance? Or was it coincidence? Did that conversation with McCarty invalidate his alibi? She didn't know, but it was something to chew over.

Eighteen

"I DISCOVERED LAMBERTVILLE and New Hope today," McLeod told George on the telephone when she got home.

"Good for you," said George. "They were completely unknown towns until you found them."

"I meant that I discovered them for myself," said McLeod.

"I know." He sighed. "Look McLeod, I'm sorry I'm so nasty lately. I'm really tired of this life."

"Did you play golf?"

"I did. At least I got some exercise. I also sent out my résumé and cover letters to three universities that had advertisements in the *Chronicle*. And the police didn't call all day yesterday or today. So that's something. Have you nailed Coales yet? Am I to be exonerated?"

"It looks like Coales has an unimpeachable alibi." She told him about her interview with Rosita Sanchez and her trip to the Rabbit Hutch.

"You pick up suspects. You lose suspects," George said. "That's the way it goes."

"Well, I'm not sure I've lost Coales. There's something funny about the way he made sure the proprietor of the Rabbit Hutch knew he'd been there all evening."

"Hmmm," said George. "But the Rabbit Hutch! I haven't been there in ages. They used to have really good food. Want to go there for supper?"

"Tonight? I just got back from Lambertville."

"I'll drive," said George.

"Sure," said McLeod. "I'm game."

LAMBERTVILLE LOOKED LIVELIER by night than it had by day. "Some of the Continental Army crossed the Delaware at Lambertville to fight the Battle of Trenton with George Washington in 1776," George said. "Washington crossed a little farther downstream at the place that's still called Washington Crossing. But Lambertville is a historic little town, too."

"Ummm," said McLeod, not interested in historical tidbits at that moment.

Like the rest of Lambertville, the Rabbit Hutch was brightly lit, and it was almost full. Clint McCarty led them to a table. "So you decided to come back?" he said to McLeod.

"Who wouldn't?" she asked.

McCarty smiled at the flattery and whipped a reserved sign off a table by the window. "For you," he said.

They thanked him and sat down. The menu looked promising, and McLeod ordered duck, which she loved but never cooked herself. She gave George the details of her talk with Rosita. "I can't believe how frankly she talked to me," said McLeod.

"Don't people always?" said George.

"I guess they do," said McLeod. "I think it's because I'm motherly. With the white hair and all."

George had a martini and cheered up considerably.

"You know," said McLeod, "I'm afraid Ken Coales's motive is not as strong as I thought. Stephanie said he stayed in Princeton on account of his girlfriend, but it turns out his girlfriend is perfectly willing to go somewhere else."

"Maybe that makes his motive stronger," said George. "Maybe he didn't want that close a connection with his mistress. Maybe he preferred it here with his wife serving as a sort of a safety mechanism. Caroline wouldn't want to leave, would she?"

"No, not at all. She has her studio and her connections with galleries, and her daughter with five children lives in Hopewell. But you never know. And if she wouldn't move with him, then if he got another job, maybe Rosita would trap him and make him take her."

"That is a bit mixed up for a motive for killing the president of a university," said George.

"I guess so," said McLeod.

THE NEXT MORNING, Saturday, McLeod decided she had better write her article on Evil Ken Coales. But first, she would run her errands: post office, dry cleaner, drive-in bank, and grocery store—three grocery stores, in fact, since she was looking for an avocado that wasn't as hard as a rock. She put the groceries away and then headed for the campus and the pool at Dillon Gym.

She noticed that the movie company's trailers, which had been absent for a few days after Billy Masters's arrest, were back, this time parked on Nassau Street, Dickinson Place, and College Road instead of University Place. In fact, University Place, the street that ran down from Nassau Street to the Dinky railroad station, was blocked off. As she walked closer, she discovered that work crews were covering the blacktop with dirt.

Max Bolt must be getting ready to film the night scene where the seniors march up University Place with the football captain leading the procession, McLeod thought. Max must have won the battle with the Borough. Or was he just defying them? No, Borough Police were manning the barricades at the ends of the street. How had Bolt done it? Maybe he had decided to film the scene without Billy Masters—could a stand-in play Avery Blaine while the seniors marched?

She looked around for Bolt and saw him in an apparently heated conversation with the mayor of Princeton. She walked over, deciding to hover nearby until the mayor, a prosperous retired businessman, left. Bolt grabbed the lapels of the mayor's jacket and held on to them while he shouted at him.

"I'm doing my very best, Mr. Mayor," he said. "This is going to be a marvelous film. Princeton is going to be famous after this. And you should cooperate with us. It will do you good."

"You don't seem to understand that Princeton is already famous," the mayor said, pulling himself out of Bolt's grasp and shaking himself as he regained his dignity. "We don't need movies made about us. In fact, we don't want any more people moving in to town."

"Elitist snob," Max Bolt sneered.

"Name-calling will get you nowhere," the mayor said, dusting off his jacket with one hand while he whipped out a handkerchief and wiped off his face with the other. "We've been cooperating with you. We're making a tremendous sacrifice for you. More than we've ever done for any movie company before. So just be out of here by five o'clock tomorrow morning. That's all I'm saying. That's all you've paid for and all you're going to get no matter what you pay."

"All right, all right," said Max. "Don't worry, Mr. Mayor, we'll be good boys. And if we aren't, then the Borough can collect that huge fine that's in the contract."

"We want open streets more than we want the money from fines," the mayor said. He walked away and Max stood in the same spot, staring at the dump trucks that were steadily hauling dirt and dumping it on University Place.

"I see you are getting back to basics," McLeod said to him. "The good earth, I mean."

Max turned, and when he saw her, he smiled. "That's right," he said. "The real nitty-gritty."

"And you'll be able to shoot the scene with a dirt surface on the street? The Borough actually agreed to closing University Place?"

"That's right. Money will accomplish wonders sometimes. We're paying the Borough handsomely, believe me. But we didn't have to take up the pavement. We'll get the same effect this way."

"And what about your star? Can you film this scene without Billy Masters?" asked McLeod.

"He'll be here by tonight. Cowboy finally got him out on bail."

"That's very good," said McLeod. "I can't wait to see the movie."

"Me, either," said Bolt. "But we have about fifteen minutes to shoot that scene." He sounded quite bitter.

"You have all night, don't you?"

"Well, yes, but you know, I'm a perfectionist. Sometimes I like to shoot a scene over and over until we get it right. And this is going to be hard. The lighting problems are astronomical."

"Hey, Max, where you want this stuff?" a crew member yelled from the back of a truck loaded with floodlights and cables, and Max turned away from McLeod. Fascinated, as always, with the moviemaking process, she watched the activity for a minute and then dutifully made her way down to the gym to swim. As she walked, she thought about Max Bolt. Was he a viable suspect? She was sure Bolt didn't have a key to One Nassau Hall, and she did not think Melissa Faircloth would have let him in. On the other hand, the murder of the president had certainly been a break for Max Bolt. Bolt was a single-minded man about his movie. If he were balked, would he go so far as to kill somebody to get what he wanted to make his movie? But maybe killing Melissa didn't solve all his problems. Was

Kenneth Coales as opposed to the film crew as Melissa had been? Still it was undeniable that the murder had drawn everybody's attention away from him and his project. Could he have foreseen that? It was pretty far-fetched, she had to admit, even to speculate that someone would kill just to draw attention away from a project like making a movie.

When she got home, she ate an avocado sandwich with great pleasure and then checked her phone messages before she started work on her article about Coales.

One message was from Sophy Robbins. "Call me at our old house," she said. And she gave her cell phone number. "I've found something very interesting."

McLeod called, reached Sophy, and asked, "What have you found?"

"Letters," said Sophy. "Very interesting letters. Come on over."

McLeod got the address of Melissa's old house on Robert Street, and drove over immediately.

"I'm so glad to see you," said Sophy, who met her at the door in blue jeans and an old sweatshirt—but still looking beautiful. "It's just amazing," Sophy was chattering. "It's amazing that I found anything. It's amazing that I'm doing this. I have all this schoolwork, and I have a million things I ought to be doing, but when I found out the tenants were leaving early, I decided to come over here and see what state it was in. Actually, the tenants left it clean as a whistle. So I thought I could get some of our stuff out of the Cowans' garage and put it here. Martha and Bruce will help me with that. I went up to the attic to see how much room there was, and I started opening old cartons and trunks and found all these letters. I think my mother saved every letter she ever got." Sophy was leading her through the downstairs and up to the second floor. "I was really surprised. I found letters that my grandmother wrote to Mom when she first went away to college. Can you believe it? And I never saved a letter in my life." She turned around and looked at McLeod. "And now I wish I had saved her letters to me. There weren't many, since I stayed here in Princeton to go to school. Oh, well. You do the best you can, I guess. You don't ever know what's going to happen, do you?"

Sophy looked so young and sounded so old and tired that McLeod's heart went out to her. "Your best is pretty good, Sophy," she said.

Sophy had opened a door in one of the bedrooms and led her up the attic stairs. "Mom saved her report cards from elementary school, and schoolwork from high school and papers from college. Can you believe it?"

This was all very interesting, but McLeod wondered what Sophy was getting at.

The attic was not large, and was filled with cartons neatly tied and labeled with a black marker. GRAMMAR SCHOOL. HIGH SCHOOL. LETTERS REC'D 1970–1975. What a woman, thought McLeod.

Some of the boxes had been opened. Some had not.

"Did you find anything to incriminate Ken Coales?" she asked. "Did she have an affair with him, or did he try to harass her when she was on the faculty?"

"I think Mom could handle harassment," said Sophy, "but I didn't find any letters from Ken Coales. I did find some from—guess who?"

"George Bush," said McLeod. "The older or the younger? They both lived in Texas."

Sophy giggled. "Mom never had any use for airheads," she said. "But Max Bolt is from Texas, too, you know."

"No! No, I didn't know. Is he from Abilene, too?"

"No, he's from Houston," said Sophy. "They met at the University of Texas."

"For heaven's sake!" said McLeod. "And did he write to her?"

"After she went to graduate school, he wrote to her. Did he ever write to her! Look at these letters." She held up two big packages of letters. "I didn't go through all of them—how could I?" She waved her hand at the cartons. "There are millions of letters here. But I did read these because they were tied with this special ribbon. Isn't that dear?" Sophy waved a strip of red ribbon with silver stars on it.

"It is, indeed. And she tied up Max Bolt's letters with that star-spangled ribbon?"

"That's right," said Sophy.

McLeod was dying to read the letters. "Which are the earliest ones?" she asked.

"I think these are." Sophy handed her a bundle that had been retied. McLeod untied the bow and took out the first letter and began to read.

> *My darling,* it began. *Austin, Texas is a darker, drearier place without you in it. Why did you have to rush off like you did? You were the only person here I cared anything about, the only person worth talking to, the only person worth looking at.*
>
> *Wouldn't September have been soon enough to get to the University of Chicago? Oh, well, I won't beat a dead horse—I know you said you'd finished with Texas and wanted out, wanted to shake the dust of Texas from your feet forever. I want out, but I have to spend another year here. The minute I finish, I'm going to do just like you did—get out of here. But now I'm thinking about the possibilities of working in the theater in Chicago. I have to be where you are—and if that's Chicago instead of New York or Los Angeles, so be it. The Goodman Theater is in Chicago and several others. . . . To be where you are instead of where you are not would be the difference between daylight and darkness, the difference between a dappled green glade and the Sahara desert, to be where you are instead of where you are not . . .*

The letter went on. Poor lovesick Max Bolt. She picked up another letter.

I'm so glad I have my photograph of you, he wrote. *I look at it the last thing before I go to sleep and the first thing when I wake up in the morning. I try to figure out what I love best about the way you look. Is it that dark hair? Those dark eyes with those incredible eyelashes? Is it that red mouth? No, it's none of these—although I love them all. What I love best is that sense of banked fires smoldering away deep inside you that drives me wild. You're such a GOOD GIRL it's maddening. I'm mad, I tell you, mad with love.*

And poetry. The young Max Bolt quoted poetry, not by the verse, the stanza, but by the mile. Excerpts from Shakespeare's sonnets, Marlowe's "The Passionate Shepherd to His Love," Yeats, Rilke. He carefully wrote out all of Andrew Marvell's "To His Coy Mistress," that plaint of a seventeenth-century man in love with a girl who was also *good*, the way Melissa had been *good.*

Thy beauty shall no more be found,
Nor in thy marble vault, shall sound
My echoing song: then worms shall try
That long preserved virginity,
And your quaint honor turn to dust,
And into ashes all my lust:
The grave's a fine and private place,
But none, I think, do there embrace.

"I hate to read these in a way," said McLeod.

"I know what you mean," said Sophy. "But in light of what happened to my mother, I thought maybe they would be important."

"It seems to me that the letters make him less of a candidate to commit murder. He obviously cared a lot about her."

"He did. But how long did he care about her? The letters get less passionate as the years go by and she kept turning him down. You know, she was very ambitious. She really was."

"After you were born, I think she was even more ambitious. But looks like she might have been glad to have a clean upstanding Texas guy for a boyfriend. Was he still writing to her after she met your father and had you and got divorced?"

"Oh, yes, but not as passionately. Still, I guess it's silly, but I thought maybe he had this kind of Gatsby thing for her. Maybe Mom was his Daisy Buchanan. Gatsby always thought that Daisy loved him still. He bought that house on Long Island just across the bay from the house where Daisy and her husband lived. He never gave up."

"And Max Bolt is such a Scott Fitzgerald enthusiast he might even enjoy seeing himself as Jay Gatsby," said McLeod. "What an interesting idea you've had, Sophy."

"I know," said Sophy. "Maybe that's even why Max Bolt decided to make a movie about F. Scott Fitzgerald. Maybe it was an excuse to come to Princeton and be near his old love. And to shoot so many scenes at Princeton—where his first love was."

"It's a wonderful reconstruction," said McLeod. "Wonderful, but it doesn't point to murder. Gatsby would never have killed Daisy. Never."

"I didn't mean it paralleled the story in every respect," said Sophy. "It's just that these letters made me think of Gatsby. I mean, there was definitely an emotional relationship—at least on Max Bolt's side."

"Your mother never mentioned him to you?"

"Never," said Sophy.

"Did she see him when he started making the movie here?"

"That I don't know."

"Didn't she have him to dinner at Lowrie House? Looks like she would have entertained a celebrity like Max Bolt, even without her early association with him," said McLeod.

"I don't know whether she did or not," said Sophy.

"Aren't there records? I'll ask Mrs. Linley. Or that social secretary lady. One of them should know."

"I've always wondered about Max Bolt and the murder—he had such a wonderful motive, but then I always had to admit that he didn't have a key to Nassau Hall and I didn't think your mother would have let him in at night."

"So now he's a hot suspect," said Sophy.

"I don't know, but let's read the rest of the letters and find out what happened to the relationship," said McLeod.

Nineteen

WHILE THEY READ the letters from Max to Melissa, McLeod resolved to ask George Bridges about encounters between those two before Melissa's death. She remembered clearly that he had told her right after the body was discovered that Max Bolt had come in and "screeched" at the president because he was being hampered in his moviemaking. Had he been around at other times without "screeching"?

Meanwhile, she read more letters. They were becoming less frequent and less passionate. Max Bolt had directed a big production of *The Madwoman of Chaillot* at the University of Texas just before he graduated. "The sets are beautiful," he wrote to Melissa, and went on to decry the stupidity of the student actors who wouldn't do exactly what he told them to do.

After he graduated, he did not go to Chicago to work at the Goodman. Instead he went to Los Angeles and started work in the movies. With great good luck he got a job as a gofer on the set of a movie that turned out to be a hit. He acted a little and finally got to direct. He never looked back. And he stopped writing to Melissa Faircloth, who also had other things on her mind.

"But you know, I don't think he ever married anybody else, did he?" said McLeod.

They had carried the last bundles of letters downstairs and Sophy had brought out bottles of Snapple with which she had stocked the refrigerator.

"Pure Gatsby," said Sophy.

"It's certainly an interesting development," said McLeod. "I do wonder what happened when he saw Melissa again here. I wonder if that was the first time since their student days. Gatsby and Daisy were still in love, but nobody thinks Daisy was going to leave Tom Buchanan for Gatsby."

"Mom didn't have anybody to leave at this point," said Sophy. "Looks like she might have been ripe for renewing the romance."

"I wonder what happened between them," McLeod said again.

"Me, too. Do you think we'll ever find out?"

"We can sure try," said McLeod.

ON THE WAY home, contemplating next steps, McLeod realized she should ask George about Max Bolt's encounters with Melissa Faircloth since she had been president. He was so taciturn about work, but surely he'd loosen up with the information if it might help clear him as a suspect.

She found a message on her answering machine from George inviting her to dinner. "I've spent the day cooking," he said. She called back to accept with pleasure and asked if she could bring anything. "Would you mind stoping at the store and getting me some of that stringy stuff that turns things yellow?" he asked.

"Saffron?" she asked.

"That's it," he said. "I couldn't think of the name. It's expensive, so I'll pay you for it when you get here."

When she arrived, she handed him the glass tube with the saffron threads in it. "They keep it behind the cash register," she said.

"I guess people steal it. It's that expensive. How much do I owe you?"

"Don't worry. I'll be happy to contribute saffron to dinner. What are you making?"

"Can't you guess?"

"Paella. That's what we use saffron for in Florida. Or chicken and yellow rice. They're Cuban dishes."

"Or Spanish," said George. "But this is paella. And it better be good. It has chicken, pork, lamb, shrimp, scallops, oysters, red snapper, lobster, and squid in it. I left out the clams. It also has asparagus, artichokes, green peas, and rice. I hope it's not too late to add the saffron. I haven't added the rice."

"It'll be fine to add it with the rice," said McLeod. "I don't think it adds much flavor anyway—it's the color, don't you think?"

"Oh, you've made it?"

"Only twice. It takes so many ingredients, and it's so much trouble to cook them all separately and then combine them. But paella's one of my favorite foods."

"I'm not sure what is not your favorite food," said George.

"I know. I do like everything," said McLeod. "Some people might call it greed."

"I wouldn't," said George.

"Thank you," said McLeod, very glad that George was in a good humor again. "I should have brought sherry. That's what you should drink before the paella."

"I know that much," said George. "I bought sherry. I even found some Tio Pepe—it's very dry. I told you I spent the day doing this."

"I certainly like it when you cook all day—and invite

me," said McLeod. "You have enough here to feed an army."

"I don't want to feed an army," said George. "You're the only person I can stand the sight of now."

"I'm flattered," said McLeod, putting her arms around him and burying her face in his chest.

"Do you want to eat or are you trying to distract me into other activities?"

"I'm in your hands," she said.

"Let's eat," he said.

"I like a man who puts his stomach first," said McLeod.

"That's me," said George. "Being unemployed beefs up the appetite and cuts down on the libido."

AFTER A COUPLE of glasses of sherry and a dozen good Spanish olives, they settled down with huge servings of paella and glasses of *rioja.*

"Mmm," said McLeod, "this is well worth a whole day."

"I had nothing better to do," said George. "No need to play golf on Saturday—when the course is crowded—when I can play on weekdays. What did you do today? I called you a couple of times and got no answer."

"I was gone all day. Went to the campus to swim and saw Max Bolt. Cowboy Tarleton got Billy Masters out on bail, and tonight they're going to film that scene from *This Side of Paradise* where the seniors march up University Place at night. The Borough closed University for him today and he was having it covered with dirt." George, wrestling with a piece of squid, nodded. "After I went swimming, I went home and Sophy called and wanted me to come over to her mother's old house and look at some letters. So I did. Guess who the letters were from!"

"They were from Ken Coales saying he was going to kill her on Monday night, April the so and so."

"No," said McLeod. "Wrong."

"From Clarence Robbins."

"No," said McLeod. "Wrong again."

"Then who from?"

"They were from Max Bolt himself. He was madly in love with her when they were undergraduates at the University of Texas," said McLeod.

"Really?"

"That's right. Sophy has this interesting idea that Max is like Jay Gatsby, *still* wildly in love with Melissa Faircloth after all these years. And I think she's on to something. Suppose that was the reason he wanted to make a movie out of *This Side of Paradise*—so he could come to Princeton and see Melissa again and win her approval now that he's a big movie man."

"That's very interesting," said George. As McLeod looked disappointed, he went on, "No, I mean it. It really is interesting. But it's speculation."

"Well, what happened when they did meet? You said he screeched at her. Was that the only time he came to the office while she was alive?"

"No, it wasn't. He came one time before that—I think it was when he was scouting the campus to see if he could make the movie. I guess it was plain that they knew each other. I had just forgotten about it. But she came out of her office to meet him in the reception area. And she brought him through my office and introduced him to me."

"She did? Did she do that often?"

"When it was somebody she wanted me to know and remember, she did."

"And so she wanted you to remember him? Did she say anything about him to you?"

"When she introduced him, she said he was an old friend, and that he wanted to make a movie on campus. I was standing there and I said, 'That's nice' or something inane, and she said, 'I'm not sure it's nice at all. But we're going to talk about it. It will be nice if he waits until June perhaps. But it won't be nice if he wants to mess up the campus while classes are in session.' She smiled at Bolt and said, 'We know what it's like, you see, Max. They shot lots of scenes for *IQ*, the movie about Einstein, on campus, as well as most of *A Beautiful Mind*, about John Nash, the Nobel prize winner, here.' "

"What did Max Bolt say?" asked McLeod.

"He just stood there grinning at her. He was clearly a man who was confident he was going to get what he wanted," said George.

"But then he didn't get what he wanted, did he?" said McLeod.

"Well, in a way, he did." George thought about this. "He took what he wanted, though. He kept on filming after Melissa was killed."

"That's what I keep coming back to," McLeod said. "He was a clear beneficiary of her death. The murder naturally distracted everyone and he just kept right on. He's the one who benefitted most from her death."

"But he didn't know it would distract everybody, did he?"

"No, I guess not," said McLeod. "But maybe he regarded her as an obstacle, and murder would get her out of the way. Besides, remember the emotional factors. He loved her, or had once loved her, and he naturally thought she would be his ally. When it turned out she wasn't his ally, but his chief adversary, he was so angry he killed her."

George frowned and looked at her. "Wait a minute. Let me get the dessert," he said. He was up and moving back to the kitchen.

"Dessert! I've had two huge helpings of paella. I don't think I can handle dessert."

"It's just flan," said George. "Thought I'd stick to the Spanish cuisine—or I guess I should say *cucina.* Anyway, you have to try my flan."

"Of course I'll try your flan," said McLeod. "I won't just try it. I'll wolf it down."

The flan was very good indeed and they both ate it greedily. When they had finished eating and were sitting on George's sofa drinking coffee, George said, "You and Sophy must have had a wonderful time with those letters."

"I wouldn't say we had a wonderful time," said McLeod. "All this is very painful for Sophy. You know it is. But she's a trooper."

"McLeod, you're a trooper, too," George said. "I'm sorry I'm such a bear these days." He put his arm around her.

McLeod shivered with delight. Was the old, cheerful, affectionate George coming back? "It's perfectly understandable," she said to him. "You've been treated very unfairly."

"I should care—as long as I have you on my side." He put his hand under her chin and kissed her gently.

Just as McLeod was settling down for what she thought would be a very pleasant interlude, he removed his arms and stood up. "It's getting late," he said.

"Are you throwing me out?"

"No, no. I'm just tired," he said. "I know I'm not good company. No matter how hard I try."

"You're good company, no matter what," said McLeod stoutly. "You'd be good company if you were in the depths of clinical depression." She hesitated, thinking that George was very likely in the depths of clinical depression right now. She stood up, too, held out her arms.

George did not respond. He held his hands in front of his face. "I'm sorry," he mumbled.

"It's all right," she said. "I can wait."

"Oh, don't be so saintly," he said. "Scream at me."

"I'm not a screamer," said McLeod. "It will be all right, George. It really will. I promise. It will be all right. I'll find the real killer and everything will be all right."

"Oh, McLeod, you're so naive. And so nice." Then he did reach out and hold her briefly. "Thanks," he said.

"Shall I help with the dishes?" she asked.

"No, I can do the dishes. Believe me. I guess I just need to be alone. I'm not fit company," he said again.

McLeod, at a loss about how to proceed with comfort and cheer, left.

As she drove home, she told herself that it was absolutely essential that she find out who the murderer was. That was the only thing that would bring George out of his funk. I have to do it, she told herself, or else the little romance we had going will be lost forever.

Twenty

WHEN MCLEOD WOKE up on Sunday morning, she had a plan of action ready. She knew she wasn't going to work on her article about Coales. She had tossed and turned most of the night, trying to think how to proceed with her investigation. She had finally dropped off to sleep about four o'clock, and she slept until seven, which was very late for her. "But I have a plan," she said out loud, to reassure herself that she was not floundering helplessly and hopelessly.

She barely glanced at the Sunday papers, and made notes on a yellow legal pad while she drank her tea.

TALK TO JIM MACY, she wrote first. She would call him at home. As director of communications, which was the way Princeton described public relations, Jim had to be thoroughly accustomed to weekend calls from the media and she need not hesitate to call him on Sunday morning.

TALK TO MAX BOLT, she wrote next. That might be a little harder, but she had two phone numbers for him and she would keep trying them both as long as it took to reach him.

Then she wrote down another instruction for herself. TALK TO NICK PERRY.

As she had predicted, she reached Jim Macy easily.

"I'm sorry to bother you at home," she said.

"That's all right, McLeod. I'm used to it," he said. He sounded harried, as usual.

"I'd like to know the exact chronology of Max Bolt's effort to make a movie about Fitzgerald on campus," she said.

"I'm not sure I understand," said Macy.

"I'm sorry," said McLeod. "I know Max Bolt came to Princeton right after the New Year to scout the campus for possibilities. He came with those two researchers, didn't he?"

"That's right," said Macy.

"Let me back up," said McLeod. "When did he first approach Princeton about shooting here?"

"Last fall," said Macy. "He went to the president's office. That's unusual—people usually come to our office first. They make an inquiry of the university, and whoever gets the letter refers them to me. But he went to the president's office, and Melissa, of course, sent him to me. He agreed to every condition that I laid down. I talked to the vice president and we both thought Bolt was going to be a jelly doughnut. When we asked him for a pretty hefty fee, he didn't even blink."

"Princeton must make money off all the movies that are shot here," McLeod said.

"We don't make money," said Macy. "The presence of a movie company on campus is very disturbing. And the cleanup costs are significant. It really is trouble, even in the summer when classes aren't in session. But we like movies that are about members of the university community that are a credit to us. Einstein and John Nash—for instance. And Princeton is very proud of F. Scott Fitzgerald. Fitzgerald did love Princeton, you know. Has anybody told you he was reading the *Princeton Alumni Weekly* when he died?"

"Not a soul has mentioned it to me," said McLeod.

Irony was wasted on Macy. "The magazine was turned to the story about a football game. Football players were Fitzgerald's heroes. He idolized them."

"I think Max Bolt is trying to capture that feeling," said McLeod. "That scene he was filming last night on University Place involved a parade of seniors with the captain of the football team leading the way."

"Yeah," said Macy.

"So all of you liked the idea of a movie version of *This Side of Paradise*? With a lot of Princeton scenes," McLeod said.

"That's right. And he told us it would be an homage to Fitzgerald, not a strict version of the novel. And we told him he could begin filming in June, after graduation. He carried on like a crazy man. He wanted to begin immediately. He said he had a schedule he had to meet. He said he wanted to get some winter shots while the trees were still bare. He wanted to start filming in March and go straight through until he finished here. We said absolutely not. He went to Melissa. He came back to me. He went back to Melissa. She was adamant. Bolt is such an overpowering personality—I'd guess he's charismatic—that I would probably have given in if it hadn't been for Melissa."

"But he did start during spring break," said McLeod.

"I think that was a mistake on our part. Melissa said finally to let him come on campus during spring break. But he was supposed to be off campus by the time classes started again. He could come back in June, we said. But he had his trucks and all his stuff poised in a vacant field over in West Windsor. He moved in the Saturday after the students left."

"And he was supposed to be out of here when spring break was over?"

"That's right. But as you know, he wasn't. And as you know, too, Melissa was not in her office the week after spring break. Nobody knew where she was. So he kept right on. I think he tried to keep a lower profile, but it's hard for a man like Max Bolt with a project like filming a movie to keep a low profile."

"You're right," said McLeod.

"Then remember that Melissa's body was found on the Sunday of the week after spring break was over and nobody had the time or the wits to run him off," Macy continued. "He just kept on. And he bulldozed the Borough into closing University Place for him yesterday. The man has guts, I have to admit."

"What about Kenneth Coales? Won't he put a stop to Bolt?"

"This is off the record, McLeod. But you'd think he would, wouldn't you?" said Macy. "A man like him. But so far, he hasn't done anything. He's got too much on his plate, I guess. And you know he doesn't have George Bridges to help him. I bet he's regretting that he put George on leave. George has provided the institutional memory for three presidents now. I don't see how Ken Coales knows what he's doing without him. But Coales has an ego a mile wide and a mile high. If you quote me, I'll kill you."

After McLeod hung up, she reflected once more that the timing of Melissa's death had certainly been fortuitous for Max Bolt. She was out of the picture when spring break was over and he had been able to keep on. Now to talk to Bolt himself.

McLeod had already decided that she would simply keep calling both his telephone numbers until she reached him. If it took all day, she would sit there by the telephone, dialing. To her astonishment, Bolt answered his home phone on the second ring. This was so unexpected McLeod couldn't think of what to say and stumbled and stuttered for several seconds. She finally got out some words: "Can I come over to talk to you? It's important."

"Sure," said Bolt. "Come on over. Have you had breakfast?"

"Yes, I have," said McLeod, who did not want to be fussing with toast and hearing about bakeries when she talked to Bolt. She wanted to have her head clear and her hands free to make notes.

"Okay," said Bolt. "When would you like to come?"

"It's nearly nine o'clock. How about if I come around nine-thirty?"

"Fine," he said.

McLeod took a quick shower, dressed in a skirt and cotton sweater, grabbed her coat—Would it never get warm again in Princeton? she wondered—and drove over to Bolt's big house on Hibben Road. Again he met her at the door, wearing blue jeans, only this time he was bare footed. He wore a Texas Longhorn sweatshirt.

"Come in," he said cordially. "Would you like some coffee?"

"No, thanks," said McLeod. "Do you have any tea?"

"Sure," said Bolt, leading the way to his sunny kitchen, where a pretty young woman was seated at the table.

"This is Natalie Longwood," he said. "My assistant. And Natalie, this is McLeod Dulaney—she's an expert on F. Scott Fitzgerald and she plays Nancy Drew from time to time."

"You don't mean she plays Nancy Drew in the movies? Or the stage?" said Natalie, staring at white-haired McLeod incredulously.

"In real life, bimbo," said Bolt.

Natalie shrugged and held out her hand to McLeod. "I'm not a bimbo," she said.

"Don't knock it," said McLeod. "Nobody ever calls *me* a bimbo."

Bolt had opened a cabinet door and brought out tea. McLeod had found that most people didn't even have tea in the house, and if they did, it was never good tea. But Max Bolt was holding up a tin of Scottish Breakfast tea from Peet's.

"How wonderful!" McLeod said. "My favorite."

"How did you know about Peet's?" asked Bolt. "Only true connoisseurs drink Scottish Breakfast."

"A friend of mine moved to Berkeley and she sent me some tea from Peet's—it was some other kind of tea—but Peet's sent a catalog with it and I saw it in there. I like Scottish things—my name is McLeod, after all—so I ordered some. And it has a little lapsang soochong in it, which I love. I've been a fan ever since. But you can't buy it in stores and I forget to order it."

"You can have this tin," said Bolt. "I don't drink it, and nobody else likes it." He turned to Natalie. "Do you?"

"Ugh," she said.

"It won't take me a minute to boil some water," Bolt said. "I believe last time you were here, you drank coffee." He looked at her with his piercing blue eyes.

"I know it's tiresome for coffee drinkers to have to make tea for somebody else," said McLeod. "I was trying to make it easy for you that time. I guess I shouldn't have asked for tea this morning."

"Don't apologize," said Bolt. "I'm happy to get rid of the tea."

McLeod noticed that he knew how to make tea. He had warmed the teapot with hot water from the tap, and emptied it before he put the tea in the pot. Now he poured the boiling water over the tea and put the lid on. "Won't be a minute," he said.

"Oh my, that's very good," said McLeod when he had poured her a mug of the hot tea. "Thanks. What a treat!"

"Ugh," said Natalie again. She got up and poured herself another cup of coffee.

"You don't like tea?" asked McLeod.

"I don't like *that* tea," said Natalie, brushing long blond hair back over her shoulders.

Bolt joined them at the kitchen table and looked at McLeod questioningly.

"I guess you're wondering why I'm here," she said. She hesitated. She had no idea how to begin, and she hadn't bargained on the presence of an "assistant." "How did it go yesterday? Did you finish up on University Place?"

"Barely," he said. "I saw the rushes this morning—"

"Already?" McLeod interrupted. "It's just now nine-thirty."

"I saw the rushes at six-thirty this morning. This is my lunch break."

McLeod, as usual, was impressed with Bolt's industry and devotion to his task. "How were they? The rushes, I mean," she said.

"All right," said Bolt. "We might have done better if we had had just one more hour. But we had to quit. I hope they have all the dirt cleaned up by now. The Borough was anxious to get the street open in time for 'church traffic.' I was surprised at that. I forget about church."

"I go to church here sometimes," said McLeod. "Lots of people do. But it's good you're out of there. The Borough won't declare war on you."

"Oh, they might still get nasty. But I'm happy. I'm going to be able to finish here, I think. Then I have to be all done before they put Billy Masters on trial."

"You mean you won't have to come back in June?" asked McLeod.

"Oh, we'll have to come back, but we've gotten more done than I thought we would. We're in good shape to do the Long Island and New York scenes. You always have to come back anyway to do something over. Fortunately the acting president has been more amenable."

"Kenneth Coales hasn't been beastly?"

Bolt began to laugh uproariously. "He was very beastly at first, but then we brought him around." Bolt was laughing so hard he could barely talk.

"How did you bring him around? What did you do?" asked McLeod.

Max Bolt finally stopped laughing, and said, "How do you think? We offered him a part."

"I can't believe it," said McLeod.

"I told him he looked so distinguished that we wanted

him to play the registrar who interviews Fitzgerald when he comes to take the entrance examination. Coales told us he had been in Theatre Intime plays when he was a student at Princeton. He positively preened. Don't tell Coales, but we shot that scene a long time ago. I talked Billy Masters into going through another take, this time with Coales."

"Was Coales any good?" asked McLeod.

"He was terrible," said Bolt. "We would have had to rewrite the part to fit him—he's one hard-assed guy, isn't he? In the movie we have a kindly old registrar who is charmed by Fitzgerald and lets him in, even though he flunked the entrance exam in math. I couldn't imagine Coales himself cutting someone slack, or even playing the part of somebody who cut anybody some slack."

By this time McLeod was laughing heartily, too.

"But you got what you wanted from him?" she asked.

"Oh, yes. He gave us tacit permission to hang around. He was thrilled with his part. He loved the costume and the makeup and the lights and the cameras and everything. The real registrar was furious. He's busy registering students for next year's classes. And we were in his office forever. But old Coales preened and pranced and had a glorious time." Bolt put down his coffee cup. "Now, listen here. Don't you dare tell anybody we're not going to use that scene with Coales. Not *anybody.*"

"I hear you," said McLeod. "I promise."

"Everybody in the world wants to be a movie star. Would you like a part, too? Is that what brings you to my kitchen on a Sunday morning?"

"No," said McLeod. "I don't recall a single white-haired woman in *This Side of Paradise*. Or in *The Great Gatsby*, for that matter. I don't think F. Scott Fitzgerald realized that women my age existed. And that brings me to why I'm here."

Bolt was looking at her expectantly.

"Have the police questioned you at all about the murder of Melissa Faircloth?"

"Sure. They talked to everybody who had been in her

office in the week or so before she died or before she went missing," said Bolt.

"You were in love with Melissa Faircloth when you were young," said McLeod, looking uncomfortably at Natalie.

"So?"

"The police don't know that you were ever involved with her, do they?"

"I don't suppose they do," said Bolt. "Are you going to tell them?"

"I don't know what I'm going to do," said McLeod. "I want very badly to find out who killed Melissa Faircloth."

"Why are you playing the Avenging Angel? Because of Melissa's daughter? I know you were staying with her right after Melissa's body was found."

"Well, there's that aspect of it, but even more compelling for me is the fact that my friend George Bridges, who was Melissa's assistant, is a suspect and has in fact been suspended from his job until he's cleared. And he's losing his good disposition and his self-esteem and everything else. I want to find the real murderer."

"Are you so sure he isn't the real murderer? I met George Bridges and he seemed quite dark and sinister to me."

McLeod laughed out loud as she realized Bolt was teasing her. "That's ridiculous," she said. "He reads Trollope. Nobody who reads Trollope could kill anybody."

"I don't think that would exonerate your friend in court," said Bolt.

"I know that."

"And so you've decided I must be the murderer since it isn't George?"

"Well, I wanted to talk to you about it," said McLeod, who was thankful indeed that Max Bolt didn't know how sure she had been earlier about the guilt of Clarence Robbins and then Kenneth Coales. "In fact, I really want to talk to you alone." She looked at Natalie.

"Sure," said Natalie. "I'll leave. I'll be upstairs." She slid out of the kitchen.

"She got kicked out of her room at the Nassau Inn, so I took her in," said Bolt.

"That was a good deed in a naughty world," said McLeod. "I don't care who sleeps here. I want to talk to you about Melissa. You and she had an emotional entanglement. You were very much in love with her."

Bolt interrupted her. "How do you know that?"

"Sophy, Melissa's daughter, found your letters to Melissa. Letters written when you both were young, I admit. About twenty, I'd say. But it's clear that you cared a great deal for her. I assume she felt the same toward you. Did she?"

"So she saved my letters?" Bolt was grinning.

"Apparently every one of them. It really is like Gatsby and Daisy, isn't it?"

"Gatsby?" asked Bolt.

"You know, Jay Gatsby. He loved Daisy to distraction when they were very young and kept on loving her. Wanted to impress her."

"Yeah, yeah," said Bolt. "Believe it or not, I have a passing knowledge of the book."

"Sophy pointed out the parallel between you and Gatsby. It sounded quite sensible when I thought about it all night, but I'm afraid it sounds insane in the light of day. Still—"

"Even if I were like Gatsby, I don't see what business this is of yours," said Bolt. "You're a nice lady, but I can't see why I should tell you anything about my private life."

"I told you why," said McLeod. "Pay attention. I want to clear my friend. And that means getting to the bottom of this. If you're not the killer—good. Then I'll go on and look for the next suspect. I'm determined to find out everything I can."

"What about the police? Are they doing anything?"

"I don't know what they're doing," said McLeod. "They've been very secretive about their investigation.

The newspapers are going crazy. I like Nick Perry, the man in charge, but he doesn't confide in me. I can take him information, however, and he listens to me. I feel like if I just go on my way, I'll get to the right answer at the end, maybe before Nick gets there. But it won't fall in my lap, I have to work at it. That's what I'm doing now—working at it. If I can eliminate you, like I said, then I'll go on to somebody else."

"Okay. 'I'll talk,' said the parrot. Yes, I was very much in love with Melissa Faircloth. She was a beautiful girl; she stood out at a school full of beautiful girls. And she was smart, too. Then she went off to graduate school, and I had one more year at Texas. I was so much in love that I thought when I graduated I would get a job in Chicago with one of the theaters there, but instead I went to Hollywood. I still wrote to Melissa, but after a time, she had met that asshole Clarence Robbins and then she had a baby. I didn't mind the baby. I was stunned, but I could have coped with anything for Melissa's sake, but she said she had to simplify her life. No romantic entanglements. She had her way to make and a child to raise as a single mother and she wanted to see no more of me. It seemed to me that she needed me more than ever but I couldn't persuade her. So I stayed in Hollywood and put her out of my mind."

"Did you really put her out of your mind? You didn't even think about her?"

"I guess I did think about her . . ." Bolt was quiet.

"How long had it been since you saw her—I mean, before you came to Princeton?" asked McLeod.

"Almost thirty years," said Bolt. "Our paths didn't cross. When I was in New York, I would think about coming down here to see her. But I didn't."

"Was the fact that she was here one of the reasons you decided to make a movie of *This Side of Paradise*?"

Bolt smiled dreamily, and McLeod thought that he was surely one of the world's most attractive men. How on earth could Melissa Faircloth have resisted him?

"You know, I guess it was." He stopped speaking and

stared out the window. "I don't think I've ever admitted that, even to myself." He turned to face McLeod. "You're some interrogator."

"Thanks." McLeod said nothing else, and Bolt spoke again.

"I guess I have stayed in love with her all these years. That's downright weird, isn't it? In this day and age? I don't mean I've led a monkish life, but I guess I've always had the feeling that—especially as the years went by and Melissa stayed single—that eventually she and I would get together."

"Well, how did you feel when you got here and saw her again?"

"She was still wonderful looking," Bolt said.

"Was that all you felt?"

"No, of course not. I had all kinds of conflicted feelings. She was obviously glad to see me. That was the good news."

"And the bad news?"

"I took her to dinner at Rat's. You know that place down at the Grounds for Sculpture that that millionaire subsidizes. Everybody said it was the best restaurant around. I had a car and driver. To tell you the truth, I was so excited I thought I might have a wreck if I drove."

"And?"

"And it was—well, different. We talked about Texas. We talked about movies. We talked about economics—as much economics as I could handle, that is. We talked about higher education. We talked about books and plays. She was still smart and good-looking and good company. I was trying to imagine a life for us together—Hollywood . . . Princeton . . . locations . . . What kind of life could we possibly have? It seemed bizarre, but I was actually trying to figure it out."

"But in the end, you couldn't? Is that it?"

"No, I could see it." Bolt stopped again. "But there was one thing. She was uncooperative about my movie. She was the biggest obstacle I've ever come up against. Jim

Macy in communications was a pushover compared to her. She wanted me out of the way. No trucks, no cameras, no Billy Masters, no Temple Jones. No quick shooting."

"Did that change the way you felt about her?"

Bolt pushed his chair back from the table and stood up. He walked over to the window as though to get a closer look at whatever it was he had stared out so often.

"To be honest, it sure did change my attitude." He was facing her, hands in the pockets of his jeans. McLeod thought he looked very sad. "I hadn't realized it until your relentless interrogation began. I was crazy about her for years. I really was. I never really got over her. I guess it was sort of Gatsby-esque." He shrugged.

Bolt walked back to the table, pulled out a chair, pushed it in again and went back to the window, then turned around to face her.

"That's me, the idiot Gatsby. Until—until she tried to throw a monkey wrench in my work. My work is important to me. That sounds fatuous, but my work is very important to me. I take it very seriously. I know it's not high art. But it's art, even if it's popular art."

"I think some of your movies have been high art," said McLeod.

"Thank you. *This Side of Paradise* might be the best movie I've ever made. But no thanks to my old friend, Melissa Faircloth."

"Her death was really a boon to you, wasn't it?" said McLeod. "There's no getting around it."

"You put it so delicately," said Bolt. "It was a real blow when I found out she was dead. It was like a part of me had been lost. And a part of me was lost. I was very sorry that she died, but I guess I took advantage of the circumstance. If somebody hands you a lemon, make lemonade."

"Harry Truman said that, and I don't think he meant use the death of an old friend to advantage."

"Why not? It saved me millions. And at that point it wouldn't have done her any good for me to stop filming, would it?"

McLeod was repelled by Bolt's callousness, but she tried to see the situation from his point of view.

"But tell me this," she said. "Did you realize ahead of time that if Melissa Faircloth were murdered, you could keep on filming?"

"Of course not," said Bolt.

"But can't you see how suspicious it looks? I wonder what Nick Perry would say about this."

"The policeman? You're the one who acts as though the police will never catch the murderer," said Bolt. "I guess he's too busy chasing petty criminals."

"What do you mean petty criminals? Do you mean like serial rapists?"

"Gotcha!" said Bolt. "I thought that would light your fuse."

"No, you're wrong. It put iron in my backbone," said McLeod. "Don't you see how it looks? You're the one who profits most by her death. And let me ask you, can you prove that you didn't kill Melissa Faircloth? What were you doing on that Monday night?"

"On that Monday night, I was working, in my so-called office at the Residence Motel on Route 1. We were supposed to get off campus, and I was trying to figure out how we could stay a day or two longer, and how we could schedule the shoots in Paris and New York and get back here when school was out."

"Was anybody with you? Natalie wasn't there? Or anybody else?"

"Actually, neither of those girls were there. There wasn't anything they could do. I was *thinking*."

"Well, think some more," said McLeod, standing up. "Think what you can tell the police when they ask you about all this."

"So you're going to the local cops?" Bolt was also on his feet.

"If you didn't kill her, you don't have anything to worry about," said McLeod. "But yes, I'm going to talk to them. I told you I want to find the murderer."

"I told you once before to be careful," said Bolt. "And now, you better watch every step you take, every bite you eat."

"Bullies threaten," said McLeod, and left.

Am I crazy? she asked herself. To talk to him like that? But he made me so mad.

Twenty-one

REMEMBERING THE THIRD instruction she had written to herself that morning, McLeod went straight to the police station when she left Max Bolt's house on Hibben Road. It was very close, and she knew Nick Perry would be there, even though it was Sunday.

She asked to see Lieutenant Perry but was told he was "in conference."

"Do you have any idea when he will be available?" she said.

"What's this about, ma'am?" asked the officer at the window.

"It's about the Faircloth murder," she said.

"Does he know you?"

"Yes, he knows me. Here." McLeod got out one of her cards and gave it to the officer, smiling in what she hoped was a very winning way. "Give this to him, please, sir, and ask him when I can see him. Thank you so much."

The officer was back immediately and handed her card

back to her. Perry had scrawled *Give me 15 minutes* on the back. "I'll just wait here," McLeod said, and took a seat on a bench.

Perry was out before the fifteen minutes were up, and beckoned her into an interview room. It seemed to her that his bald head was shinier than ever. "Good to see you, McLeod. Have you solved the mystery yet?"

"Maybe, but probably not," said McLeod. "Have you solved it?"

"Probably, but maybe not," said Perry.

"Who is it?" asked McLeod, wondering if Perry's head shone brighter as he got closer to a solution.

"My lips are sealed," said Perry.

"Your lips are always sealed."

"They have to be," said Perry. "What can I do for you?"

"I have some information that I feel duty bound to give you," said McLeod. She realized belatedly that she was truly reluctant to tell Perry about Bolt's longtime attachment to Melissa Faircloth. Bolt was one of the most magnetic, interesting men she had ever known. She liked his movies, and she loved his devotion to his work. And although she had been a little annoyed at Natalie's presence in his house, what on earth did she expect of an attractive man?

"Information?" prompted Perry.

"Yes," said McLeod, hesitating. This was hard, harder than she had thought it would be. "It's about Max Bolt."

"Max Bolt. He's your new suspect? He's a glamorous movie man, not a ne'er-do-well like Clarence Robbins or a tough administrator like Provost Coales."

McLeod grinned ruefully. "I know he is. And I wouldn't say he's truly a suspect. I don't feel strongly about him the way I did about the other two. I was pretty Lucy-goosey, wasn't I? No, I just have some information I feel duty bound to lay before you."

"Lay away," said Perry.

First she explained about Max Bolt's situation vis-à-vis Princeton University. He was allowed to film for one week during spring vacation and then he was supposed to be off campus until after Commencement in the middle of June. He was desperate to finish filming the Princeton scenes in one fell swoop. But it was Melissa Faircloth who was absolutely refusing to allow him to remain on campus. When she was missing, Bolt kept right on filming. And was still at it.

She told Perry about the letters.

"Pretty hot stuff, were they?" asked Perry.

"They were sweet, they were *love* letters," said McLeod. Then she told him about her conversation with Bolt. Perry listened, as he always did, until she'd finished. "You know why I never considered him seriously as a suspect?" she asked him. "I knew he didn't have a key to the president's office, and I didn't think Melissa Faircloth would let him in. After all, she had been resolutely determined to keep him from doing his work, carrying out a mission as he saw it. And so I didn't think there was any way possible that she would have opened that office door to him on a Monday night."

Perry stared at her silently.

"But when I heard about their fling in college, I realized she might very well have opened her door to him. Especially at night."

Perry still said nothing. "What do you think?" McLeod asked him.

"I'll tell you what I think, McLeod," said Perry. "First I want to remind you that Wednesday you were sure the murderer was Kenneth Coales. Last week it was Clarence Robbins. And something else, I think Sophy Faircloth should have called us the minute she found those letters. And you should have called us the minute she told you about them."

"I guess you're right. In a perfect world, I wouldn't be curious or impulsive. I'd do nothing about anything," said McLeod. "And I would call the police every time I turned around."

"It's not a perfect world. I realize that. Anyway, thanks

for telling me at last. We'll talk to Bolt. But, McLeod, let me say something. I'm very serious. You have to be more careful. You're going to get hurt if you keep this up."

"I hope you're not right. I still think Clarence pushed me down the stairs, and Coales tried to halfway drown me. I wonder what Max Bolt will do?"

"Let's hope nothing. What else is new with you?"

"Not much," said McLeod.

"How's George? Has he got his job back?"

McLeod looked at Nick Perry sharply. Sometimes he astounded her by what he could remember. "No, he hasn't. But he's still getting paid. He's not in the best humor all the time, but that's understandable. I'd sure like it to track down the real murderer so he'd be the real George again."

"I know you'd love to track down the real murderer," said Perry. "That's only natural. But why don't you leave it to the professionals? In fact, I'll put it more strongly: Stop trying to find the murderer. The police will find out who it is. We may be slow, but we're sure."

"Are you?" said McLeod.

"We always get our man," said Perry.

"Okay," said McLeod, standing up. "Thanks for seeing me."

"Anytime, McLeod," said Perry, also standing. "But stop investigating. I don't want to hear any more reports of evidence you've stumbled on. I don't want to see you in the hospital again." He paused. "I guess I'd better talk to Sophy Robbins and we'd better take a look at all of Melissa Faircloth's correspondence that's stored in that house."

"Do you have the manpower to do all this? And still keep Princeton safe for its residents?"

"Don't be sarcastic, McLeod," said Perry. "We have resources we can draw on from the State Police and the prosecutor's office—believe me, we can handle it. And we will."

"I know you're capable personally," said McLeod.

"And I know you'll get it done. I just hope it's sooner rather than later."

They shook hands, and McLeod left.

Outside Borough Hall, she looked at her watch. It was nearly noon. She decided to walk uptown and get something to take home for her lunch—maybe at Panera, a new place on Nassau Street. Should she call George? He was so moody lately. Did he want to be left alone—or did he want company and attention? It was hard to know what to do where he was concerned.

McLeod decided it was better to pay too much attention than too little, and she sat down on a bench on the sidewalk and pulled out her cell phone. She called George, who answered immediately.

"Where have you been?" he asked angrily. "I've been trying to call you all morning."

"I'm sorry," said McLeod. "I went to talk to Max Bolt."

"You're like everybody else," he said. "You've got a crush on those movie people."

"No, I don't," said McLeod. Now wait a minute, she said to herself. What is this all about? Why am I defending myself? What if I did have a crush on Max Bolt? Am I tied to George Bridges? I like him a lot. A whole lot, but he hasn't committed himself to me in any way, and lately he's been cross as a bear. What is going on? All this raced through her mind. "I don't have a crush on the movie people," she said. "They're a different breed, believe me. It's like Scott Fitzgerald saying the rich were different from you and me—"

George interrupted her to point out that Fitzgerald had said it to Hemingway and Hemingway had replied, "Yes, they have more money."

McLeod plowed on. "The movie people *are* different. Anyway, I wanted to talk to him about his previous relationship with Melissa Faircloth."

"And what did you find out?"

"I don't know what it all boils down to," said McLeod. "I don't think he killed Melissa Faircloth, although he had a very strong motive. That is, he had a motive if you think somebody would really kill an old sweetheart because she was preventing him from filming scenes from a movie that he could film two or three months later anyway."

"Does he have an alibi?"

"No, he doesn't. He said he was alone that Monday night."

"Like the rest of us," said George.

"Clarence wasn't alone," said McLeod. "And Ken Coales wasn't alone."

"Yeah," said George. "Would you like to ride over to the shore?"

"Oh, George, I do love the beach. All beaches. I just can't do it today." A car on Nassau Street honked at a bus.

"I gather you're not at home . . ." George said.

"No, I'm sitting on a bench on Nassau Street using my cell phone. My car's at Borough Hall. I'm going to get something to eat and then drive over to Sophy's mother's house. We'll finish the letters."

"Oh, all right, McLeod."

McLeod lost her temper. "Don't be such a martyr," she said. "I'm trying to prove you're innocent. And you don't do anything to help."

A long silence followed. "You're right," said George, and hung up.

McLeod turned her phone off and went to Olive's for a sandwich and a bottle of tomato juice. She took them back to the bench on Nassau Street, sat down, and began to eat.

She was tired of George's bad temper, no matter how justified it was under the circumstances. She was tired, and she was hungry.

"Oh, hello, m'dear. I didn't see you in church this morning. In fact, I haven't seen you in church lately. I thought you were going to be different from those other atheistic professors."

Fletcher Prickett, in his dark suit, had sat down beside her. She smiled at him. His skin was so rosy, his hair so white, and he was always cheerful. "I *am* different,"

McLeod said. "I'm not a real professor, you know. I'm officially classified as a lecturer."

"A mere technicality," said Fletcher Prickett.

"Anyway, I didn't get to church today. How was it? What was the sermon about?"

"It was about Jesus," said Fletcher vaguely. "How are you? You don't look as cheerful as you usually do."

"I'm not," said McLeod. "I'm not cheerful at all. My friend George Bridges is under a cloud about this murder—I think I mentioned it to you before—and nobody seems to have a clue as to who the real murderer is. In fact, this morning I went to talk to Max Bolt, the man who's doing the movie on campus—you know some sort of version of *This Side of Paradise*—"

"I know about that moving picture," Fletcher interrupted. "I just hope it will show Princeton in a favorable light."

"How could it not?" asked McLeod. "Fitzgerald loved Princeton."

"I know. But everything seems to go wrong for Princeton these days. And why did you talk to Max Bolt?"

"It seems he knew Melissa Faircloth—"

"That Woman!" Fletcher interrupted her again.

"Yes, That Woman, as you call her. They knew each other in college at the University of Texas. He was madly in love with her. But she didn't want him to make the movie. I mean she didn't want him to shoot on campus when classes were in session. He was supposed to be here for one week during spring break, then leave and be off campus until he came back in the summer."

"But he didn't leave," said Fletcher. "Did he?"

"No, he didn't leave, because That Woman, as you call her, was missing, then murdered, and everyone was distracted so nobody made him leave."

"Well, you are a busy little girl, aren't you?" asked Fletcher. "You know, m'dear, I really do suggest you stay out of this investigation. You had best leave it to the police—and I know you'll laugh at this—leave it to men, men who know what they're doing."

McLeod thought that when Fletcher tried to look stern, he merely looked sad. She smiled at him. "Thanks," she said. "I appreciate your concern. But just for the record, where were you on the Monday night That Woman was killed?"

"M'dear, I don't have the slightest idea. Can we have another lunch one day this week? I've been longing to further our acquaintance."

"I'm sure we can," said McLeod. "I don't have my calendar with me, but I'm pretty sure I'm free tomorrow. Call me at the office, if you will."

"I certainly will," he promised. "Lovely to see you." He got up from the bench, took her hand and shook it warmly, then left.

Twenty-two

ON MONDAY, MCLEOD went to her office early and finally started work on a draft of her article on Ken Coales. It was tough going. The trouble was she knew too much about Coales, too much that she couldn't put in the paper. It was a relief to shove that problem aside when Fletcher Prickett called.

"Can you have lunch with me today, m'dear?" he asked her.

"You know, I really can't," said McLeod. "I've got to finish this article I'm working on. I'm sorry. I'd love to otherwise."

"Well, how about taking time off some time today for a little stroll. I want to show you something on campus. I think you'll like it."

"Sure," said McLeod, who thought a stroll with that maniacally sexist old gentleman would be a relaxation. They finally settled on ten o'clock that morning.

"Why put it off?" asked Fletcher. "If it's worth doing, it's worth doing soon, I always say."

"That's right," said McLeod.

"I'll come by your office in Joseph Henry House," said Fletcher.

"Fine," said McLeod.

"COME ALONG, NOW. What I want to show you is just a step away," Fletcher Prickett said when she opened the door to his knock, promptly at ten o'clock.

"Still, it's chilly outside, let me get my coat," said McLeod.

"All right, m'dear, although I don't think it's really chilly, but then I'm a cold Yankee fish. Isn't that right?"

"You're hardly a cold fish," said McLeod, "although you are undoubtedly a Yankee. Where are we going, incidentally?"

"Just over here to the chapel," said Fletcher. "Just a step or two away, but I think it's something you have to see."

They passed the statue of John Witherspoon, crossed the plaza between East Pyne and the chapel, and walked up the steps to the narthex of the huge Gothic cathedral–like building. "It's big," Fletcher said to McLeod. "Look at the nave." He waved his hand toward the alter and chancel, which seemed to be miles away.

Stepping from the narthex, with its low ceiling into the nave, where the vaulted ceiling was seventy-six feet high, was always a dramatic, even breathtaking, experience for McLeod. "It is beautiful," she said to Fletcher.

"Yes, it is. Did you know that pulpit came from France and used to be bright red?"

"No, I didn't. I love facts like that. How did you know that?"

"I like to find out everything I can about Princeton. I guess I read it in some pamphlet about the architecture on campus. You've seen the balcony, haven't you?"

"No, I've never been up there."

"We'll go." Fletcher led her back to the narthex and to a winding stone stairway to the south of the front door. He whisked away a cord that was blocking the stairs, ignored a sign that said BALCONY CLOSED, and led McLeod up the flight and into the balcony, where they could look down on the nave.

"It's fabulous," said McLeod.

"And now for something I know you haven't seen," said Fletcher, leading her out of the balcony and back to the stairway. A few steps up was a heavy oaken door. Fletcher whipped a key ring out of his pocket, fitted a key into the lock, and opened the door.

"How do you have a key to that door?" asked McLeod.

"It didn't used to be locked," said Fletcher. "When they started locking it up, I—shall we say—procured a copy of the key. I like to roam around the campus and I love the chapel. Come on, m'dear, and I'll show you the most beautiful view on campus."

Up and up, round and round, they climbed until they reached the top of the stairway on the south side of the main, or west, facade. Fletcher unlocked another door and led her out onto a narrow—no more than ten inches wide—space that ran just behind a gallery of seven small Gothic arches on the facade above the great west window.

"Look," said Fletcher, pointing out one of the tiny arches. "Just look at that. Isn't that something?" The sill of the arches was waist-high, so there was no danger of falling, yet they could still see beautifully.

And what they saw was indeed "something," McLeod agreed. Through one small arch, she could see the whole campus laid out below like a model town on a sand table. She was looking down at the squat brownstone towers of East Pyne, the green dome of Chancellor Green Hall, the Georgian cupola of Nassau Hall, and farther away, the spire of Holder Hall. It was an aerial view of Princeton University.

"I feel like a bird—a bird with an eye for a view," said McLeod.

"I love it up here. Don't you?"

"Who wouldn't?" said McLeod. "Thank you so much for bringing me up here. I really appreciate it." She turned back toward the door through which they had come out of the building.

"No, no, m'dear," said Fletcher. "Tour's not over yet."

McLeod, for some reason, began to feel uneasy. What were they doing up here behind locked doors in the first place? She was sure it was absolutely forbidden to be up this far. And hadn't there been some accident last year, when a student had fallen down the shaft of a tower?

"I should go," she said. "I have work to do."

"Just one more thing to show you." Fletcher was taking out yet another key and unlocking a door in the center of the narrow little gallery. McLeod had never noticed the door up high on the facade behind the row of arches.

"How many people ever come up here?" McLeod asked him.

"No one," said Fletcher softly.

"No one else has keys?" she asked.

"No one but the sexton," said Fletcher. "Come along." He gently pushed McLeod through the little door. He found a light switch, pressed it, and closed the outside door. The sound of it crashing closed was like a crack of doom, McLeod thought. They were facing a catwalk that ran right under the slate roof of the chapel, above the top of the vaulted ceiling of the nave.

"This way, m'dear. Wait till you see the north tower." Fletcher led the way down the catwalk and then turned left onto another catwalk. This whole space was shadowy and McLeod felt it had an extremely ominous atmosphere. But she was always curious, ready to see the next thing, and she walked carefully, following Fletcher.

"How did you know about this?" she asked him.

"When I was an undergraduate, I explored all the buildings on campus. They were not locked up the way they are now. And I guess it all started with stealing the clapper."

"Stealing the clapper?" asked McLeod.

"You know, it used to be a tradition for the freshmen to steal the clapper of the bell in the belfry on Nassau Hall. It was supposed to mean that classes couldn't meet if the bell didn't ring. So every year, all of the freshmen tried to be the first one to get up there and steal the clapper. I was the one in my class—the Great Class of 1940—that's my biggest claim to fame. I got a key to the cupola of Nassau Hall and I stole the clapper in 1936."

"Do they still steal the clapper?"

"No. The university put a stop to it. It was too dangerous, they said. Truth is they were afraid of lawsuits. Another great tradition bit the dust."

They were making their way slowly along the catwalk that led to the east end of the nave. "Thank goodness the catwalks have railings," she said.

"Oh, yes, perfectly safe, m'dear." Fletcher led her onto another catwalk that branched off to the left. "Now be careful of your head here. Duck way down to go under this beam."

McLeod almost had to crawl to get under the beam. When they were able to stand up again, they had reached a door on the north side of the chapel. Fletcher was pulling out another key and unlocking the door. "Come along," he said, smiling at her. "Wait until you see this view."

The door opened inward, and he almost pushed McLeod inside a tiny room, a round room obviously at the top of a tower. It had an iron grill for a floor, but no windows.

"Where's the view?" asked McLeod.

"Oh, it's over here," said Fletcher. He reached out and pulled her toward him, and McLeod noticed for the first time an open shaft in the grill of the floor. "Actually, the view for you is down there." He pointed down the shaft.

Not realizing what he meant, McLeod peered helplessly down the shaft. Nothing but shadows, and the hazy outlines of more grilled floors, one under the other.

"Yes, m'dear, you're going down that shaft. You won't

find anybody down there to ask questions of. You do know you ask too many questions, don't you?"

"Fletcher, what do you mean?" McLeod asked him. He was much stronger than he looked, and his grip was bruising her arm. "What on earth are you talking about? Why do you care how many questions I ask?"

"You're the only person who's ever asked me where I was that Monday night," said Fletcher. "The police have never come close to me. I never heard a word from them."

"Why should you?" asked McLeod.

"Hah!"

McLeod's brain felt fuzzy. She was frightened and she couldn't think clearly. Fletcher wasn't saying that he was a murderer, was he? "Let's go, Fletcher," she said and tried to pull away toward the door to the tower. Fletcher stopped her. His arm was hard. McLeod remembered that he worked out regularly at the gym.

"Come on, Fletcher. Don't tease me anymore. Let's go back downstairs. I have lots of work to do."

"Oh, no, m'dear. You don't understand. You're going down but you're not going down the stairs." His eyes glittered. "I tried to get That Woman up here, you know, but she wouldn't come. She wouldn't even see me. But I fixed her. I told you I'd do anything for Princeton. And I got rid of That Woman."

"You didn't," said McLeod. "You couldn't have! How did you get in her office? She would never have let you in—" And then her hand flew to her mouth. Of course he could have gotten in. He had keys to all the nooks and crannies in the chapel, and he had once had keys that enabled him to get to the cupola of Nassau Hall. He undoubtedly still had keys to Nassau Hall. He could have gotten in that Monday night and strangled Melissa Faircloth.

"Yes, m'dear, I could get in. People always underestimate me. I strangled That Woman. And I put my mark on her. I showed her that men are meant to lead, to be on top."

"You mean you—" McLeod could not get any more words out.

Fletcher smirked. There was no other word. "I did indeed. Now, as I said, you're going down but not down the stairs." He nodded again toward the shaft. McLeod looked at the shaft again, and then looked at Fletcher. He pushed her toward the shaft. She tried to leap over it, even as Fletcher pushed her, but one foot slipped and then the other and down she went.

As she fell, she heard the door to the tower close with a sound that was even louder than the crack of doom.

WHEN MCLEOD BEGAN to notice things again, she realized, first, that she was alive and, second, that it was very dark. She was lying on a grilled floor. One leg was dangling down a hole of some kind. It was the shaft. She carefully felt the floor around her and then tried to shift her body so that she could pull her leg out of the shaft. This was a simple task but it seemed to take forever. At last it was done.

I can't have fallen all the way down to the bottom of the tower, she thought. If I had, I'd be dead. That would be seventy-six feet. I must have fallen a much shorter distance than that. But where am I?

Then she remembered Fletcher, who had certainly tried to kill her. There was no doubt about it. He had pushed her down the shaft and left her falling down the north tower of the chapel at his beloved Princeton University. And he had apparently turned out the light before he left, slamming the heavy door.

She felt bruised and shaken, but she had survived. And there had to be some way out of there. Then she remembered the tortuous trip up to the top of the chapel and all those steps. They had edged sideways along that little gallery on the outside. And then they had made their way along catwalks and ducked under the beam. There were locked doors all along the way. Maybe there wasn't a way out. Maybe she was going to die in the chapel.

Holy ground, she thought. It was cold comfort. Why on earth had Fletcher pushed her down the shaft? And then left her—left her to die? So jolly old Fletcher Prickett, Class of 1940, was the murderer. It was as simple as that, and nobody had suspected him. Nobody at all. And he must be as loony as a—well, a lunatic, she thought. Did he really think it was worth a murder to get rid of Princeton's woman president?

She certainly had not suspected him. If she had, she wouldn't have been foolish enough to come up in the upper regions of the chapel with him. Not a soul knew where she was, either. There was no hope that any one would come looking for her. She would die here in this dark tower, and she would never know whether Rosie wrote her book about Nadine Gordimer or whether Harry finished his dissertation. She herself would never write a book about the Bartrams, father and son botanists from Philadelphia.

Twenty-three

HOW LONG SHE lay there, unmoving, she did not know, but finally she decided to take action. Better to die trying to get out than to die passively lying on the floor, she thought. Trying to assess her present situation, she decided that she must have landed on the grill floor one level below the top floor of the tower. Maybe she could get back up to the top and get out. It had apparently never occurred to Fletcher that she wouldn't fall all the way down. Or maybe, he knew she was securely locked in the tower and it didn't matter what level she was on.

Her right knee throbbed—she had apparently hurt the same knee she had injured at Lowrie House—and her right shoulder was very painful. Nevertheless, she felt all around herself and located the shaft again. She nudged her body until she was a few inches away from it and finally managed to sit up. Well, her back wasn't broken. Still feeling all around in the dark, she turned over and got herself into a position to crawl. She carefully began to creep toward the wall, feeling ahead of her before each movement, aware of the shaft that she knew was there and afraid of other shafts that might be around.

She found the wall of the tower, and carefully crawled all the way around its circumference until she came to the shaft again. Feeling the wall above the shaft—it was tricky here, to stay safely on the grill floor and reach the wall above the shaft—but she managed. And she was rewarded. She felt the rungs of a metal ladder set into the wall above the shaft. I thought I remembered seeing that ladder going down, she said to herself.

Cautiously, she began the painful act of standing up, careful to avoid the shaft and stay on the grill. Now could she swing onto the ladder from the grill and climb up to the next level, surely the level she had fallen from? She had to try; that was all there was to it.

She put both hands on a rung above her head and felt a stab of pain in her right shoulder. She swung her left foot, the one below the uninjured knee, out until it landed on a rung, and then carefully placed the right foot next to it on the same rung. Despite the pain in her shoulder and her knee, she hung there and reached for the next rung, then moved first one foot and then the other. And so, painfully, slowly, she climbed up, and up. It wasn't far before she reached the next level, but it seemed like miles.

Oh, if this was the level where they had been, she thought, then there would be a light switch—and maybe the door would open from the inside. She inched onto her stomach on this grill floor and finally was clear of the shaft. Now, to find the switch. She was afraid of falling down a shaft again, so she proceeded with extreme caution. She crawled a foot, stood up, and felt the wall for the light switch. Then she got back down on her hands and knees and crawled another foot, stood up, and searched the wall for the switch again.

It seemed to her to take at least two days before she found the light switch and clicked it on. She felt the way God must have on the first day of Creation, the day he made light. When God said, "And it was good," he understated the case, McLeod thought. Light was better than good. Light was fantastic. She looked around her. Solid stone walls, and an iron grill floor with a shaft in it. But she was standing right beside the door. She tried the knob. The door was tightly locked. She pulled on it. She pushed on it. She pounded on it and screamed as loud as she could: "Help me! Help me! I'm stuck in the north tower! Help!"

Nothing happened. Of course, no one could hear her way up here. And no one ever came up here. Ever. She looked all over the surface of the door for a latch that would open it from the inside. Nothing. She walked around the wall looking for a way out. Nothing but stone wall, iron grill floor, and a shaft. Time was passing.

Looking down the shaft, she saw the grill floor below, the one where she had fallen. The shaft went down and down and down, and McLeod thanked God that she had somehow landed on the grill below the top level and had not fallen all the way down the shaft. Then she noticed that the ladder bolted to the stone wall apparently went all the way down to the bottom of the shaft.

She sat down on the grill floor and considered her options. They were not attractive. She could sit there and die. She could waste her breath yelling and die. Or maybe—just maybe—she could climb down and get out on the main floor of the chapel—and not die.

She rested a moment. She prayed. She took a deep breath and thought of Rosie and Harry. And then she got up and went to the shaft and with some difficulty started down the ladder. At least she had a little light and could see where she was going. She slowly climbed back down to the second level—it seemed easier to go down than it had been to go up—then down to another, then another, and another . . . and then one foot coming off the ladder hit a stone floor. It was very dim down here but she could make out a door across the room. She prayed again, limped across the stone floor, and waited a second before she tried the knob. It turned. Thank God, it turned. She turned it again and pushed hard and the door opened. But the room she entered was very dark. She waited, trying to see the room better. Finally, she started around the wall and realized the wall was no longer curved. She was definitely out of the tower. She kept moving and ran into what turned out to be a stack of cartons. This was a storeroom. Let's hope it's not locked, she thought. There was more junk in her way as she searched for another door. She either pushed things aside or skirted them carefully and finally came to another door. This was the crucial door. Would it open?

She turned the knob. It opened. And she stepped out of the dark store room into a lighted room and what seemed to her a scene of incredible coziness and domesticity. In a stone archway, two men and a woman sat at a small table covered with a white tablecloth, set with dishes and cutlery and glasses. Behind them was a tiny kitchenette. The three people were obviously having lunch.

The trio paused, held their forks motionless before open mouths, and stared at McLeod. The white tablecloth, though, was what McLeod would always remember. It looked so classy that she nearly fainted at the sight.

"Who are you and what were you doing in the storeroom?" the woman asked her.

"I'm McLeod Dulaney, and I teach a writing course . . ." she began. She reached out and put her hand on a stone pillar of the arch. "Can I sit down?"

The three people unfroze. One of the men leaped up and took his chair to McLeod. "I'll get a better chair, but sit down in that for the moment." He disappeared through a door beside which hung a sign that said CHAPEL CHOIR DIRECTOR, and reappeared with an upholstered chair. He helped McLeod up out of the straight chair and into the softer one, and introduced himself as Mack, the chapel choir director.

"Would you like a cup of tea?" asked the woman, who said she was Millicent, the organist.

"Or brandy? We actually have some brandy down

here," said the second man, who was Larry, another member of the music staff.

"I'd love a shot of brandy, and then a cup of tea," said McLeod. "Where am I?" McLeod asked. "Is this the crypt?" She was thinking of cathedrals.

They explained briefly that she was in the basement of the chapel, not exactly the crypt, which was a couple of rooms away. But they were anxious to know what had happened to her.

It took McLeod some time to explain, and before she'd finished, Mack said, "We have to call the police. This is serious." He headed toward his office. "I'll call 911," he said.

"Don't call 911," said McLeod. "They'll get here with lights flashing and sirens keening. Call Nick Perry at the Borough police."

"No, we need 911. We want the Rescue Squad. You have to see a doctor and get some X rays," said Millicent.

"I'll go upstairs and wait for the police then bring them down here," Larry offered.

"Now who was it who pushed you down the shaft?" asked Millicent.

"His name is Fletcher Prickett and he's Class of 1940 . . ." McLeod had barely taken up her tale, when the police and Rescue Squad arrived. Protesting feebly, she went once more in an ambulance heading to the emergency room at the Princeton Medical Center.

Twenty-four

"HIS NAME IS Fletcher Prickett and he's Class of 1940," she was explaining again to Nick Perry sometime later. Perry had come to the emergency room, where McLeod was still lying in a curtained booth, waiting for X rays. "He pushed me down a shaft in the north tower of the chapel on the university campus."

"The north tower—that's where that young woman fell down the shaft a few years ago," said Nick. "Tell me exactly what happened."

"Fletcher Prickett called me and said he wanted to show me something on campus. He took me to the chapel and he had a key to the door in the tower in the west front." She told him about the climb upward, the narrow little hidden gallery they'd crossed the facade on, the little door in the middle of the chapel, the catwalks, the beams, and Fletcher's key to the door of the north tower.

"He said he wanted to show me the view, and of course there is no view from that tower. Just stone walls, and a metal grill for a floor—and a shaft. He pushed me down the shaft, and left. I fell to the floor below and somehow landed on that grill floor instead of going on down the shaft. I think I was unconscious for a while. What time is it?"

"It's two-fifteen," said Nick.

"We went up there about ten o'clock this morning," said McLeod.

"And then what happened?"

"I managed to feel around and pull my leg out of the shaft and find the ladder and get on it—although I hurt my knee when I fell—and climb back up to the top. I turned on the light—"

"You mean you were in the dark up there all that time and you crawled up that ladder?" Nick asked.

"I did," said McLeod. "I had to do something, didn't I? But when I got the light on, I still couldn't get the door open. It was locked. Anyway, I pounded on the door and screamed but nobody heard me. I finally decided to try to go down the ladder in the shaft and see if I could get out at the bottom. And I did. I came into a storeroom and then into this room in the basement of the chapel and three people on the music staff were having lunch down there. It was the most amazing thing. And they called 911."

NICK WAS SILENT a long time, then he asked, "Why would Fletcher Prickett want to push you down the shaft in the tower in the chapel?"

"I think he wanted me to stop asking questions about the murder," said McLeod. "I—"

Perry interrupted. "*Everybody* wants you to stop asking questions about the murder, especially me."

"I think I will. I asked Fletcher questions, but I ask *everybody* questions. I never suspected Fletcher of anything but sexism. I thought he was a diversion, a quaint old buffer. But he's full of anger, furious that Princeton changed, that it wasn't the way it was when he went here in the thirties. For some men, college is the best time of their lives. And it must have been that way for Fletcher. He loved it when he was a student, and he wanted it to stay the same. He hated coeducation. He detested 'diversity' in the student body. He was beside himself with rage at all the women that were hired as professors and administrators. And then having a woman president drove him over the brink. I didn't take him seriously. Nobody did. But he really tried to kill me. He pushed me down that shaft and left, and locked the door behind him. He must have thought I fell all the way to the bottom and was either dead or would die soon. And for all his knowledge of the chapel and its towers, he may not have known about that door at the bottom."

"Look, we'll pick this guy up. But you'll have to be prepared to testify against him."

"I certainly will," said McLeod. "Sweet old guy with rosy cheeks and white hair he may be, but I will testify against him."

"I wonder why he was so worried about your questions. Is there any connection between him and Melissa Faircloth that you know of?"

"None that I know of except that he hated for her to be president. But he murdered her, you know. He said he did. He apparently has keys to everything on campus, including Nassau Hall."

"He said he killed Melissa Faircloth?" Nick had risen and pulled out his cell phone.

"Didn't I tell you?" asked McLeod. "I guess I didn't. And he raped her too—"

But Nick had left, and the orderly came to push her gurney to X-ray.

MCLEOD WAS ADMITTED to the hospital. "You've damaged your right knee," a doctor told her, "and sprained your right shoulder. We'll have to wait to see what happens with that knee, but I think the shoulder will heal by itself.

Stay in here overnight, and we'll let you go home tomorrow."

GEORGE BRIDGES APPEARED just as McLeod's supper was brought in—it was only five o'clock, but supper was early in the hospital.

He carried a bottle of champagne.

"I assume you can have a sip of this," he said. "Nick Perry called me. He told me you caught another murderer—can't you find a way of catching murderers without almost getting murdered yourself?"

"I guess not," said McLeod. "I'm so stupid I never suspect the real murderer until it's too late."

George popped the cork and poured champagne into two plastic cups.

"Have they arrested Fletcher?" asked McLeod.

"They have," said George. "Or at least, he's at the police station being questioned. Everybody is agog. What happened? Nick didn't have time to tell me anything much."

"I was exploring the chapel with Fletcher Prickett," she said. "He thought I suspected him—and I never once thought of him as the murderer. But he thought I was on his trail, I guess. Anyway, he took me to the chapel this morning. He told me he wanted to show me something. . . ."

McLeod told the story of the steps in the tower, the catwalks, and the north tower. "And he pushed me down that shaft in the tower." She told him about the grill floors, the shaft, the ladder, her climb up, and her climb down, and her emerging into the basement of the chapel and finding the music staff at lunch.

George was quiet when she finished. "You know, Fletcher Prickett is literally mad. I remembered that a few years ago he was actually in a fancy mental hospital for some time. But you know, you do have a thing for making men push you down steps," he said.

"I thought about that," said McLeod. "Clarence Robbins at Lowrie House, and I think Ken Coales certainly wanted to push me down the steps at Dillon. Then I thought about *The Thirty-Nine Steps.* I wondered if I could make a connection."

"You mean the Hitchcock movie?"

"I was thinking about the book. It's the best spy story I ever read," said McLeod. "The hero finds out the German spies are going to leave England with all this secret information on a certain date from a place on the English coast where there are thirty-nine steps down to the water and where the tide is high at ten-seventeen P.M. They find the place and catch the spies. Nobody gets pushed down the stairs. No analogy. There are forty-two steps from the locker room in Dillon Gym to the pool—I've counted them several times—and at Lowrie House, I guess there are about twenty steps. I was trying to figure out how many steps there would be in the chapel—about ninety, I guess. Then I realized that Fletcher didn't try to push me down stairs, but he pushed me down a hole with a ladder in it. Like a well."

"You're babbling," said George kindly. "Have some more champagne."

"I'm about to pass out from the few drops I've had."

"All right, darling. I'll see you in the morning." George leaned over and kissed her lightly and left.

He never called me darling before, thought McLeod as she went off to sleep—without her supper.

WHEN SHE WOKE up at six o'clock the next morning she was, naturally, ravenous, and wondered how she'd last until her breakfast came at seven-thirty or eight. Hospital meal times were odd, she thought.

But she didn't have to wait. George came in with a basket that contained breakfast—orange juice, two still-warm croissants, and a thermos of hot tea.

"Oh, George, thank you. How did you know how hungry I was?"

"I figured you would be—I saw you weren't going to eat your supper and I knew you hadn't had lunch. So I bestirred myself on your behalf. About time, too. And I want to apologize for the grouchy mood I've been in the past two weeks."

"At least you're not under suspicion anymore."

"Fletcher Prickett has been charged. He'll be arraigned today. He says he strangled her with her own tights. The kinky part is he says he 'demonstrated his male superiority' over her."

"He told me that," said McLeod. "The feminists are right—it's a sign of male hegemony."

They were quiet while McLeod munched on a croissant. From a paper bag, George pulled his own croissant and a container of coffee.

"They still don't have the DNA results but I'm finally cleared of suspicion," George said. "Ken Coales even called me last night when he heard about Fletcher. He said he couldn't wait for me to come back. Said nobody in the office knew anything. When he asks them about something, they all say, 'George took care of that.' "

"Hurray! Didn't that cheer you up? And you're going back?"

"I told you I didn't want to work for Ken Coales. But it won't be for long. He's had an offer—a good offer apparently—to take effect as soon as Princeton names a new president. And he's accepted the offer. He told me that frankly he no longer wanted to be president of Princeton, that he would be glad to leave town."

McLeod thought about what that would mean for Caroline and Rosita Sanchez. But George was still talking.

"So I'm going back. Going back today, actually."

"Congratulations!" said McLeod.

"Thanks. I owe it all to you, you know."

"I'm not sure—" began McLeod.

"The police would never, ever have arrested Fletcher, if you hadn't rattled him."

"I was just being nice to an old man," said McLeod.

"And oh, yes, Sophy Robbins called and she was trying to find you to tell you that Max Bolt did go to dinner at Lowrie House. She found out from Mrs. Linley."

"That doesn't matter now, but I do hope Max finishes his movie."

"He will. I told Sophy about Fletcher, and she said she wanted to thank you for finding the murderer. And I want to thank you. The whole world thanks you."

"It was nothing," said McLeod.

McLeod's Dinnner for George

Ginger Chicken with Prunes and Olives

1 teaspoon ground ginger
1 teaspoon dry mustard
1 cup orange juice
2 tablespoons Worcestershire sauce
2 cloves garlic, chopped
1 cup pitted prunes
1/2 cup ripe pitted olives
1 3-oz. jar capers, with juice
6 small chicken breasts, poached and cut into strips
8 oz. sliced mushrooms

Combine ginger and mustard in saucepan. Add orange juice and Worcestershire. Stir over low heat until blended. Add all other ingredients. Simmer 20 minutes and serve over rice. Serves six.

Crême Brulée

4 cups heavy cream
pinch of salt
1 teaspoon vanilla
8 large egg yolks
3/4 cup plus 2 tablespoons sugar
8 tablespoons light brown sugar

Preheat oven to 300 degrees.

Combine cream, vanilla, and salt in saucepan. Warm over low heat for 5 minutes.

In a large bowl, beat egg yolks and combine with granulated sugar. Pour in the hot cream and stir gently. Pour custard into 8 6-ounce custard cups. Set custard cups in roasting pan. Pour warm water into the pan until it reaches halfway up the sides of the custard cups. Bake until set, about 1 hour and 15 minutes.

Remove the custards from the oven and let cool. Cover and refrigerate for at least 3 hours. When ready to serve, top each custard with brown sugar. You can put the custards on a cookie sheet and run them under a hot broiler for a short time (30 seconds to 2 minutes) to caramelize the brown sugar, or you can use a chef's tiny blow torch. Serves eight.